GW00771472

A
ARRIVAL
IN BORTEEN
BAY

A brand new and utterly heart-warming feel-good romance

MORTON S. GRAY

The Secrets of Borteen Bay Book 7

Choc Lit

A JOFFE BOOKS COMPANY

Choc Lit
A Joffe Books company
www.choc-lit.com

This edition first published in Great Britain in 2024

Cover art by Dee Dee Book Covers

ISBN: 978-1781896747

To our own precious arrival, our grandson, Roman!

CHAPTER ONE

Skye knew it was time. If she was ever going to go through with her plan, it had to be now or never. What had seemed simple in her head, a way to get revenge almost, now felt stupid and maybe even childish, but then it was the child in her that needed to do this.

She forced herself to put one foot in front of the other and walked down the high street of this unfamiliar seaside town and onwards towards the beach. Now or never, Skye, now or never.

* * *

Buzz tried to swallow down the disillusioned feelings that were flooding into his mind. No one really understood what he was trying to achieve with the labyrinth on the sand. He was raising money for charity, yes, but there was a higher meaning to his efforts.

He should have known by now that it was all in vain. Most of the people living in and visiting Borteen didn't care about ancient teachings; they only cared about the fastest broadband and where they could get a mobile signal and cheap beer.

'I'm getting cynical,' he said to himself, and laughed. It was nothing new to feel like this, nothing new to have conversations with himself either. He brushed some grains of sand off his tie-dye jacket.

The tourists who came into his shop, Crazy Crystals, were exactly the same. They oohed and aahed over the pendants and ignored his psychic insights into which one would better suit their needs for healing and energetic cleansing, buying instead the one that matched an item of clothing or caught their eye.

It used to make his blood boil. These days, he was just resigned to it.

Resigned and alone . . .

The labyrinth on the beach was proving popular today, but as a sort of fairground attraction, not as a way to cleanse the aura and expand the body's energy field. Still, did it really matter? Walking the path on the sand would have those effects anyway, regardless of the mindset or belief systems of the participants, and the bonus was that at the same time Buzz was raising money for the homeless charity he supported.

He mustered a smile for the family of four in front of him. They each threw a pound coin into his pink heart-shaped donations bucket, before beginning to walk around the spiral path, giggling, the children skipping. He couldn't help his sigh of despair, but then he saw *her* and all other thoughts fled from his mind.

To begin with, Buzz thought the woman was a mirage, a figment of his imagination, but no, she looked pretty real and just as he remembered her. Wynn stood at the far side of the labyrinth, her long plaits laced with feathers and her fringed dress edged with beads.

His heart performed a strange skippety beat and he clutched at his chest. But his reaction to Wynn went beyond the physical. It always had.

A flashback launched itself from his memory. Wynn in his arms, dancing up close to him, their laughter combining with the promise of passion in the air. Their wedding day. He closed his eyes to examine the remembered scene and when he opened them again moments later, she'd gone, seemingly having evaporated into thin air.

Buzz ignored the man trying to pay for his two daughters to walk the labyrinth and searched the beach with frantic eyes. Had he imagined it? Had the energy of the sacred path conjured Wynn from his subconscious? Panic rose in his throat, because he couldn't see her anywhere now and he had so badly wanted to believe she had actually returned.

Back to reality, Buzz, you old fool.

He turned to the man with the two little girls, dressed in identical blue dresses and pink cardigans, waiting for his attention. 'I'm so sorry. I thought for a moment that I saw someone I knew many years ago, but I must have been mistaken.' He crouched down to allow the girls, both blonde, blue- eyed and eager, to put money into his bucket. 'Thank you for your donations, beautiful ladies.'

The girls giggled, their father lurking warily behind them.

'Walk the path and then come back and tell me how it makes you feel.'

Not many people bothered to speak to him afterwards, of course, but Buzz liked to hear the occasional person say that they felt lighter and strangely free.

He felt anything but light and free since glimpsing Wynn, be she real or imagined. Was it a sign? Maybe he needed to walk the sandy path himself today, before the sea destroyed his handiwork when the tide surged up the beach.

He'd always known that Wynn was a free spirit . . . thought that they both were . . . He'd never dreamed she'd up and go, leaving him a brief scribbled note asking him never to contact her again. Just . . . disappeared, apparently into fresh air, leaving no trace or clue about where she'd gone. The absolute heartbreak of losing his soulmate was still raw and not far under the surface either, if the unexpected jolt he'd just received was anything to go by. It had been well over eighteen years now. Nearly nineteen years living, or rather existing, without the love of his life. He told himself that he was an example for the philosophy of living for the moment each day, but was he actually deluding himself, just kidding himself to survive?

Technically, they were still married — after all, there had been no divorce. Was she perhaps dead? Had her spirit visited him here today? Had she come to see him one last time before entering the spirit world? On this occasion, he wasn't sure, wondered if the sighting of her was all a product of his overactive imagination and a fond longing to see Wynn again.

He must have stood thinking for a long time, oblivious to anything or anyone, as he was 'woken' from his thoughts by sea water running over his sandaled feet. The tide had crept right up to him while he was absorbed in the trance-like state. Three lads sitting on the sea wall were laughing at him as he made his way up the steps to the promenade clutching the pink donation bucket, his signs and his sand shovel and feeling bewildered by his troubled mind.

On the way up Borteen high street, Buzz felt every one of his forty-nine years. His muscles screamed at him as if they had taken on all of the remembered pain of loss. Stumbling through the door to Crazy Crystals, which was set midway up the high street, he locked the door behind him and made sure that the shop sign was turned to 'Closed'.

There was a large rose quartz crystal on the shop counter that was for display only, most definitely not for sale, as it had been his wedding present from Wynn. Buzz grabbed the large pink stone and sank to his knees out of sight from the door and windows, hugging the crystal to his chest with tears streaming uncontrolled down his face, splashing onto the floor and soaking into the neck of his T-shirt.

Why today? Why had she come today? It was his birthday of all days, but maybe that in itself was significant.

Eventually, he calmed down and sat up with his back against the shop counter, still clutching the pink crystal as if his life depended on it.

The unexpected assault on his emotions had shaken him to the core. He'd never really healed after being seemingly abandoned by Wynn, and his reaction today confirmed that if he didn't know it already. There had been repercussions to her disappearance. He had to declare her missing and had been astounded that the police immediately questioned him. The investigation had been harrowing, but there had been, thankfully, no grounds to charge him with anything, especially as she'd left a note.

It had been a long time to live on his own, but he could hardly replace his soulmate, so he'd been damned to a solo existence ever since Wynn had gone.

Buzz had eventually, philosophically, decided that the Universe had decreed he be alone on this life's journey, so that he could concentrate on his work as a healer and clairvoyant. He could strive to help others, but would anyone ever be able to help him?

He'd thought of every possible scenario about what might have happened to Wynn, where she might have gone and why. He'd pictured her abducted and murdered, seduced and enticed away by a travelling salesman, having a breakdown and living on the streets in a faraway city. He worried that she was lost, maybe in pain, and that hurt him to the core, or was it the thought that she was happier away from him, maybe even with a new lover? The habit of scanning faces wherever he went had never left him, but without any success at all, until today.

He hauled himself up from the floor, using the shop counter for support, feeling old, despite his fitness regime of running, yoga and tai chi. He retreated to his flat above the shop, the same flat he'd once shared with Wynn. He'd never had the heart to move just in case she came back to find him. He fingered the now worn tassels on the curtain tie-backs and remembered the joy on her beloved face at being able to decorate this small space especially for the two of them.

It wasn't until later when he was preparing his evening meal, simple flatbreads with houmous, avocado and tomatoes, that the inconsistencies of what he thought he'd seen on the beach hit him. He'd been too emotional earlier in the day to analyse the situation logically.

The Wynn he believed he'd seen on the beach today was the same Wynn he'd been married to all of those years before. As he thought rationally about it, absent-mindedly popping a stray half-tomato into his mouth, she would now have the appearance of a woman over eighteen years older than she'd been back then.

He examined his own wrinkles and crow's feet in the reflective glass of the oven door. He came to the conclusion that the woman he'd seen earlier couldn't possibly be his wife, unless of course she was a spirit visitation from Wynn or else a double of the woman she'd been all those years before, maybe even looking a little younger than that. An uneasy thrumming set up in his chest as he considered the possibilities. Maybe he was finally losing his marbles.

* * *

Her mother was going to kill her.

Skye took off the beaded dress very carefully. She now knew that it had been her mother's wedding dress and had always been in the box on top of the wardrobe at home, cushioned in tissue paper. Glancing again at the photograph of her mother wearing the dress on her wedding day, which Wynn had only shown to her for the first time a week ago, Skye couldn't quite believe how closely she'd managed to replicate the image from the photograph, right down to the correct positioning of the feathers in her hair.

She undid the plaits now, letting the feathers fall to the patterned carpet of the guesthouse bedroom. Her newly loosened hair had a wavy appearance that looked extremely odd, given she was used to her raven-black hair falling in a sleek curtain around her face.

What exactly had she achieved from her theatrical performance? She questioned her motivation. It had all seemed so clear before she'd arrived here. She'd seen the light of recognition in Buzz's eyes from across the sand labyrinth and the dawning of his disbelief, but then her courage had deserted her and she'd run away as fast as she could.

Her mother had recently finally given in and supplied answers to her questions, telling her about Buzz and his crystal shop in the small seaside town of Borteen, with the flat above where they used to live together. Skye had peered through the windows when it was closed and guessed it was like a time capsule, still selling the same crystals and incense as when her mother had been involved in the business all those years before.

Her mother had been less forthcoming about her reasons for leaving Borteen and Buzz, clamming up completely with tears in her eyes. Skye was confused and frustrated, especially as her mother appeared to treasure the wedding dress and her wedding photograph from the way they were kept safely and separately in the box on top of the wardrobe.

With no further information, Skye had decided to come to Borteen to try and get answers for herself. She had another reason for travelling to England after all.

The guesthouse bedroom was large and comfortable, if old-fashioned. She'd booked it for two weeks and defiantly paid the bill with her mother's credit card before she'd left home. She'd spent a couple of days building her courage, silently and stealthily watching Buzz, like a private investigator. The fact that he'd set up the labyrinth on the beach had been a bonus.

She guiltily knew that by now her mother would have found the credit card payments for her flight and the accommodation at Rose Court guesthouse. She'd know that Skye was in Borteen, England, and she wouldn't be at all happy.

Curiosity might yet kill the cat . . .

As she'd run up the stairs to her room dressed as her mother, impersonating her mother in fact, she'd nearly bumped straight into the dishy guy who was staying in the opposite room. He'd introduced himself to one of the other guests at breakfast as Adam. She knew it was Adam, because the elderly man had repeated it as Alwyn and had been corrected.

Adam had apologized for getting in her way, even though it was really her fault they'd almost collided. He'd looked at Skye and the strange dress with curiosity and, dare she imagine it, interest in his blue eyes. She made an effort to try to remember that look of admiration, as given her current predicament, she was unlikely to have the time or inclination to think about men or romance for the foreseeable future.

CHAPTER TWO

Dust was a big problem at Crazy Crystals. Buzz fought a seemingly never-ending daily battle with it. With lots of small items in the shop and it being such an old building, he often thought that the dust had well and truly won and he'd spend the rest of his life dusting ineffectually.

The sound of the shop door security chime made him turn to see who was there, an onyx turtle in one hand and his duster in the other.

The turtle shattered at his feet as it hit the tiled floor, but he didn't look down, instead he clutched the duster to his mouth in an attempt to stop the scream that was threatening to escape. He immediately regretted the action as a dust cloud rose around him and filled his eyes and open mouth, making him cough.

The girl was dressed in jeans and a purple tunic today, with a long, colourful ethnic cardigan on the top, but she was unmistakably the woman he'd seen on the beach the day before. She hesitated in the doorway as if unsure whether to come in or go out again, and cold air rushed into the shop.

'Wynn?' Buzz's voice didn't sound anything like his own.

She smiled and shook her head. 'I do look like my mother, don't I?'

'Absolute spitting image. I thought you were her yesterday on the beach, or maybe her ghost. Your mother, you say? Wynn is your mother?' Buzz was aware he was almost stuttering.

'Yes, Wynn is my mum.'

She took one step inside the shop and let the door close behind her. She paused to finger a colourful embroidered bag hung on an old wooden hatstand near to the door.

Buzz didn't know what to say next and it seemed the girl didn't either, as the silence stretched on.

Then suddenly she faced him, her eyes flashing with incandescent rage, her hands clenched at her sides. 'I wanted to come to Borteen to meet my father and to find out once and for all why you scared my mother away!'

With that last statement hanging in the air of the dusty shop, the girl flew out of the door, leaving it creaking on its hinges and the door chime on stuttering repeat.

Buzz debated whether to chase after her, but decided against it. His hands were now shaking and his mind reeling with confusion. Wynn's daughter? And what on earth did she mean — scared Wynn away? Meet her father? Then the truth dawned. Did she think *he* was her father?

In shocked autopilot, he took his drum down from its hook on the wall behind the shop counter, a large bodhran with a wolf's face painted on it, and took refuge in humming and drumming rhythmically to try and calm the dangerous maelstrom swirling within him.

The questions kept coming, but he had no answers to any of them. Had he scared Wynn away? Had it really been his fault she'd left? Had his intense younger self been too intent on a spiritual path, evangelical in his thinking? He liked to believe he'd mellowed with time and become more accepting of human nature. Had his youthful enthusiasm and zealousness scared his wife off? But where did a daughter fit into this picture? Why hadn't Wynn told him? How could she not have told him something so monumental? Why was the girl so angry? It was all too much, too overwhelming.

10

He continued to chant and drum, allowing the beat to resonate through his body, but the pain grew more intense rather than receding. Desperation made him drum faster, louder.

Nothing was working and he found his thoughts drifting to putting his fist through the drum. This urge alarmed him almost as much as his questions, as he'd been a pacifist all of his life.

How could he have a daughter? A daughter he'd known nothing about for all of this time. There was no doubt she looked like Wynn, but was she his too?

It was bewildering to think that Wynn wouldn't have told him that she was pregnant. He'd once thought their love and the trust between them indestructible and everlasting, even perhaps existing over more than one lifetime. He was still at a loss to understand what had changed all of those years before.

He gave up any thought of opening for business again that day, locked the shop door and made his way up the narrow steep staircase to his flat. The living room still smelled of the incense stick he'd set burning that morning — sage and frankincense. It was one of many rituals in his ordered life. Rituals he'd built up to help him survive despite the overwhelming pain of loss. The unabating ache that never went away whatever he did, even after all of this time.

Rummaging through the bottom drawer of the old-fashioned teak sideboard, he found a crumpled photograph of Wynn. His favourite photograph of her, which was why it was so dog-eared. She had a flower in her hair and was grinning in a slightly manic way, but somehow the snapshot captured the essence of her. The woman he loved. The woman he still loved despite everything. The woman he would always love.

He'd never really been the same since she'd left.

Now he recognized that he had to pull himself together. He'd have something to eat and a sugary tea, then he had to go in search of Wynn's daughter to finally get some answers.

* * *

11

Skye stumbled down Borteen high street towards the beach. Vision blinded by tears, she walked straight into someone.

'Sorry, sorry.' She didn't even look up and made to go past the person.

'Hey, hey.' Strong arms enveloped her.

For a second she gave in to the need to be held and slumped against the solid chest in front of her. Then she remembered. Men weren't safe. Men lured you in and hurt you.

She pushed herself away from the chest she'd been leaning against, so hard that the stranger lurched backwards. That's when she realized it was Adam from the guesthouse.

Their eyes grew wide as they recognized each other, quite unsure how to react in this strange situation.

'You!' exclaimed Skye.

'Hey! Yes. You okay? Can I do anything to help?'

'No, I'm not okay. Why do you think I'm running down the street in tears? Fun?'

He had his hands defensively in front of him now, as if he feared she might hit him.

She actually wanted to hit him. She could even imagine pounding her fists against his chest.

'Look, I wasn't trying anything. You ran into me, remember?'

'Sorry. I did, didn't I?' Skye wanted to lie down on the pavement and die with embarrassment. None of this was Adam's fault. Now the adrenalin was abating, she had begun to feel cold and shaky.

'You don't look too good. Will you at least let me buy you a coffee?'

'No!'

'A tea?' He had his head on one side. She was annoyed that she liked his face, especially the way his eyes seemed to hold a sparkle of challenge.

'No!'

'Herbal tea, maybe?'

Despite everything, she found herself grinning back at him. 'Oh, okay. Yes. Thanks.'

They walked the short distance to the beach café. There was only one other couple inside. The heat and smell of coffee made her feel even more sickly than she was already.

Adam seemed anxious to get her sitting down, herding her almost, but trying not to actually touch her, and she guessed her features had taken on a deathly white pallor as she had become so shaky.

'I'm not very experienced with herbal tea, I'm afraid. What do I ask for?'

'Chamomile, or if they haven't got that something with ginger, please.'

'Oh, and I'm Adam by the way.'

She didn't let on that she knew his name already. 'Skye.'

'Nice name.' He turned away after smiling at her.

She took the chance while he was at the counter to check her face in her little handbag mirror. It confirmed she looked as white and stressed as she'd thought.

Adam wasn't away long. He came back with obvious concentration on his face as he balanced their drinks on a tray. She watched his long fingers unload a strong dark coffee on his side of the table and a cup, spoon and teapot in front of her. There was a plate with a Danish pastry and a spongey-looking cake on another.

'I know I shouldn't make assumptions, but I got this gluten- and sugar-free almond thing for you.'

Skye laughed then, a real belly laugh that reduced her to tears again. Adam looked rather uncomfortable and perplexed when her vision cleared sufficiently for her to see him once more.

'Am I that predictable, so much of a stereotype?'

'I don't know. I didn't want to do the wrong thing, but it seems I have . . . again.' He went to pick up the plate from in front of her.

'No.' She stayed his hand. 'I laughed so much because you're spot on. It's probably what I would have chosen for myself anyway.'

He took a sip of his hot coffee and grinned. 'So, I had got it right?'

She nodded, giving him a smile, and proceeded to pour a small amount of herbal tea into the cup to see if it was strong enough. It wasn't as yet.

Adam was cradling his coffee between his palms as if he needed to warm his hands.

She decided to stir the tea to hasten its readiness, fumbling with the teapot lid to insert the spoon.

'Am I allowed to ask why you were so upset? Why were you running?' The way he was now holding on to the table suggested that he was ready to push his chair back and run himself, depending on how she reacted to the question.

Skye sat back and looked at Adam properly. He had deep-blue eyes framed by dark lashes. His hair was short and receding a little at his temples, even though he must only be in his early twenties. As his words brought her thoughts back to why she was in Borteen, tears threatened to bubble up once more. 'I'd rather not talk about it.'

'Okay, but I'm here if you change your mind. I mean here, as in staying in the same guesthouse.' He moved his plate closer to him and stared at his pastry.

'Thank you. That's thoughtful.' She decided she may as well try her odd-looking cake.

'Are you staying in Borteen for long?' asked Adam.

'Depends. Might ask around for a job.'

'I imagine there are lots of those when the holiday season starts.'

'It's November!' Skye couldn't help feeling disheartened, because she couldn't stay too long in the guesthouse before her funds ran out.

'Excuse me for having rather big ears and listening in.' The woman cleaning the nearby table called over to them. 'If you're any good at café work, I've been badly let down and need help. You can start straight away.'

'Right now?' Skye couldn't quite believe it. She knew her mother would say that she'd just asked the universe for a job and it had been manifested.

'Yes, if you can. I'd be very grateful. I'm Christine, by the way. I'm the owner.'

'Skye.' She smiled at Adam, finished the last bite of her almond cake and slurped the last drop of chamomile tea from her cup. 'Well, it seems that's me sorted. Thank you again for being so kind to me, Adam.'

She got up and went over to the counter and explained to Christine that she wasn't totally sure if she could work in England without a permit, as she was from Dublin.

'I believe you can, but I'll pay you cash for now, until we've checked.'

Skye took the proffered apron from Christine's hand, smiling again at Adam, who was still at the table they'd shared, as she put it on.

* * *

Adam didn't really want to leave the café just yet, even though he'd effectively been dismissed from "looking after" Skye. The pretty girl with amazing hair seemed fragile, and not only because she'd been crying. He could almost feel the pain, the struggle going on within her, probably because he recognized someone going through a similar thing to himself.

There was something about Skye he couldn't quite put his finger on. She seemed familiar even though he knew instinctively that their paths had never crossed before his visit to Borteen. And he was sure she was shielding some inner turmoil, a problem much larger than getting a job here.

Why did he even care? Maybe because he'd vowed never again to ignore another human being who appeared troubled. He'd learned his lesson on that one, but then it was impossible to be there for absolutely everyone.

As she smiled over in his direction, he saw that the new job would provide a good distraction from her worries. It was lucky she would be working in a public place, as it meant he didn't need much of an excuse to casually check up on her. But he needed to be careful that his desire to help others didn't take over; he had other reasons for being in Borteen that were more important than getting involved with this girl, however attractive he found her.

Skye waved as he left the beach café and moved to clear the table they had shared just a short while earlier. What was she thinking? Did she want to see him again, or was she celebrating that he'd gone?

Adam walked along the promenade, a long, paved area fronting the sea wall above the beach. The wind was bracing as it headed up from the sand, over the promenade and onwards up the steep hill on which Borteen was laid out. He could see the church at the far end, a little off the main promenade, in a wooded area behind what must surely have been a school at one time, but now sported a sign saying 'Owl Corner Crafts'.

He thought he might explore the crafts too, when he'd had a look at the outside of the church and the churchyard. He wouldn't go inside the church yet; he was saving that exploration for the right moment. He wished it was just a simple break at the seaside that had brought him to Borteen, but it wasn't. He had things to sort out and someone to see, but first he wanted to learn more about the town.

CHAPTER THREE

After the two encounters with the mystery girl he now knew was Wynn's daughter, one on the beach and one in the shop, Buzz had great difficulty regaining his equilibrium and feeling strong enough to face whatever was going on. Maybe he was finally getting old. He began to feel stir-crazy with his circling thoughts. It wasn't helping to be enclosed by the walls of the small flat above his shop, so he decided to go out for a walk and a coffee. He couldn't hide away forever.

It wasn't until he was sitting at a table in the little beach café that he realized the waitress was the same girl who had earlier claimed she was his daughter.

He tried to shrink into the corner, but she'd spotted him. Visibly tensing, she grabbed a menu and stalked over to his table, slapped it down and stood over him with her pencil poised over her notepad.

'I'm a regular. I know the menu off by heart.' He couldn't believe he was explaining himself to her. 'Americano, please.'

'Milk?'

'No, thank you.'

'Sugar?'

'No.' An odd question, since there were sugar sachets in a little pot on the table. Maybe she wanted to know how her

17

supposed father took his coffee? The thought shook him to the core again, as questions bubbled up inside of him.

She struggled to pick up the laminated menu, which seemed to have welded itself to the plastic tablecloth. She appeared desperate to get away from him, so he took pity on her, picked up the laminated sheet and handed it over.

Most of his coffee ended up in the saucer, as she virtually threw it at him on her return with his drink. She went to move away.

'Can I at least know your name?'

She hesitated mid-turn. 'Skye.'

He smiled, suppressing the gurgle of laughter which rose inside of him. 'Skye? That makes perfect sense.'

Her hands were on her hips now, her look indignant. She'd obviously misconstrued his comment as a negative statement.

'What exactly do you mean by that?'

'It was my mother's name . . . your grandmother's name.'

The shock on her face made her eyes wide and her mouth worked like a goldfish for a moment, but she didn't say anything apart from a strangled exclamation.

Buzz was sad that Wynn appeared never to have told Skye about the origin of her name and the grandmother on her father's side. If indeed he was her father after all, but didn't the name give a positive clue?

'Skye, maybe we should talk properly?'

'I'm working till five.'

'Then would you let me treat you to an evening meal? That way we could start from the beginning and you can tell me everything. I promise to answer any questions you have as best I can.'

He could see indecision clouding her expression.

Eventually, she half smiled. 'Yes, please.'

'Meet me outside the café at seven.'

She nodded and went to give menus to an elderly couple on another table. Buzz noted that Skye didn't slam their menus onto the tablecloth.

* * *

However angry she was feeling, Skye had so many questions to ask this man who she believed to be her father. She still didn't totally understand the overwhelmingly negative surge of emotion she'd experienced when she approached Buzz. Was he really her father? Did he share her blood? Had she quirks and mannerisms in common with this man who had lived apart from her all her life? Why had her mother seemingly shielded her from him?

She was angry with her mother too for never having let her have the opportunity to know her father, for not giving her any information at all. It cast some doubt over the authenticity of her supposed parentage, but then he'd said she'd been given his mother's name — her grandmother's name. It was all so bewildering.

She'd always told herself that it didn't matter if her dad wasn't on the scene, that Wynn was a wonderful mother and, up until recently anyway, her best friend. But somehow the stigma of not having a father had wormed itself into her heart. She always called herself half an orphan if anyone asked and her mother had infuriatingly never shared any information about her birth father, clammed up completely if she had raised the issue, until last week when Skye had finally refused to accept her mother's silence on the matter and forced her mother to confess his name.

* * *

That evening, Buzz, for once, was unsure what to wear. He didn't normally think about what he wore at all, but he wanted to make a good impression for Skye — in case it was true. Could he really be her father? He'd trimmed his greying beard and cleaned his teeth twice. His clothes looked suddenly scruffy as he viewed himself in the mirror, but it was too late to buy anything new. He shrugged into his denim jacket, lamenting the fact that he appeared this evening to look far too old for it.

Skye was waiting outside of the café as they'd arranged. The girl looked tired and the way she shifted from foot to foot suggested she was nervous too.

She spoke first. 'What should I call you?'

He shrugged. 'Most people call me Buzz, short for Buzzard.'

'Have you got other kids?'

'No, none. Never really been with anyone since Wynn left. She was my life, my soulmate, my everything. I've never really got over her loss.'

'So, my mother left you?'

'Yes.'

Skye turned away. Maybe she didn't believe him. He began to walk slowly along the promenade towards the Ship Inn. Skye followed to the side of him warily, half a step behind. He could tell he would need to win her trust.

'What do you like to eat?'

She caught up to him before replying. 'Anything veggie or vegan. I'm a bit of a vegetable and fruit addict.'

'Figures.'

'Why do you say that?'

'You've been brought up by Wynn after all.' He smiled, and after a small hesitation, she smiled back.

Buzz led the way into the Ship Inn. Lally Kensington was behind the bar chatting loudly to two men sitting on the bar stools. He saluted Buzz and Buzz nodded a greeting.

They found a table in the dining part of the pub. Skye sat to the side of him and seemed to relax a little as she looked at the menu.

Buzz went up to the bar to order their food and drinks, having first checked the table number.

He'd gone for fish and chips with mushy peas and half a pint of lager. Skye had asked for halloumi and chips and an orange and lemonade.

When he sat back down at the table, the energy around them appeared to shift. Skye was full of curiosity. He was curious too. What had Wynn said about him? Why hadn't she told him she was expecting his child back then? Was this girl actually his daughter?

'Is your mum in good health?'

Skye pulled a face. 'She's well, but I would imagine right now she's hopping mad. I didn't tell her I was coming to Borteen . . . to meet you . . .'

'What! I bet she's worried sick.' Buzz felt goosebumps rise on his skin as he imagined how he would feel in Wynn's position.

'We had a bad, bad argument, so we weren't speaking to each other by the time I packed.' Skye scowled.

'Surely no argument is that bad. What was it about?'

'You.' She put her forehead down on her hands on the table, so all he could see was the top of her head.

'I haven't got her number anymore, but you must have it. We need to ring her right now.'

'She's in Dublin.' Skye sat up again and looked wary as if she might run away.

Now Skye's lyrical accent made sense.

Her skin tinged red. 'Would you call her, please?'

'Let me have the number then.'

He really didn't want to make this call, but his conscience told him he had to regardless of his own emotions and feelings. It wasn't fair to leave Wynn frantically worrying about the fate of her daughter.

When he finally got through, it was weird to hear Wynn's voice after all of these years, but sounding exactly the same. He'd wondered about her all this time and now reaching her was as simple as pushing a few numbers on a keypad.

Wynn was silent for a short while when he announced who was calling.

'Thank you for ringing me, Buzz. I'd already guessed where Skye had gone and she's forgotten I can track her on her iPhone. She's been ignoring all of my messages and calls, so I've actually booked a flight for tomorrow morning.'

'You're coming here — to Borteen?' He was stunned, and more than likely sounded it too.

'Yes, I'm coming back to Borteen after all this time. There are things I need to discuss with my daughter.' She paused. 'And with you too, of course.'

'I think maybe it's about time.' He deliberately tried not to put any emotion into his voice.

'I know.'

'If you text the flight details, we'll pick you up from the airport.'

'There really is no need.'

'Wynn! We'll pick you up. I insist.'

'Okay, I'll send the arrival time to Skye.'

'See you tomorrow.' It was just three words, but words he hadn't been able to say for so long, and he found tears in his eyes. He should surely feel angry with Wynn, but unbelievably he didn't. A layer of tension dissolved from his body knowing that she was safe and well, and questions that needed to be answered filled his mind instead.

Skye was looking at him curiously when he finished the call. He wiped his eyes, now wet with unshed tears, with the back of his hand.

'She's coming here?'

He nodded, unable to form any words.

'Yikes!'

* * *

Skye was glad of the distraction of the food arriving from the pub kitchen as it gave her time to come to terms with the fact that her mother would be arriving the next day.

Sitting here with Buzz, who appeared — on the surface at least — to be a calm, gentle guy, it was hard to summon the anger that had been coursing through her mind and body ever since her mother had finally admitted who her father was and that she had left him when she was first pregnant to go and live in Ireland. She had refused to explain exactly why she had left Buzz, causing Skye to imagine that domestic abuse or some other horrible reason had driven her mother to leave Borteen and this man.

Buzz was also making a good show of being totally absorbed by his plate of food. They ate in silence, glancing at each other from time to time, and it wasn't until both of them put down their knives and forks that Skye had decided what to say.

'I've been very angry since I found out about you.'

His eyes widened and he froze with his glass halfway to his mouth, then he put it down without drinking from it. 'I think it would be good to clear the air and tell me about this anger.'

'Nothing to tell really.'

'I don't believe that for one minute.'

Skye took a deep breath and launched. 'Okay, I've spent my whole life being upset that I didn't know my father. My mother is fantastic and I've never wanted for anything. If Mum couldn't buy it, she made it. If I was stuck on something at school, she educated herself so she could help me. But . . . I've always felt that there was something huge missing in my life . . . a father-shaped hole, I suppose.'

'That sounds like the Wynn I know. But I'm not sure I like being described as huge.'

His attempt at humour missed the mark, but Skye half smiled.

'I was just so angry when I found out you were actually alive and living in England but you'd never been near me.'

'And Wynn actually told you that I'm your father . . . you're sure about that?'

'Yes, but only when I pushed her to the limit. I've let her fob me off for years, but she promised to tell me when I turned eighteen, so last week I was determined.'

'You have to understand that I had absolutely no idea about your existence . . . absolutely no idea that Wynn was even pregnant. Do you honestly think I wouldn't have wanted to know you and be involved in your life?'

Skye rubbed her eyes with her sleeve. 'Until I met you, I'd pictured some horrible man, probably angry and bad-tempered, who had driven my mother away . . .'

'And now?' Buzz lifted his eyebrow in question.

'Despite how I reacted when I arrived in Borteen, I can see you aren't at all what I had imagined and Christine speaks very highly of you too — she says you're one of the nicest guys she knows.'

* * *

Suddenly alarmed at Skye's words, Buzz straightened in his seat. He knew how the gossip grapevine worked in Borteen. 'Did you tell Christine about our connection?'

'No, I only asked her casually who you were when you left the café earlier.'

Buzz smiled and breathed a sigh of relief.

He and Skye needed to sort out their possible relationship before it was the talk of the town. 'Let's order dessert — I think we both need sugar. The way I see it, as a first step, we have to ask your mother to explain what happened back then, or at least I do, and as for you and me, I'd like to take the time to get to know you and I hope that you feel the same way.'

In answer, Skye extended her hand and they shook on the deal to give each other the benefit of the doubt and find out more about each other. Buzz liked the girl and liked even more the idea of having a daughter, but some inner sense was telling him not to get too excited just yet.

CHAPTER FOUR

Buzz stood next to Skye in the arrivals lounge at the airport. Skye was hopping from foot to foot again. But he wasn't nervous. No, he wasn't. Oh, who was he trying to kid? He was completely terrified.

He pulled at his pigtail, which he'd brushed until the hair glistened before he left home. His hair had been jet black just like Skye's the last time Wynn had seen him. He experienced a moment's irritation that he still wore his hair in the same style he'd had for years despite the slight bald patch that had appeared on top of his head and the grey streaks that made it look as if he'd peppered his head.

Why did it matter what Wynn thought of him after all of this time? She'd not cared enough to get in touch with him before, to find out if he was alive or dead. It bothered him a lot that it *did* actually matter to him. He could see his reflection in the glass screen in front of him. What he saw was an older guy trying to be hippy. Or was that hip? Skinny jeans, cowboy boots, pigtail and a face lined by life.

Wynn's face was still clearly etched in his memory. High cheek bones, dark straight hair, petite with her eyes bird-like, almost black — intense, knowing, insightful. Those eyes burned into your soul and left you with nowhere to hide.

Of course, he was imagining Wynn as she'd been all those years before and he had no way of knowing what time had done to the woman he'd loved . . . did love . . . still loved. For in truth, there had never been anyone else for him, not really, and although he didn't understand what had happened to make her go away, he knew there must have been a good reason.

He focussed back on the reflection of himself and Skye in the glass screen and realized all at once that he was now matching her nervous side-to-side foot shuffle. Dammit!

The arrivals board said that Wynn's flight had landed twenty minutes ago, she couldn't be far away from them now in the endless corridors of the airport, although he knew it took time to get from the plane to the arrivals hall.

Surprising him, Skye grabbed hold of his hand and it was all he could do not to jump. He looked down at her.

'I'm getting worried. Mum's going to be so mad with me.'

'I think she's more likely to be relieved to see you fit and well, to be honest. She's probably been imagining all sorts of unthinkable tragedies.'

Buzz had a strange feeling that Skye meant her mother would be mad about something other than her coming to Borteen, but he dismissed the thought.

And then, just like that, after so many years of heart-ache and missing her, that beloved face he knew so well was coming towards him. It was surreal, but the woman coming down the corridor was unmistakably Wynn, even if some-how smaller, broader, more lined. Her straight black hair peppered with grey, her eyes tired-looking and her mouth set in a serious line. She stopped a few feet away from them and put her hand up to her mouth.

'Mum, don't.' Skye released Buzz's hand and took a step forward.

Wynn was crying openly and Skye moved to envelop her mum in a hug.

'I'm sorry . . . sorry I've made you come all this way. Sorry I've worried you so much. Sorry we argued. But I found Buzz exactly where you said he'd be.'

Buzz hovered behind them, trying to give them space, his foot shifting increasing in speed and intensity as he was unsure what to do, how exactly to react, what to say.

Wynn fought her way loose from her daughter's embrace. She nodded at Buzz.

He nodded back, feeling the nods were totally inadequate, but neither of them appeared to be able to do anything more demonstrative.

'You look like two peas in a pod.' Her voice had an unfamiliar Irish lilt over certain words. She scrubbed at her face with her hand and linked her arm with Skye's. Buzz picked up her small case and led the way out of the terminal building.

* * *

They were all quiet in the car, with conversation brief and short. Wynn had insisted that she sat in the back seat and that Skye took the front, mainly because she couldn't face being that close to Buzz as yet.

Wynn clutched the seatbelt until her knuckles were white, and it was nothing to do with Buzz's driving. She was trying to deal with the overload of emotions she was experiencing.

She was so happy to see Skye safe and well. And Buzz still looked like *her* Buzz despite the passage of the years. She had never dreamed that she would be back in England. Forced to confront her choices and decisions, she didn't feel any better about herself. It had been unfair and unrealistic to think Skye, her beloved daughter, wouldn't want to know about her origins, but how could she tell the girl the absolute truth even now?

Buzz was exactly as she remembered. Kind and gentle with that calm air in everything he did, he was still the man she had fallen in love with, had loved and, she realized with a jolt, still did love. She'd had flirtations over the years, of course, but never let anyone become a serious item in her life. Now the truth hit her that she'd never stopped loving Buzz.

She'd been a fool and made the wrong decision, but all of that was well and truly water under the bridge.

Having had many years to analyse why she had left Borteen, she realized that she'd followed a pattern shown to her in childhood by her mother, and that made her even more irritated with herself. When her own mother found difficulties in her life, she up and left — and not just once. Wynn could recall three times that they'd packed up and moved, often at night, to a completely different place, only for her mother to set up home with yet another man who treated her and Wynn badly. Her mother stood dreadful situations for longer than maybe she should have before repeating the pattern and running away yet again. Wynn knew that her mother's first flit had been from her own father, whom she'd never known.

Faced with her dilemma and its associated complications over eighteen years ago, Wynn had unfortunately done the same as her mother would no doubt have done, and she'd had all of those years to regret it.

Looking at the back of Skye's and Buzz's heads in the front of the car, she could see that they had already established a relationship of sorts. Guilt and fear flooded into Wynn's body.

As they came over the hill and began to descend into Borteen, she exclaimed at the familiar but long unseen view, and Skye turned and smiled at her.

Buzz had offered her the use of his spare room and she had felt dreadfully awkward about it. Thankfully, she had booked ahead at the Rose Court guesthouse having seen where Skye was staying from her own credit card entries.

Buzz dropped the pair at Rose Court and carried Wynn's case up the entrance steps. She promised to call at Crazy Crystals later that afternoon for a herbal tea.

What must he think of her? She was surprised that he could even muster a smile, but then he had always been so tolerant. What a pickle she had got herself into then and now. Somehow, once she had left Borteen, she had been able to distance herself from the mess. She had made her choice back then to run away. Had blanking things been better than facing the music?

Well, there was no getting away from it now. She had to face her demons. There really was no escape anymore. Confession time. She had to at last be honest with Buzz about why she had gone away and then she would have to have another difficult conversation with her daughter regardless of the consequences. Her fictitious world hadn't really made her happy at all, had it? How had she ever imagined that it could? Fool!

* * *

Buzz rushed home to tidy his already tidy home and to make sure he had a selection of the type of herbal teabags his wife used to like, hoping that her tastes hadn't changed since he knew her before. He was bursting with questions, but was determined not to scare Wynn away by voicing them all at once. Nonetheless, they buzzed around his brain like angry wasps. Why had she left? Why had she never let him know she was okay? How could she have left it this long to let him know he had a daughter? Or did that mean Skye wasn't his after all?

He kept reminding himself he had to bide his time. He may be upset, confused, even betrayed, but aware that he would only get the answers he needed if he listened rather than confronting Wynn straight away. Strong reactions, getting angry, would most likely result in her going away again without answering his burning questions. And yet, despite any negatives, he was also relieved that Wynn appeared okay and healthy and his heart felt lighter for having seen her again despite everything.

When Wynn and Skye finally arrived at the shop, Buzz turned the sign to 'Closed' and led the way up to the flat, hoping that it wasn't too obvious that he'd hurriedly cleaned and tidied and that his heart was beating a million times faster than normal.

Skye soon left Wynn and Buzz alone together, Buzz guessed on purpose, with the pretext that she needed to discuss her shifts with Christine at the café.

It was unreal and he would never ever have believed it could ever happen again — they were sitting in the same spot by the fireplace just as they had done all those years before. It was almost as if time had stood still, or else been rewound.

They were awkward to start with, beginning conversations and not quite knowing how to continue them. She asked after a few of the people that she'd known in Borteen. Buzz bit back the barrage of questions, biding his time, afraid of scaring Wynn away.

'A full moon tonight, Buzz. I looked it up. Would you join me on the beach tonight?'

'Like old times?'

'Kind of . . . although I'm not taking my clothes off this time.'

'Spoilsport.' He winked. The tension was only now beginning to leach from his body, but it was an effort.

They laughed together and it felt gut-wrenchingly good, despite everything that lay unanswered between them.

He would need to have those answers tonight or he would surely go mad.

* * *

Later that evening, Buzz and Wynn stood side by side on the beach, watching the moon rise over the horizon. They'd done this together many times in the past and usually, euphoric after the experience, they'd gone back to the flat and made wild, passionate love.

What was Wynn thinking? She must know that he had questions, resentments, disappointments, hurts? How could he still think of her as his Wynn? She wasn't. She'd lived so many years without him. Was she even the same person? How could the woman he'd fallen in love with have left him in such a painful limbo for so long? Maybe she never loved him in the same way as he had loved her.

The contrast between his thoughts and emotions, compared to the reaction of his body to Wynn, bewildered him. Buzz badly wanted to hold her hand, but it didn't feel right to do so, even though just standing next to her felt companionable and right. He needed some sign from Wynn before he attempted to touch her in any way.

Wynn pointedly hadn't invited Skye to join them at the beach, so Buzz hoped that she might be ready to talk, to explain about what happened, explain about Skye. He badly needed to understand, even though he knew the explanation had the potential to break his heart all over again.

The moon appeared over the horizon and began to rise, tentative at first, and they stood in silence as it tracked up the sky, bright, huge, amazing. Buzz didn't think he could ever tire of watching this natural phenomenon, but being with Wynn again made it all the more precious. He didn't tell her that he'd done this every year since she'd gone, on the full moon closest to the date of her leaving, as if still following their ritual might bring her home one day. And at last, here she was.

Was he acting like a complete fool? He could feel the tension building in his body once more as Wynn continued to remain silent. She stood next to him. So near and yet still so far away.

Eventually he could be patient no longer and he knew he had been far more patient than most people would have been.

'Why?' The word sounded stark on the clear cold air. 'We could have had such a good life together, you and I.'

When he looked across at her, Wynn already had tears tracking down her face, but still, infuriatingly, she didn't speak.

'What did I do wrong? You have to tell me and put me out of all of these years of misery, please. And I can't believe you didn't tell me about Skye.' He had to make an effort to unclench his fists and the muscles of his face.

Her voice when it finally came sounded breathless. 'It wasn't you that did anything wrong; it was me.'

'What could you possibly have done that I wouldn't have forgiven?'

'I slept with your brother . . .'

All of the air disappeared from his lungs and the crushing pain in his chest was so intense that he doubled over on the sand.

Wynn knelt down next to him, her face contorted. 'Buzz, Buzz. Are you all right? You're not having a heart attack, are you?'

He curled up into a tight ball, hugging his knees into his chest and crooning, a deep, primeval sound of despair. He knew Wynn was next to him, but he couldn't speak to her, not yet.

The cool dampness of the sand was seeping into both his clothing and his bones. After rocking and sounding out his emotion, he eventually rolled over, sat up and rested his arms on his knees, facing the moon. Wynn came to sit down next to him in exactly the same pose. This time, it took all of his willpower not to push her away. This hurt so, so badly.

'See, I knew I had to go . . . to leave. It was something unforgivable, even for a completely generous soul like you.' She shifted sideways, putting some distance between them. 'Of course, when I went I didn't know that I was expecting a baby.'

'And . . .' He almost couldn't voice his next question. 'Skye? Is she mine or his?' He couldn't bring himself to even use his brother's name.

'Who knows? She could have been fathered by either of you, I'm afraid.' Wynn's voice was almost a whisper on the cold air.

'We could do tests to find out.'

'But then we'd have to explain to Skye why she needs to take a test . . .'

'I think we have to have that conversation with Skye, in any case. She's an adult now, you can't in all conscience leave the girl thinking I'm her father if I'm not.' Buzz gulped as the enormity of what Wynn had just told him struck him anew. 'But given he's my brother, if you'd stayed, I would never have known, probably never have suspected she wasn't mine . . .'

'But I would have known . . . Even if I'd come back when I realized I was pregnant and confessed what had happened, there would always have been, always has been that doubt, and I knew that I couldn't possibly live with you with that huge deception between us. It would have . . . has . . . eaten away at me, and heartbreakingly, it's affected my relationship with my daughter.' Her face was glistening with tears again in the moonlight.

Buzz was amazed that his voice could sound so calm given the circumstances. 'I can understand all that. But I have to know — was it a full-blown affair with Ed, or just once?'

'We only slept together one time. But then again, once is enough.'

Buzz ran his hands over the sand, making furrows where his fingers dug into the grains. 'Oh, Wynn!' It came out more like a shuddering sigh than a comment.

'Do you know just how many times I've said those words to myself over the years? How much anger I've shown to myself about what happened?'

'Have you ever told Ed about Skye? Skye about Ed?' His mind was still cartwheeling.

'No!' she wailed. 'I hated myself and Ed from the very moment we'd . . . I've never seen him since that day. I've always prayed that Skye was yours. Begged the universe that she was yours.'

'The poor girl thinks she's mine now.' Buzz rubbed his face. 'We have to speak to her. She's old enough to understand that relationships aren't straightforward.'

Even though it had been a complete shock when Skye had turned up in Borteen and declared that she was his daughter, it now hurt deeply that there was a possibility that she might not be his after all, that she might instead be his brother's, of all people.

Wynn's face changed. 'Do you think we could possibly keep it that you are her father? Not cast any doubt on her parentage. I mean, whatever you think of me after all this time, Skye doesn't deserve to suffer any more than she has already.'

'I'm really not comfortable with lying to the girl. We need to find the right time to discuss all of this with her, including why you've been so secretive and kept her away for so long. This isn't just about you anymore, Wynn.'

'You're right, Buzz.' Wynn hung her head.

'My brother has five kids already.'

'Five?'

'Yes, five. From three marriages.'

'Can we at least pick the right moment to speak to Skye? I've made such a mess of things.'

'I agree we need to be sensitive about how we approach this.'

'Thank you, Buzz.' She slowly put her hand over his to stop him from digging grooves in the sand.

They sat quietly for a few moments, Buzz enjoying the warmth coming from the contact with Wynn, his thoughts again warring with his emotional reaction to her.

'Why did Skye really come to England?'

'We argued, and I guess she wanted to meet you.' Wynn removed her hand.

'But why now? Why after all this time?'

'We've had an awkward summer, since she started asking questions again. We'd argued, had words about her father, about you, and she's been going through a difficult phase and floundering around since she didn't get the exam results she'd been predicted.'

'That must have been disappointing.'

'Yes, and totally unexpected. She's always worked hard and been top of her year. Her dad's genes, I'm guessing.'

Wynn was referring to Buzz's early life, before everything had changed for him, before she'd met him. No one asking Buzz for a tarot reading or a crystal recommendation in his shop would ever guess he had a PhD in automotive engineering.

It was something he pondered often — the fact that people only saw the surface of an individual. All of the achievements and disappointments, loves and losses were usually invisible when others formed opinions about a person.

Buzz had a thing about life-defining moments. He spoke to clients about them when he was working as a therapist. You could let these moments dictate the rest of your life, or you could use them as a catalyst for rebellion and/or change.

His own first such moment had been when the driver of a prototype car made to Buzz's design had been killed. Everyone had told him that the accident wasn't his fault, but Buzz wasn't convinced. He felt that he'd taken that man's life just as surely as if he'd put a gun to his head.

A short while later, he'd turned his back on the career he'd worked towards for years and wandered around in his own wilderness, where he'd served in bars, waited tables, anything to drown out his thoughts. That proved impossible most of the time; those sorts of thoughts dogged you, creeping into the crevices between activities. He'd always been a hair's breadth away from living on the streets, maybe taking mind-numbing drugs.

It wasn't until his late mother had persuaded him to see a hypnotherapist, and insisted on paying for the therapy, that he'd turned a corner. His mum had spotted the signs of him careering headlong towards self-destruction. The hypnotherapist had helped him to get the car crash incident into perspective, turning it somehow from vivid colour into muted greys and boosted his confidence enough for him to seek a new way forward in life.

A new life where he'd met Wynn on a course about crystal healing. The next life-defining moment had been when she'd left him. Buzz shook his head to clear the thought process.

'So, if Skye is a bright, high-achieving student, how come she flunked her exams? I know you say you'd disagreed, but was she ill? Stressed? I could understand her having a bad day maybe, but failing? Suggests something else catastrophic or a conscious decision.'

'You don't think that I've wracked my brains trying to work it out? I've analysed the weeks leading up to the exams in great detail, but apart from our rows, I've drawn a complete blank. She had spent a lot of time out of the house, staying with friends, but Skye won't give me any more clues about what happened.'

'It must have been something big. Maybe she couldn't cope with you not talking about her father?'

Wynn rose to her feet, her movement graceful despite her age and bearing testimony to someone who had practised yoga daily all of her life. 'Yes, probably my fault. My return flight to Dublin is tomorrow.'

He'd done what he'd vowed not to do — he'd pushed her too far. The shock jolted him, and despite what she'd told him about her leaving in the first place, he really didn't want her to go again, not now.

'So soon?'

'I think it's best.'

'What about Skye? We need to talk to her.'

'We'll try in the morning. She said she wanted to stay until the new year at least. Says she wants to get to know her father. And after we talk to her and cast doubt on that, she'll no doubt hate me even more. How do you feel about her staying in Borteen for a while — if she still wants to?'

'As long as we speak to her about the possibility I might not be her dad, it's fine. I'd like to get to know her too, but she can't stay indefinitely at Rose Court.'

'Not unless she finances herself. I recognize that I need to let her do this, need to let her fly free, however hard it may be for me as her mother. Can you keep a good eye on her for me? Maybe try to get her to talk about her exams and what on earth went wrong? I'm still hoping she'll resit at some point.'

'Of course, you know you don't even need to ask. I've not known her long, don't even know if she's mine, but I care about her already. She's a lovely girl.'

'Buzz?'

He struggled to his feet and brushed the sand from his clothing. 'Yes?'

'I'm sorry. So terribly, dreadfully, heart-squeezingly sorry that I messed up.'

He pulled her against him then, breathing in her scent, absorbing the warmth of her, grieving once again for all of the lost years and might-have-beens.

'Don't go tomorrow, Wynn. Not yet.' He breathed into her hair.

'I have to. I really believe I have to.' She stiffened in his arms.

'No, you really don't, because despite everything, unbelievably, I think I still love you.'

She made a strange huffing sound. 'You carved your name on my heart long ago, Buzz.'

'I wish you'd been able to cope with the guilt.'

'Even if I could have coped with the guilt and stayed here with you, do you really imagine that your brother would have been able to resist the opportunity to gloat? To get one over on you? You two always had such a strange relationship.'

'You're probably right, and now I know what happened, some of his cryptic comments over the years are beginning to make sense at last — he's definitely been dropping hints about what happened between you two.'

'Do you still see Ed?'

'No. If I'm honest, even though he's my brother, I avoid him like the plague. I still meet up with some of my nephews and nieces when they're over in Borteen. Ed has a high-flying job, bought one of those mansions overlooking the cathedral in Sowden. You picked the wrong brother . . .'

'Don't you ever say that, Buzz. You're worth ten of him.'

The accumulated years of despair threatened to overwhelm Buzz. 'Then why? I still can't get my head around it properly, why did you and Ed, erm, happen?'

She wriggled out of his embrace, as if she'd only just realized what she was doing. 'Alcohol, a joint of weed, curiosity, foolish impetuosity.'

He could hear the rich vein of self-disgust in her voice.

She whispered 'goodnight' so quietly he could almost have believed he'd imagined it, and he sensed rather than saw her slip away into the darkness.

Buzz stood still for a while, seemingly rooted to the spot, half listening to the waves coming onto the beach. Pain enveloped him as he realized that he'd lost Wynn once again and it was no less excruciating than the first time. Except that now he knew the truth. Why did it have to involve Ed — he could have taken almost anyone else more easily than his brother. The brother who always tried to go one better than Buzz. The brother for whom one-upmanship was a way of life. It was still a betrayal, full stop, but somehow magnified because it had been with Ed.

He'd speculated over the years, of course, embroidered fantastical possibilities and missed Wynn . . . missed her still. Was he really going to let her walk away forever? But then could he ever get past the enormity of what she'd done, even if the betrayal was so many years ago? Could he forgive something like this? It was a huge obstacle. And then there was Skye . . . Wynn had told her daughter that Buzz was her father.

He forced himself to follow her footprints up the sand. His heart leaped when he realized that she hadn't yet returned to the guesthouse, but was sitting, head in her hands, on one of the benches by the sea wall.

'Wynn?'

She looked up, eyes glinting with tears in the moonlight.

He decided to try again. 'I still love you.'

She sobbed out loud then. 'And I still love you, that's the big problem. I could sort of deny it to myself in Dublin, but having seen you again . . . I can't.'

They had both paid a heavy price for one act of alcohol-fuelled temptation. If, of course, that was the full story. He dropped down onto the bench next to her. He had to try to make her see sense or else he would never forgive himself, let alone her.

'Look, Wynn, why don't we try to start over? As if . . . as if we've only just met? I mean, if we had met now, just think, we'd have plenty of baggage at our ages, plenty of lost loves, past history . . .'

'I guess so.' Her voice was quiet and hesitant.

'Then why not? What have we got to lose?' He extended his hand towards her. 'Hi, I'm Buzz, short for Buzzard. I run a new-age gift shop in Borteen, sell crystals and I do tarot readings. I draw walking labyrinths on the beach to raise money for a homeless charity whenever I can.'

She giggled and put up her hand to shake his. Neither of them could deny the spark of electricity that passed between their fingers.

'Hi, I'm Wynn, a single parent from Dublin.'

'That's a strange way to describe yourself. You're much more than that. And you didn't need to be that.'

'Am I? It's how I see myself. It wasn't easy raising Skye alone, particularly in the early days, but I felt so ashamed that I didn't see that I had a choice.'

'Have you relatives in Dublin?'

'A friend of my grandmother's. She took me in . . . thankfully.'

Buzz bit back the words he wanted to cry out. He could have helped. He would have enjoyed all of the stages of Skye's life, but then what if he'd been going along happily, enjoying parenthood, and had suddenly found out Wynn's secret . . . what then? Would the knowledge have destroyed him, destroyed them? Would he have ended up being the one to run away instead?

Wynn had become very still, as if she could see the thoughts rippling through his mind in the darkness. The moon had gone behind a cloud. He felt her shiver. 'It will always be between us, Buzz. Ed will always be between us. Now you know, you would never be able to forget what I did. It would never work.' Her voice sounded wretched.

Buzz experienced the same gut-wrenching sense of loss from the first time Wynn had left, but this time layered with new feelings. He still loved her, goddammit. She still moved him like no other woman he'd ever met before or since. Even despite her wrinkles and slightly more rounded figure, even despite her terrible confession. He knew he didn't want her to leave. Desperately searching for reasons to make her stay, he spoke almost against his will. 'Would you like me to give you a lift to the airport tomorrow?'

'That's awfully kind, but I don't think it would be a good idea, do you?'

'Don't go, not yet . . .'

'I have to, Buzz. Please understand that I just have to.' She laid a hand on his arm, the warmth of it burned through his coat and shirt to his skin, his longing for her rising up once again.

'Why? Why do you have to go? Do you have someone to return to in Dublin?'

'I don't have a man in my life if that's what you mean, but I do have a business to run.'

'Business? You haven't told me about that yet.' He was clutching at straws, hoping that if he kept her talking she'd maybe change her mind about going.

'Oh, Buzz, I've got a little shop exactly like yours, almost identical in fact, as if someone had picked up Crazy Crystals and planted it in a back street of a Dublin suburb.'

He stared at her for a moment, then gulping back raw, painful emotion, he tried to disguise his reaction by retying his shoelace.

'Buzz?'

'Sorry. I'm finding all this just as hard as the first time.'

'Me too, love.'

She pulled his face gently around and pressed her lips to his. His instinct was to deepen the kiss, to hold on to her and never let go, but she was too quick, pulling away, leaving him puckered up in mid-air — alone.

'Goodnight, Buzz.'

And then she really was gone, away into the night. His heart went with her yet again.

CHAPTER FIVE

The next day, Buzz was still reeling from his grief at being about to lose Wynn yet again. He hadn't slept well, tossing and turning, as he wondered what else he could have said to keep her in Borteen, to win her back. The ache inside of him was set to be his constant companion.

He'd sent a text to Wynn in the early hours of the morning to suggest she and Skye come to his flat for breakfast, so that they could *discuss what they needed to discuss* with Skye.

Wynn had replied this morning and he was expecting the pair any time soon. He had just polished the breakfast spoons for the second time when the doorbell rang.

Wynn looked as if she was going to an execution rather than breakfast and Skye was quietly following in her wake, no doubt aware of her mother's strange mood.

Once they were settled at the table with toast, jam, cereal and fruit, Skye sighed loudly. 'You two have obviously planned this to say something, so come on out with it.' She glared at Wynn and then turned her gaze onto Buzz.

Wynn showed no sign of speaking, so Buzz began. 'Your mother and I had a long conversation last night about why she left me to go to Ireland before you were born.'

'And did you discuss me too? About why she's only just told me about Borteen and you?'

'About that too. Wynn?'

Wynn put down her spoon with a clatter — as far as Buzz could see she hadn't eaten anything anyway, only stirred fruit and cereal around in her bowl. 'Okay, I'm going to say this quickly, so it might not come out right, but I'm just going to say it.' She paused. 'Buzz might not be your father.'

'Might not be? But . . . but . . . you told me that he was.' Skye's face was full of pain and Buzz would have done anything to save the girl from her anguish.

'I know what I said before, but I'm not actually, totally sure. You see, and I'm not proud of this, I slept with two men about the time you were conceived.'

'Two men? But you were married to Buzz, weren't you? You mean you were having an affair? Sleeping with someone else? I don't understand, Mum. You and Buzz seem so perfect together even now, so why would you even need anyone else?'

'It's a question I've asked myself many times over the years and I'm ashamed that I gave into stupid temptation. It doesn't make it any better at all, but I only slept with Ed once.'

'Ed? *Ed*? Is that the other man who could be my father? Who is he? Where is he? How can we find out who is actually my dad? After I got over my anger that he'd not been part of my childhood, I was so pleased to know Buzz was my dad. I really like him.'

'Ed is my brother,' said Buzz. 'I knew nothing about any of this, or I would have told you when we first met. He lives in Sowden, near here, and he has five other children.'

'So, if he's your brother, we wouldn't even know on looks if he's my father or not?'

'No, exactly that. A DNA test could probably tell, but I'll need to find out more about that,' said Buzz, reaching out his hand to touch Skye's arm.

Skye looked at her mother. 'Have you nothing else to say?'

'Just that I'm so truly, awfully sorry. This is the reason why I've not told you anything about your father before and why I knew I had to leave Borteen and my lovely husband behind back then. I now recognize, of course, that I only repeated a pattern my own mother followed in my childhood — to run away if things got difficult — but to say it's a learned behaviour doesn't excuse it and hindsight is a wonderful thing. It doesn't help at all.'

Suddenly, Skye got up from the table, grabbed her bag and dashed out of the room and down the stairs.

Wynn and Buzz looked at each other. 'I'll say goodbye, Buzz. I'd better go after her and then get to the airport.'

'Aren't you just doing the same again, Wynn, and running for the hills?'

Wynn shrugged. 'Habit of a lifetime, I'm afraid.'

And with no kiss or hug goodbye, she was gone.

* * *

Buzz somehow didn't expect to ever see his wife again, but unbelievably she appeared at the shop door after lunch.

He was aware that he had his mouth wide open in surprise and he had to make a real effort to close it. Wynn came into the shop and held the door open for a young man Buzz vaguely recognized from about town. His heart had momentarily soared at the sight of Wynn, but the expression on her face didn't suggest she had changed her mind, or was now intent on a blissful reunion.

She came toward the counter, the young man close on her heels.

'This is Adam. He's staying at Rose Court too and says he spoke to Skye in the hallway earlier when he realized she was leaving.' Wynn's eyes seemed overly wide open.

'Leaving?' Buzz felt confused. 'But I thought she was staying here for Christmas?'

'So did I.'

Adam looked warily at Wynn and then addressed Buzz. 'She said there was someone else she needed to see, so she was going south for a while. Said it had all become a bit intense in Borteen since her mum had arrived here too.'

'Sorry, Adam, I should introduce myself. I'm Buzz . . . Skye's, erm . . . father.'

'I gathered that you were her dad from the little she's said to me. We've chatted a couple of times at the beach café.'

'Did she by any chance say who the other person she wanted to visit was?' asked Wynn.

Wynn had gone a deathly white colour and Buzz thought he knew why. Had Skye gone to seek out Ed after the revelations of this morning?

'No, she didn't elaborate. Sorry, I should have asked her really.'

'Not your fault. Thank you, Adam. If you hadn't spoken to her, we'd know nothing at all. Can you let one of us know if you hear or see anything else of Skye? Or remember anything else at all?'

'Of course.' Adam dutifully copied their mobile numbers into his phone.

Buzz thanked Adam too and he left, again repeating his promise to alert them if he saw Skye or heard anything about her whereabouts.

Wynn sat down heavily on one of the tall stools behind the shop counter and Buzz sat on the other one. It was as if she'd never gone at all, as if all of the years had melted away. He reached out his hand to her and she clasped it tightly for a few moments.

As she let go of his hand, Wynn jumped off the stool and rushed to the door.

'Wynn?'

'I just want to go and see if she left a message for me at the guesthouse. Back soon.'

And she was gone.

* * *

45

Wynn walked as fast as she could to Rose Court guesthouse. By the time she reached reception, she had worked herself into such a state that she sat on a chair in the hallway and sobbed.

As soon as she had control of her emotions, she pressed the bell on the counter and asked Pippa who ran the guesthouse about Skye.

'Ah, yes, Skye told me that she'll be away for a short while and she left you a note.'

It was an effort for Wynn to control her impatience as Pippa turned away to search the guest mailboxes. And it was all she could do not to snatch the folded piece of paper from Pippa's hand once she had found it.

Somehow she managed to politely thank Pippa, take the note and return to sit on the chair. Her heart thudded as she opened it.

Hi Mum, I have to go to see a friend. Need some time to take in what was said this morning. Please give me space. Be in touch soon, Skye x

Wynn took in a huge shuddering breath. How could she blame Skye for going? After all, she was only following Wynn's own pattern. Things too difficult? Then leave.

Pippa was sorting papers on the reception desk.

'Is it possible to extend my stay by a few days, please?' asked Wynn.

'Of course, it's a quiet time of year so there's no problem at all.'

Wynn thanked her and then rang to see if her flight could be changed too.

She felt much calmer as she walked back to Crazy Crystals. She couldn't help but notice Skye leaving this time ironically meant she would have to spend more time with Buzz, but maybe it wasn't a bad thing to face her demons completely before returning to Dublin.

There was no way she would go back to Ireland until she knew Skye was safely settled back with Buzz in Borteen.

She was also bursting with curiosity about who on earth Skye could be visiting.

* * *

After her aborted breakfast with Buzz and her mother and the brief conversation with Adam that morning, Skye had hurried to the bus stop. The last thing she needed was for Buzz or her mother to spot her leaving and to stop her going.

She had very mixed feelings. Adam had definitely looked disappointed that she was going away with her backpack hoisted on her shoulders. But then, he had no idea about her predicament. She'd been so stupid. So classically, timelessly stupid.

At that moment, she'd felt the life inside of her stirring, as the baby kicked or turned in her womb.

History repeating itself perhaps? But she still didn't completely understand why her mother had run away back then. Had she even discussed things with Buzz?

Having seen both of her parents in the same place for the last few days, she was even more baffled about why they weren't still together. They seemed perfect for each other and both of them looked at the other with what she could only describe as adoration in their eyes. It was a strange situation, and she knew there must be much more to their story and the brief affair with Buzz's brother Ed than she yet knew.

Could she judge, when she had given in to the urge to run away too, when she'd left Dublin, wondering and hoping that her father would possibly support her through her pregnancy? She should have guessed that her mother would follow her to Borteen.

One of her ideas had been to have the baby in England, then to get it adopted before returning to her life in Dublin to retake her exams without her mother being any the wiser. She could see now that this plan would never have worked.

She also felt very lucky that Buzz had been willing to accept her and had taken her under his wing, until they had dropped the Ed bombshell. She could only assume that Buzz truly hadn't known about it when Skye had first met him. But despite everything there was something she needed to do before she decided whether to have her baby in England or to return to Dublin with her mother, and she couldn't put it off any longer. The awful revelations at breakfast had just given her the excuse to precipitate her mission. Besides anything else, she needed time to think things through.

By the time she got to the railway station in Sowden after the jolting bus ride across Pink Moor, Skye could feel sweat running down her back. Why was she so hot? The people around her seemed to be bundled up in coats and scarves, whereas she had taken off as much as was decently possible.

When she'd bought her ticket and made her way to the right platform, a quick glance at the little mirror from her bag confirmed she was bright red. She began to feel very odd and flustered.

'Are you all right, my dear?' An elderly lady, who for some reason looked vaguely familiar, was peering strangely at her as she leaned back against the station wall for support.

'I . . . very kind of you to ask . . . I'm not really sure. I feel very hot and a little sick, but then I'm pregnant.'

'Well, I don't like the look of you at all, dearie. Have you far to go? Maybe you should sit down?' The woman's voice became squeakier and higher pitched.

'I'm going to . . . Birmingham. Thank you for asking about me.'

Skye moved further down the platform. The words of the train announcements began to swirl around her dizzy head and she was suddenly lying on the ice-cold platform, awkwardly positioned because of her backpack.

* * *

Skye lay back and winced at the coolness of the gel the nurse squeezed onto her stomach. Her heart rate accelerated. Was the baby okay? What if she'd made all of this effort to come to Borteen and she lost the baby anyway?

Lord knew she'd denied initially that she could be pregnant — after all, her monthlies had never been regular monthlies. Then, when she could no longer pretend that something wasn't going on, she'd prayed it wasn't true. And when she'd finally taken the pregnancy test, or rather tests, she hadn't believed the result.

All that was before she'd felt the baby move for the first time, before she'd realized that inside of her was a life as precious and unique as it could be. Even if ultimately she didn't think she could keep the child, she would do her best to make sure it was safe. Tears oozed out of her closed eyes. She couldn't bring herself to look at the screen — just in case.

The nurse put a hand on her arm. 'Baby's fine. Nice strong heartbeat.'

Skye opened her eyes. The image on the screen was most definitely a baby. And inside of her? It seemed incredible and unbelievable. The heartbeat was evident as a fluttering on the screen. She felt a grin forming involuntarily on her face.

The nurse smiled back. 'Do you know yet if your baby is a girl or a boy?'

'No. I'm afraid I haven't been to any check-up appointments yet.'

'Now, you must make sure that you register with a maternity unit. Please promise me?'

Skye nodded sheepishly.

'Do you want to know?'

'No . . . erm . . . yes.'

'Are you absolutely sure? You can't unknow the information, remember. But some mothers find it easier to relate to baby, to bond even before it arrives, if they know whether to think pink or blue, so to speak, although I know that's considered terribly old-fashioned these days.'

Skye wiped her tears from her face with the back of her hand. 'Yes, please. I'd like to know. It's just . . .' She shuddered. 'I was so scared that there might be a problem with my baby as I was feeling so weird.'

'A very common worry for pregnant mums. I'm pretty sure you've just picked up a virus and that's why you've been feeling awful. You and baby will be fine after a rest and some fluids. We'll keep you here overnight at least to make sure. Is there anyone you want us to call for you?'

'No, thank you. I have my mobile with me.' Skye had no intention of calling anyone.

'Have you been eating properly lately?'

'Not really, I'm afraid. I've had a lot on my mind.'

'Well, now is the time to make sure that you pay attention to your diet. You need to keep healthy and strong for your daughter.'

'Daughter?' Skye experienced a strange unfamiliar sensation in her chest.

The nurse nodded. 'You have a little girl on the way.'

Skye craned her neck to look at the screen, trying to see the baby's shape, her facial features.

'You can have a photograph. I'll print it in a moment.'

'Really?' A rush of protective feelings filled her heart, but she also had some doubts. Could she love her baby if she looked like her father . . . looked like Declan? But then she knew that this baby was hers . . . her daughter.

The nurse handed her a wad of tissues. 'Happy tears, I hope?'

Skye nodded, not trusting herself to speak, as she mopped at her face.

'It's a very emotional time and your hormones will be all over the place.' She handed Skye a printed photograph of the screen and Skye stared at it for a very long time, before clasping it to her chest. She now knew for sure that there was no way she could ever consider giving up her baby.

CHAPTER SIX

'I want to do a labyrinth on the beach today.'

'Why today? We still don't know where Skye is. I still think I need to try to find her, despite her asking me to give her space.' Wynn had appeared at Crazy Crystals early that morning with desperation in her voice and a disapproving look on her face. Deep rings were etched beneath her eyes due to lack of sleep.

'I know, but she left you the note and, reading between the lines, I think she was asking you to trust her. She did say she would be coming back, so I suppose we have to wait. She'll be in touch if she needs us, I'm sure. I'd like to get back to a feeling of calm so that I can tap into my intuitions about Skye. I'm no use to her or us in this state. The labyrinth will help to calm me and I raise a fair amount of money for my homeless charity each time too — I can't let them down. And it might do you good to walk the path with me.'

Wynn shrugged. 'I'm really not in the mood. I can't rest until I hear from Skye; she didn't answer my texts. She's even switched off the tracker on her phone this time.'

'Trust, Wynn. In a way, the labyrinth might help.'

Tears appeared in Wynn's eyes. She turned away. 'Sorry, it's just so hard.'

'I know, but it's been less than twenty-four hours, remember.'

'Feels like a lifetime. I wish we knew where she's gone and who she wanted to see so urgently.'

Her tears began to flow again and she looked so miserable that he pulled her against him for a supportive hug.

'Come on, let's lay out the labyrinth together. It might help. At the very least we can collect a little for charity while we're waiting for news.'

'Oh, all right. Come on then. Show me how to do it. I'll wash my face before we go.'

Buzz was concerned about Skye too, especially as she'd left so soon after they'd told her he might not be her father, but he was trying to stay calm for Wynn's sake.

Losing himself in the familiar ritual, first he drew the pattern of lines on the sand, then he rhythmically dug small banks around the lines with his ancient shovel, before erasing the original drawing with his bare feet. Wynn was pacing up and down and he just had to ignore her frantic energy and get on with what he was trying to achieve without getting distracted by her mood.

He positioned his usual 'Walk the Labyrinth' sign together with his pink heart-shaped bucket and prepared to collect donations with a silent plea to the universe for Skye's safety and well-being.

* * *

Wynn watched Buzz as he worked intently in what had obviously become a ritual for him. She politely asked questions about when he started to do this, about how he became involved with the homeless charity he'd mentioned.

As he began to welcome people wanting to walk the sand labyrinth, she returned to her own dilemma — why had she left in the first place all that time ago? After all, she still had feelings for Buzz, they had never gone away. But she still believed that her deception, however brief, even if it was only one single encounter with Ed, would have damaged her in time, shattered her equilibrium, eventually wormed its way between Buzz and herself and destroyed their marriage.

In reality, it hadn't been any better leaving, but at least she had spared Buzz her anguish and circular thoughts. He would undoubtedly have wondered what was going on. At least she had been relieved of lying to Buzz every day, even if she was still left with her constant tortuous thoughts and heartbreaking regrets.

The great pity was that she could still see exactly why she had been attracted to Buzz in the first place — was still drawn to him now. His presence, his way of holding himself and speaking to others whatever their level of education or status in life as if they were equally important. She now bit her lip as she watched the intent look he had on his face as he laid out the labyrinth. She had never been far from tears since she had returned to Borteen. The regrets were multiplying. What a waste of loving feelings, what a waste of potentially happy shared years.

And had she now lost Skye as well? She checked her phone for the millionth time that day, but no messages had appeared. Had the truth fractured her relationship with her daughter, maybe completely? She clung to the fact that Skye had still put a kiss after her name on the brief handwritten note.

Wynn had been able to ignore the past, almost, when Skye was a child, but now she was an adult and not satisfied by platitudes and distractions. Wynn had known what she had done would come out eventually, but she prayed that her traumatized daughter was safe.

* * *

When he was finally satisfied with the labyrinth, Buzz looked around to see where Wynn was. She hadn't helped him with its construction in the end. He had a momentary panic that she'd gone, but then he saw her sitting on the bottom of the beach steps, staring out to sea with a blank look on her face, her hands grasping the fabric of her skirt in a distracted way. He walked towards her and plastered a wide smile on his face that he didn't really feel.

'Right, come on, you. Time to walk this labyrinth and meditate. Refresh your troubled soul a little.'

'Buzz, I thought you were clairvoyant. Why haven't you had any inner knowing, any visions about where Skye has gone?'

It was the question he'd been asking himself too, ever since his daughter had left. But then was she actually his daughter? Did that matter anyway? He cared about Skye full stop.

'I think I'm maybe too close to this situation to have any clear thoughts, too emotional . . .'

She stood up and took his hand. 'To the labyrinth!'

They smiled at each other and walked together hand in hand into the path he had created on the sand.

Despite their worries about Skye, they walked slowly and deliberately around the path, arriving at the start again to be met by five bewildered-looking children, who must have been watching the two engrossed adults. Each child was holding a pound coin in their sandy hands.

Wynn and he made a good team. It reminded Buzz all too painfully of what they had been like in the good old days. A unit. A pair of like-minded souls who communicated seemingly telepathically. The bond between them, which he'd believed unbreakable. Until . . . she went.

The tide was coming in. Desolation crept over Buzz, even though the pink donations bucket had a healthy number of pound coins in it. He'd somehow hoped Skye would have contacted her mother during the morning, but the distraction of the labyrinth was almost over.

He could see that Wynn was talking to an older, grey-haired lady near the steps up to the promenade. Buzz watched as her face suddenly lit up and she beckoned Buzz over. He almost fell over his feet as he rushed towards the pair.

'This is Liz, we've talked a couple of times at breakfast at the guesthouse. She saw Skye yesterday at Sowden station.'

'Really?'

The older lady smiled at him. 'I went to Sowden railway station to wave off my niece, she's been staying in Borteen with me for a few days.'

Impatience gurgled up inside Buzz. 'But you say you think you saw Skye? At Sowden railway station?'

'Yes, it was definitely your daughter. I've seen her with you at the guesthouse. She wasn't feeling too well at the station, which is why I spoke to her to ask if I could help. She told me about her baby. You must be so thrilled to be expecting a grandchild.'

Wynn turned to Buzz, shock written all over her face. 'Pregnant?' They both voiced the question in unison.

Liz looked confused. 'I'm sorry, you didn't know?'

'I expect she was going to surprise us soon,' stuttered Wynn.

Buzz tried to focus. 'Where exactly were you when you saw Skye?'

'The station platform in Sowden. She said she was going to Birmingham.'

'Birmingham?' Again a joint exclamation.

'Sorry, Liz, we had a bit of a misunderstanding with Skye, but I'm sure your information will help us to sort it out.'

Buzz thanked the woman and Wynn gave her a brief hug.

Wynn and Buzz looked at each other when Liz had gone.

'Pregnant,' said Wynn.

'Birmingham,' said Buzz.

Buzz watched as Wynn fired off another text message to Skye asking her to get in touch.

He glanced quickly over the sea wall. At least the tide had washed away the labyrinth so there was little clearing up to do.

The couple walked back from the beach in silence for a while, both lost in their own thoughts. Wynn carried the signs and donations bucket, Buzz the spade. He felt almost uncomfortable walking next to Wynn, just because it was so comfortable, so natural. Had she made the right decision all those years ago? Had all of the years of pain and wondering really happened? Walking up the high street, he could almost let himself imagine that it had only been a nightmare and hadn't been his solo-living reality at all.

'At least we know that she had a plan, that she wasn't forced to go anywhere with anyone.' Wynn's quiet tones broke into his thoughts.

'But pregnant?'

'Even though I hate the thought of it, I suppose that makes sense of the running away . . . but I've been wracking my brains as to who could possibly be the father.'

'I hope she's okay. That lady said she wasn't feeling well.'

'She could just have been overwhelmed by the stress of everything.'

'Why Birmingham? Does she know someone there? Maybe someone at one of the universities? The father of her baby perhaps?'

'I've no idea. It's made me realize how out of touch I've become with her friendship groups.'

Buzz pulled Wynn to a stop. 'Now, don't you go feeling guilty. You couldn't have known that this would happen, couldn't have second-guessed what Skye would do.'

Wynn turned her face into his shoulder for a moment, then pulled away and shook herself, squaring her shoulders. 'Right, that's the self-pity done. Let's find her.'

* * *

Buzz looked suddenly doubtful. 'Birmingham is a huge place. Can you maybe try to get in touch with some of her friends to see if they know anything?'

'I'll try, as I said I'm not even sure who she's friends with anymore.' Wynn knew he was watching her closely as she made a few notes on the back of a discarded envelope on the kitchen worksurface. Then, she scrolled desperately and unhopefully through her phone contacts. She typed some messages and pressed send.

Buzz was still watching her. Sitting here, it was a mystery why she'd ever left. He was a good man. They would have remained together had she not been tempted elsewhere for one brief stupid moment — a couple of drinks, a joint of weed and the high sex drive of her younger self had a lot to answer for. The pain in her chest became intense all of a sudden.

She had an overwhelming need to draw. She asked Buzz if she could use the felt tip and marker pens in the jar by the toaster. He nodded and soundlessly gave her a pad of paper from the bookcase. Was she the same back when they lived together before? Either that or he could read her mind. She wouldn't put it past him, but decided it was the former.

Wynn had a strong connection to Celtic art and soon had an outline of a pregnant woman on the page — her dress decorated with Celtic patterns and a border of interlocking shapes — the baby outlined in her distended stomach.

Buzz was watching her again. 'Are you hoping your image will manifest Skye?'

'I felt an irresistible urge to draw the picture, so I hope so.'

She put down the pen she was holding and checked the messages on her phone — no replies, nothing at all.

Buzz touched her hand so that she looked directly at him. 'If I can be serious for a moment, we need to decide a clear plan of action. There's no point heading to Birmingham if we have no idea where she was intending to go. It would be pointless. It's a big city with lots of suburbs. Can you send another message to Skye's mobile? Maybe if she realizes that we know she's in Birmingham and that we understand she had a reason to go there, she'll reply.'

'I'm going to have to think very carefully about the wording of the message — can't exactly blurt out that I know she's expecting our first grandchild, can I?'

CHAPTER SEVEN

Birmingham was a huge city. Compared to Borteen, even Dublin, it was enormous and unknown. Skye began to question the sanity of her actions when she finally arrived in the centre. She could tell straight away that she had been monumentally stupid. The streets outside of the station were a seething mass of humanity — all nationalities, ages and accents. How on earth could she find Declan here? Her head began to swim again, despite her rest in the hospital overnight.

She walked blindly away from the station, wondering which way to go. She followed the signs pointing towards a museum and art gallery. At least there should be somewhere to sit, toilets and maybe a café.

She'd been ignoring her mother's messages. The number of them were increasing and she began to long for her mother's reassuring voice. But how to admit where she was and why? It seemed impossible. She'd let her mum down and got into a mess.

Just then her phone screen lit up with an incoming call — her mum.

Skye sighed, time to face up to things. She pushed to accept the call.

'Skye?' Wynn's voice was excited, emotional, but wary.

'Mum? I'm so sorry, Mum.'

'Where are you, love? We're really worried. Are you okay?'

'I'm fine, miserable but fine. I'm sitting in an art gallery café in Birmingham right now and I think I've been very silly. I'm lost and a bit scared, but yes, I'm okay really. You'd love the pictures in this gallery and the Staffordshire Hoard exhibition.'

'Maybe we can visit again one day. Do you want us to come and get you?'

Skye could hear Buzz talking in the background.

'If she's feeling up to it, it would probably be much quicker for her to come back by train, we could meet her at Sowden railway station.'

'Did you hear that, love?'

'Yes, and I know it makes sense, I really wanted to try to find Declan first.'

'Declan?' Wynn glanced meaningfully at Buzz.

'A friend . . .'

'Can't you just ring him?'

'We lost touch — I think he's maybe blocked me, or else changed his number.'

'There's always social media?'

Skye went quiet for a moment. 'We've lost touch in lots of ways . . .'

'Look, Skye. Come back to Borteen and I promise we'll all try to find this friend of yours together.'

'But I thought you were going back to Dublin?'

'I'll stay here a while longer.'

'You'd stay in England to help me? Really?'

'Yes, love. Of course I will if it's important to you. Just don't go disappearing on me like that ever again.'

'Okay, Mum, I promise I won't. I'm going to get something to eat because I'm feeling a bit light-headed, and then I'll head back to the station. I promise I'll let you know my arrival time by text.'

'Skye? You do know I love you whatever, don't you? Please be safe.'

'Yes, Mum. I love you too. And I'll be careful, promise.'

As the call ended, Skye cried tears of relief. It was time to head back to Borteen.

She couldn't help but scan the crowds as she retraced her steps and made her way back to the station. She was convinced that she saw Declan every few yards. She even called his name aloud one time. But it was hopeless. She could see that now. Why had she ever imagined anything else?

Declan wouldn't want to know her again anyway. He didn't care about Skye at all, she was sure she'd just been a notch on his bedpost, one of his conquests. She'd known that really, but still she had a tiny ridiculous hope.

They'd argued. He'd walked away. The last time she'd seen him, he'd been wrapped around another girl — a taller, blonde girl with curvy hips. And then she'd found out she was expecting his child.

She began to cry as she walked along the never-ending pavement past the bustling shops. Her hormones were working overtime today and she felt pathetic. How had it come to this? Right now all she wanted was a big hug from her mum. Guilt crowded in that she'd worried Wynn and Buzz unnecessarily, but then they had dropped the whole *we don't know who your father is* thing on her.

She took a pause from battling against the flow of jostling people, leaning her forehead against a cool shop window of a rather interesting vintage jewellery shop and that was when she experienced it — her baby moved inside of her. It was just a fluttering feeling but unmistakably in her womb. She jolted upright and put her hands on her stomach. The baby moved again.

Her tears came more freely now. 'You and me, little one.' This was it. This was real. No more childish ridiculousness. She had to 'man' — no, 'woman' up. There was more at stake here than her feelings. She mopped at her tears with her coat sleeves, adjusted the tie in her hair and hitched up her backpack.

She would return to Borteen, confess all to her mother . . . and get on with the business of growing a baby, of being a single mother. Declan be damned. She didn't need him.

CHAPTER EIGHT

The forlorn figure of Skye stepped off the train and launched herself into Wynn's arms. She looked exhausted. Wynn clung on tightly but released her hold a little when she remembered the baby — the baby she wasn't yet supposed to know about.

Skye let Buzz take her backpack and the three of them made their way back to Buzz's car. It wasn't lost on Wynn that to onlookers they would just look like normal parents meeting their daughter from the train. No one would see the maelstrom of emotions, tensions and unknowns inside each of them.

'Let's get you back to the guesthouse and into a hot shower.'

For once, Skye didn't argue. Wynn felt intensely maternal and protective. Skye didn't normally allow her to play mother these days. She'd been an independent soul seemingly ever since she could toddle.

Buzz drove steadily towards Borteen. He dropped them at the Rose Court guesthouse and made Wynn promise to keep in touch to let him know how Skye was faring after her adventure.

Skye was biddable until she'd showered and lay snuggled up in bed. She hadn't even argued about being moved into her mother's twin room at the guesthouse. Wynn smoothed damp hair back from her daughter's forehead.

'I'm pregnant, Mum.' Skye pulled a strange expression and closed her eyes.

'I know.'

Her daughter's eyes opened wide. 'How do you know?' A flash of alarm sparked across Skye's face.

'The lady who tried to help you on the railway platform the other day, Liz, was staying here at the guesthouse. She didn't think you'd recognized her, and she told us you'd said you were pregnant.'

'Ah.' She fell silent for a moment. 'I'm sorry I didn't tell you before.'

'I wish that you'd been able to confide in me, but I can understand why you didn't.'

'Yes, I was rather scared of your reaction. I knew you'd be disappointed in me.'

'Especially as I don't feel old enough to be a grandma.' Wynn winked.

Skye laughed.

The fact was that her daughter was pregnant and mother and daughter would need to deal with the fallout from that now. There was no choice really.

'It maybe isn't the path I would have chosen for you, but I will admit to being rather excited now I've got used to the idea.'

'You'll be great with your granddaughter.' Skye smiled.

It took a few seconds for Wynn to register what Skye had said and then she squealed and did a lap of the room. Skye sat up in bed laughing and Wynn returned to squeeze her gently.

'She heard you scream,' said Skye, and guided her mother's hand to her stomach. 'Can you feel her?'

Wynn sensed the small vibration and a tear of joy ran down her cheek as she realized how precious this little girl was going to be. She was so protective of this new life already and knew that she would do anything for Skye's child.

'I wish I knew that Buzz was actually my dad. He feels like he is already and I think he'd like being a grandad.'

'There is a fifty percent chance.'

'Can I be the one to tell Buzz it's a girl?' Skye's face was serious again.

'Now? On the phone?'

'I think I'd like to tell him face to face tomorrow. If you don't mind?'

Wynn was disappointed. 'The only thing is, I promised to give Buzz an update this evening. I'm not sure I can keep something so momentous from him, if I'm honest.'

Skye sat up and swung her legs over the edge of the bed. 'Let's ring him together then.'

In the end, they video-called Buzz. He looked a little bit bewildered to begin with as neither Wynn nor Skye were able to contain their excitement long enough to speak coherently. At the end of the call, his grin was just as wide as theirs.

'That was the right decision, Mum. Thank you.'

'I think Buzz is as thrilled as we are.' She knew that Buzz would be wondering if the baby was his grandchild or his great niece, but she had a feeling he would have a role in the baby's life regardless.

Skye got back into bed. Wynn noticed that she was now not trying to hide her baby bump as she must have been before. As she pulled the duvet up around her shoulders she asked Wynn a question. 'Mum, why did you ever leave Buzz?'

Wynn felt as if a chasm had opened up at her feet. They'd discussed this before, of course, but somehow in Dublin, with no Buzz close by, it had seemed better to give glib responses to satisfy a girl who'd not met her potential father. Wynn crossed her fingers behind her back hoping Buzz was indeed Skye's dad. Buzz was now known to Skye, he was real and someone she so obviously liked. Wynn's usual responses were totally inadequate.

'Please remember I was younger. Things seem different when you're younger — you should know that — sharper somehow. The edges get worn off your principles and ideals the older you get and things you got so worked up about in the past seem somehow less significant.'

'It's only that seeing you two together, you seem like a great couple — like you belong together.'

Wynn found it difficult to breathe for a moment. 'Maybe we do. I think with the benefit of that wonderful thing called hindsight, I made a huge misjudgement. Ed and I were a complete mistake, a fumble that developed into something it shouldn't have, but I'd had a drink and . . . well, it happened. I'm not proud. I think now I should have told Buzz and hoped that he could forgive me, but I couldn't face the pain I knew he would feel.'

'Does Ed know about me?'

'No! No, and I think I'd rather keep it that way for now if we can. I know it's a lot to ask but let's see if we can prove Buzz is your dad and take it from there.'

Wynn felt sick at the thought of actually knowing rather than imagining, but it would need to be tackled now that Skye wanted to know, and who could blame her? This couldn't be about Wynn herself anymore, she'd run away for far too long.

'Buzz is a good man and he's had a very lonely life thanks to me. I've had a lonely life too, thanks to my misguided actions and decisions, but at least I had you. He was on his own.'

Skye's expression changed. 'So, do you think I should continue trying to find the father of my baby?'

'Is that what you were trying to do in Birmingham, love?' Wynn had guessed that it was, but wanted to hear what Skye would say.

'Yes, but like a fool, I didn't imagine that Birmingham would be like that — that big. I somehow thought I'd find him easily.'

'And then what? What are you hoping for if you find him?'

'The fairy tale, I guess — that he'll scoop me up in his arms, tell me everything's okay and that he wants both of us, but I know that's delusional. I suppose I just need him to know that he's fathered a child.'

'How did you part in Dublin?'

'I was rather grumpy that he was planning to go to university in England. We argued. He walked away and the next time I saw him he was kissing someone else. I couldn't believe we'd broken up. I was obsessed by him, couldn't think of anything else when we were together. It's why I didn't really bother with studying — too busy mooning over and trying to please Declan. I never even imagined that we'd made a baby.'

'But before the argument, did you get on well with him?'

'Yes. Well . . . mostly. I thought to begin with that he was "the one".'

'And now?'

'I think, if I'm totally honest, if I wasn't carrying his child I would hardly have thought about him again. He hurt me too much. And besides, I didn't much like his temper.'

'Then you still have a dilemma.'

CHAPTER NINE

Skye noticed the bobble hat first, then long bare legs. Adam had obviously been running on the sand and stopped for a coffee at the beach café. She busied herself with the early morning jobs — replenishing the coffee beans, putting out the sandwiches freshly made by Christine, getting crockery and cutlery out of the dishwasher, wiping down the surfaces. Her eyes kept straying back to Adam. His phone rang and he answered the call with deep hushed tones. She couldn't tell what he was saying — it would have been rude to listen anyway — but his voice, even quietly spoken, did something strange to her insides.

Eventually she was left with the job of wiping the tables and tidying the chairs, so she had to venture out from behind the counter.

'Skye, you're back!' Adam almost dropped his phone.

She smiled broadly at him, delighted at his reaction to seeing her. 'What can I get for you on this bright, cold morning?'

'An Americano and a croissant, please. Are you okay? I know your parents have been worried sick, frantic to find you.'

'I'm back. I wasn't away long. Feeling rather stupid, but that seems to be normal for me at the moment.'

'Oh dear. Have you time to join me for a drink, maybe tell me what you've been up to and why you think that?'

Skye wasn't ready to share that much, so she made an excuse about working and went to get his breakfast. His delight at her return made her feel warm and happy. She wasn't ready to admit her pregnancy and the possible confusion about her own parentage, not until she'd got her own head around it anyway.

* * *

What was it about this girl? Adam didn't understand his reactions. She was so unlike any girl he'd ever shown an interest in before, and maybe that was his answer. Or maybe he was trying to distract himself from the real reason he'd come north to Borteen. His mother had just called to check up on him.

Adam relished his early morning routine in the seaside town. It was his most relaxed time of day. It gave him purpose to get up and put on his running kit. The beach at Borteen was great for runners, being flat and smooth. He'd even begun to recognize some of the other people who ran regularly and got some cheery waves this morning, which he'd returned with a smile.

He was disappointed that Skye couldn't spare the time to have a chat with him. He wondered whether to try to arrange a meet-up for later in the day — not a date, of course, only a meet-up — but he lost his nerve when a lad came in and began to shamelessly flirt with her over the Danish pastries. Adam went back to the guesthouse for a shower a little deflated.

* * *

After her early morning shift at the café, Skye went to see Buzz at the crystal shop. She sat on one of the high stools behind the counter. Buzz was dusting as usual. She'd begun to get to know him a little more, especially as he was now less shy with her than when they'd first met.

As she'd left the guesthouse, Wynn had been talking animatedly on her phone to the lady who was managing her shop while she was in England.

'You know it is uncanny how similar this shop is to Mum's in Dublin,' Skye remarked to Buzz. 'Almost an exact copy.'

'Well, we did set Crazy Crystals up together originally, so I expect she just followed the same pattern when she arrived in Dublin, especially as most of the ideas we used were hers in the first place.'

Buzz looked terribly sad whenever he talked about the old days with Wynn. He and Skye had yet to develop the sort of bond that allowed her to probe his relationship with her mother. It seemed too personal for such an early stage of their own fledgling connection.

The baby moved at that moment and she forgot her train of thought as she focussed on the small flutterings inside of her. She placed her hands protectively over her stomach. Her daughter was awake and probably listening to the sound of their voices.

The door chime sounded and Skye jumped a little at the noise. A youngish thin woman came into the shop and nodded at Buzz as if she knew him and had been in the shop before. Buzz stopped dusting and came to sit next to Skye behind the counter to allow the woman full access to the sales stock on the shop floor.

The woman picked up a colourful pair of ethnic print trousers in rainbow colours. 'Ooh, I love the colours of these trousers so much, but they're much too long and the waist is too big for me. Do you possibly have them in another size?' She held up her hand with her fingers crossed.

'Sorry, that's the last pair. I don't think I can get that style anymore, unfortunately,' said Buzz frowning.

Skye stood up. 'If you like them that much, I'm sure I could alter them to fit you.'

'Really?' The woman looked surprised, as if she had only just noticed Skye was there at all.

Skye went around the counter. She took the trousers from the woman, who said her name was Connie, and after asking permission, she held them up against her. 'A couple of inches off the bottom and a few inches out of the waist and they'd be perfect on you.'

'Would it take you long to alter them?' asked Connie.

'Not long at all, but as I've only recently come to Borteen, I'd need to find a sewing machine I could use.'

Buzz joined them in front of the counter with a big smile on his face. 'Don't worry about that, I have a sewing machine upstairs in the flat.'

Connie took the trousers over to look at them in the light from the window. 'I do really love them. If you're sure you can change them to fit me, I'll buy them right now.'

Buzz spoke again. 'How about we say that if you're not completely happy when they're done, I'll give you your money back?'

'Deal.'

She bought the trousers and said she would pop back in two days to try them on. 'I'm excited already,' said Connie as she left the shop and the trousers on the counter.

Buzz turned to Skye after the door had closed behind her. 'I've been debating something with myself today and this conversation has made up my mind. If you're set on staying in Borteen for a while, why don't you move into my spare room rather than staying at the guesthouse?'

'Really? You'd let me do that? You'd like me to do that, even? Despite us not knowing for sure about us?'

Buzz's smile said it all. 'Come and have a look at the room first. Then you can make up your mind. And I like you a lot regardless of what we eventually find out about our relationship, so there.'

Skye put her hand on his arm and a spark of excitement ignited inside of her. Buzz turned the shop sign to 'Closed' and locked the door. He led Skye through the heavy velvet curtain at the back of the shop and up a short flight of steep stairs.

She was curious to see more of Buzz's home. The building was long and thin. The lounge was over the shop area and its windows looked out onto the high street, opposite a shop Skye intended to visit called Polka Dot Paradise. The sign said it sold vintage clothing. Behind the lounge and the stairwell was a kitchen above the shop storeroom, beyond that was a bathroom and Buzz's bedroom. Another flight of stairs led to an attic room with sloping ceilings. There was a bed, but it had been set up mainly as a workroom, with a couple of bodhran drums hung on the wall, an easel with a half-finished painting of a tree and a wooden desk with an old-fashioned treadle sewing machine on it.

Skye's eyes stood out on stalks. Admittedly everything was old — the furniture, the wallpaper, the curtains — but the room had a homely feeling and smelled of sage smudge sticks just like her mother used back in Dublin.

'If you'd like to stay with me for a while, this can be your room,' said Buzz.

Skye was speechless. She flung her arms around Buzz's neck, hung on and sobbed against his chest.

'Hey! I hope those are happy tears?' Buzz sounded choked with emotion himself as he patted her shoulder.

'Most definitely and yes, please, I would love to stay here, if you're willing to put me up, and put up with me. Does the sewing machine actually work?'

'It might be a little dusty. I should have covered it up really, but with its enamelled pattern, it's nice to look at. It worked last time I used it to shorten my own trousers.'

Skye went over and ran her fingers over the beautiful patterns on the side of the old sewing machine. She turned to Buzz and smiled. All was right with her world.

'Move in whenever you like. Rearrange the room however you like. I'll take my drums and art stuff out of your way, because I use those nearly every day.' He moved to take the decorated drums from the wall and collected the beaters from the table.

'Thank you. This means so much.'

'You're more than welcome. I think it'll be exciting to share the house with you and get to know you better. After all, we've missed out on quite a few years.'

Skye's face changed. 'If it's okay with you, for now it might be best if I just use the sewing machine to alter Connie's trousers. I think I'll have to find the right moment to tell my mother that I'm moving in here with you, especially now she knows about my baby. She's had a lot to deal with concerning me, so I don't want to drop this on her suddenly. Is that okay? I'm sorry if you wanted me to move in today. I really don't want to upset you either.'

'You are wise beyond your years, dear girl. I understand completely — you want to be sensitive to your mother's feelings. Take your time and if it's meant to be, you can bring your things over here when you're ready. The room is yours if you'd like it and for however long you want it.'

Skye moved in to give Buzz another brief hug. It still felt strange, but she knew implicitly that he was completely on her side. Though she still didn't know him very well and even his incensey smell took her by surprise when she got up close to him. She guessed it must be as odd for him, and neither of them knew if they were just developing a friendship or a father–daughter relationship. The possibility of a DNA test seemed to hang in the air, but Skye didn't want to spoil the happy moment by mentioning it.

They went back down to the shop and Buzz sorted out some cleaning cloths and polish for Skye to use from the storeroom.

Excitement bubbled up inside her. It appeared that volunteering to alter a pair of trousers might have heralded a new start for her. Could she really support herself working at the beach café and doing clothing alterations? She rather believed that she could, and her mother always said that if you imagined something clearly enough, you could make it happen for real.

Going back up the stairs alone, at first it was odd to be in the attic room without Buzz, but it didn't take long to sink into the calm atmosphere of the unique space. She sat on the bed for a long moment while she pictured living there, trying to visualize a cot and a baby chair and lots of rainbow-coloured toys on the shelf. Then she looked out of the tiny window. There wasn't much of a view, only rooftops really and the promise of the sea to the one side. She took a deep breath. This felt right — for now anyway.

She began to clean the old sewing machine and explored the sewing box next to it, which seemed to contain all she would need for the time being. She'd ask Buzz about where to get more cotton and material in the nearby bigger town of Sowden.

When she'd cleaned the dust away, she used a piece of scrap cloth from the sewing box to experiment and get to know how the machine behaved when it was sewing. The tension was perfect; Buzz must have used it recently.

She went back down to the shop to retrieve Connie's trousers.

'Is it all right if I use things from the sewing box by the machine?'

'What's mine is yours,' said Buzz, one hand on his chest. 'Use what you need and I'll take you to Busy Pins in Sowden next week to get anything else you want.'

'Busy Pins?'

'It's the small sewing shop I like to patronize. You can get everything from the supermarket or Amazon these days, but being as I run a small shop, I know the importance of using local stores or else they just disappear.'

'Yes, Mum always says the same. It's important to build up a group of loyal customers to stand any chance of surviving in today's market conditions. All too easy to place an Amazon order.'

'When we've time, I'd like to tell you more about what I do here at Crazy Crystals too.'

'How did the shop end up with that name?'

'It was what your mother originally called it, when she thought my idea for the shop was a bit mad. It kind of stuck, even though the sign was originally supposed to say Second Amethyst.'

'Oh right. I think I like Crazy Crystals much better.'

'Me too. And it was as if I kept a small part of Wynn close to me. The name has had some sad associations for all of these years, but now we're finally talking again, I can smile again at the sign.'

'I look forward to helping you with the shop when I can.'

'I would really like you to be involved.'

As so often happened now, it appeared as if the baby had been listening to them talking, because when Buzz stopped speaking the flutterings inside of her intensified and she gasped.

'Baby moving?'

'Yes, she's getting stronger. Would you like to . . .' She pointed at her tummy, suddenly shy.

'Only if you're happy for me to put my hand on your stomach.'

She pushed her bump out towards Buzz and pulled her cardigan out of the way. The baby seemed to respond to Buzz's touch and Skye sensed an undeniable dart of warmth coming from his hand.

Buzz smiled. 'She likes the Reiki energy.'

'You practise Reiki too? Mum's assistant at the Dublin shop used to give treatments in the back room. I'm curious but don't know much about it.'

'Another thing we can discuss. Goodness, this baby is having a good kick.'

'I kind of get the impression that Iona is going to be a feisty free spirit. I think I'm going to have my hands full.'

'Is that the name you've chosen for your daughter? Iona?'

'I change my mind almost every day, the poor mite is going to be very confused. She's been Daisy, Willow, Rose and Iona so far.'

'That's not unusual. I believe it's difficult to name a child or indeed an animal until you've looked deeply into their eyes, their soul even, and then the right name becomes clear.'

'I won't worry about changing her name all the time then. I'll just try them out for size, so to speak. Names are so important, aren't they?'

'They definitely get linked to your identity. But you can always change them if you feel they don't suit you — I changed mine, remember.'

'Another tale for a cold winter's night by the fire. I must start keeping a list of things we need to discuss.' She laughed.

'I think you and I are going to muddle along together very nicely.'

'Me too.' This time when she hugged Buzz, it was heart-felt and she relaxed into his warmth for the first time. She sent up a fervent prayer that Buzz was her real father. She heard Buzz sigh and knew it was because he was happy and probably having similar thoughts too.

CHAPTER TEN

Skye held her breath and crossed her fingers behind her back while Connie Hutton was in the shop changing room trying on the trousers she had altered to fit her.

'They're absolutely perfect,' announced the delighted woman, giving a twirl. 'You are so clever. And to think I wouldn't have bought these lovely trousers because of the size. Do you do alterations normally?'

Skye glanced at Buzz and crossed her fingers even harder. 'I'm thinking of starting up my own business here in Borteen, doing clothing alterations and making clothes to order.'

She couldn't really believe that those words had come out of her mouth, but why not? She'd excelled at textile lessons at school in Ireland and had made lots of clothes for herself in the past. She had the skills to use and would need something to do to earn money that could fit around the needs of her baby when she arrived.

Connie told her that she was a therapist at a retreat centre called Lucerne Lodge just outside of Borteen and she promised to spread the word about Skye's new business and was also happy to have some business cards in her therapy room to give out to her clients as soon as Skye had had some printed.

When Connie left Crazy Crystals, having gladly paid the modest alteration fee Skye had requested, Buzz came over and put his hand on her shoulder. 'I'm proud of you. Where did you learn to sew like that? As far as I remember, Wynn's abilities stretch to sewing on buttons.' He laughed.

'I took to it at school. Then I experimented at home and made some clothes for myself and friends.'

'So, you enjoyed your studies?'

'You're trying to ask why I didn't do well in my exams?'

'Well, in the short while I've known you, I've found you to be bright and intelligent, so what Wynn told me didn't seem to make sense.'

'When I got together with Declan, I went off the rails, got sort of obsessed by him. I was in a phase of being annoyed with Mum too, so I never brought him home or anything. She thought I was going to the library, but I was hanging out with him. I switched off from studying, couldn't see the point anymore. Ironic, really, when he's ended up at university. Now, I can't believe I was so stupid to react like that over a boy.'

'Infatuation, love, they're strange but strong emotions.'

'Of course, I now realize I should have worked harder for myself and, if I'd known about her then, for my baby too, but I guess I've got to do things the hard way and study alongside working and bringing up a child.'

'I suppose the relationship happened at the wrong time, but it truly is never too late if you want something enough. You can always retake exams or study something completely different.'

'Do you know, when things settle down, I think I'd like that, but for now I can work in the café and discover if this sewing business has any legs.'

'We'll have to see if we can find more customers for you then. Maybe we can design a poster for the shop window and get those business cards printed too.'

* * *

As it was, neither Buzz nor Skye had to do much to get her new business off the ground. The very next day, Sorrel from Polka Dot Paradise, the vintage shop across the street, came over to the shop.

Skye and Wynn were talking to Buzz about the crystals on the shelves, when the bell on the shop door sounded and they all turned to look at the new arrival.

'I've just had a visit from Connie Hutton. She says your daughter alters clothes?' Sorrel addressed Buzz.

Wynn looked first at Skye and then at Buzz with a puzzled expression. 'What's this?'

Buzz ignored her and spoke directly to Sorrel. 'Have you some business to put Skye's way by any chance?'

'I most certainly have. That's if you're up for it, Skye?'

Skye couldn't look at her mother yet. 'What sort of thing did you have in mind?'

'I recently lost the lady who altered clothes to fit my customers and mended any damaged garments to make them suitable for sale. She's moved away. Would you be interested in taking over her jobs?'

'Most definitely. Shall I come over to your shop and talk about my rates and turnaround times?'

'Yes, could you possibly come now? It just so happens I have a pile of lovely things with tiny problems that need attention — mending, fraying, loose buttons, hems that have come down, that sort of thing.'

'Let's go,' said Skye, winking at Buzz and still pointedly ignoring her mother.

* * *

As soon as the shop door had closed behind Sorrel and Skye, Wynn pounced. Buzz had known full well that she would.

'What's going on?'

It was all Buzz could do not to laugh as Wynn had taken up her characteristic pose of hands on hips when she was challenging something.

'Hasn't Skye said anything to you yet?'

'No!'

Wynn looked hurt and Buzz knew he had to defuse the situation quickly.

'Skye asked me to let her find the right time to tell you. I suppose she hasn't found that right time yet.'

'Well, you might as well tell me now.'

'Skye is going to stay with me for a while. We've discussed her moving into the attic room. She's already got the part-time job at the beach café and she's sort of fallen into a business mending and altering clothes. Maybe even making them from scratch eventually. She's going to use my mother's old sewing machine.'

Wynn let out a huge shuddering sigh. 'Thank goodness for that. Thank you, Buzz. It seems you've managed to pull her out of her terrible lethargy and got her fired up about something at last.'

'Now that has taken me by surprise. I never imagined you'd react like that to the news and I know Skye has been scared to mention it to you. I can't really take any credit. She seemed to come up with the idea all by herself. I just happened to be able to supply both the room for her to stay in and the sewing machine.'

'Obviously meant to be, but are you happy with this? Given we still don't know for sure that she's yours?'

Buzz nodded.

Wynn's face changed and he could see that she was battling not to betray her true emotions.

'What's the matter?'

'Nothing. Silly really. It just feels as if I've somehow lost my daughter.'

'We've not discussed anything long term. I guess if the business takes off, then she might want to stay here.' He paused and then added, 'You could stay here too . . .'

'Don't tempt me, Buzz. I still need time to think about this and I can't believe you would be so generous after what I've put you through.'

'I know you thought what you did was unforgivable, but having you here . . . well, it's made me realize how much we've missed.'

'It was easy to leave all those years ago, but it felt as if I could never come back, until Skye came here and I saw you again.'

'Absolutely no pressure, but do think about it, please. A lot of water has gone under the bridge and we're not getting any younger. We deserve some happiness.'

Wynn nodded and Buzz sensed it was time to change the subject. Best not press the issue.

'Has Skye discussed the future of the baby with you yet?' Buzz asked. 'Does she want to keep it, adopt it? Have it here, have it in Dublin?'

'She's still very touchy about the whole subject. It must feel a huge thing to make decisions about. It's daunting to contemplate that far into the future.'

'What about the father of her baby?'

'Some toerag who knocked her up and left her for someone else, by the sounds of it. I don't think I've ever met him. Declan.'

'She did say that she'd kept the two of you apart when you were going through a sticky patch. Does he even know about the baby?'

'I don't think so. He was long gone before she realized she was pregnant. Last heard of heading for Birmingham University.'

'Hence the Birmingham escapade?'

'Yes, exactly. But I don't think Skye knew how big the place was . . . is.'

'She's a lovely girl. Looks so much like you.'

'I'll take that as an inferred compliment.'

Before they could say any more, Skye came back into the shop smiling, with her eyes shining and a bag of clothes in her hand.

'My first jobs.' She looked at Wynn. 'Has Buzz told you about my idea for a business?'

'Yes, darling. It sounds wonderful. Perfect, even. Exactly what you need to fit around the baby when she arrives.'

'You're not mad at me?' Skye hid for a moment behind the bag of clothes.

'Why on earth would I be mad?'

'Because I didn't tell you I was thinking of staying in Borteen, moving in here with Buzz, starting a business?'

'I think it sounds like just the fresh start you need. It'll be excruciating to return to Dublin on my own and leave you here, but at least I'll know where you are and that you have Buzz to help you. And I can always come to visit.'

Skye flung her arms around her mother and hugged her tightly. 'Thanks a million, Mum. It means more than you can ever know to have your blessing.'

Buzz looked at the two women who meant so much to him and found that he had tears in his eyes — one would stay and the other would go.

CHAPTER ELEVEN

It seemed to Buzz almost as if Moira had taken up residence at Crazy Crystals. He reckoned she must have examined every crystal and every necklace in the shop twice over at least.

Moira was a widow. Her husband had been one of Buzz's best friends, the person he would put the world to rights with at the Ship Inn on Friday nights. He knew that Moira had always hoped he would take Frank's place after a suitable period of mourning, but unfortunately Buzz didn't fancy her at all. It would only ever have been a relationship of convenience, and Buzz wanted so much more.

The *more* he actually wanted was to feel the same way he'd felt when he was with Wynn, the thing he'd been missing all of these years. Poor Moira, she was trying so hard to attract his attention and had been doing what she could to capture his heart. He knew that, but it just wasn't working. There was no spark or magic between them, or at least Buzz didn't feel it from his side. They would only ever be friends.

The shop door chime sounded, and Buzz looked up from the figures he'd been intensely studying to avoid talking to Moira and saw Wynn coming into the shop. His face lit up with a smile. You couldn't really put these two women in the same category at all. Chalk and cheese.

Wynn glanced at Moira, scanned the rest of the shop and smiled back at Buzz. Just that simple smile tugged at his heartstrings in a way he didn't believe poor Moira ever could, no matter how long she lingered in his shop.

Moira came to the desk at that very moment, and he felt embarrassed even though he didn't believe she could see into his heart and mind. Nevertheless, his friend's widow looked at him quizzically, a pendant exactly like the one she'd bought on her last visit to the shop balanced on her palm.

'Moira, do you remember Wynn, my . . . wife?' He gestured unnecessarily towards Wynn. Then a thought struck him — was she truly still his wife? They'd never formalized their parting, after all. There had been no divorce, so, he realized with a jolt, she was still his spouse.

Moira stood open mouthed. Wynn's expression was unreadable.

Eventually, Moira replied, 'Yes, I think I remember, but it's been a while since I've seen her.'

Buzz reflected that the face Moira was pulling right now was one of the reasons why he'd never warmed to the woman. Looking as if she was chewing wasps was an understatement. He supposed he should be flattered that she even cared enough to show an interest. His ears extended on stalks, listening to see if Wynn would comment.

Wynn just smiled at Moira and said, 'Lovely to see you again.'

In a move that surprised him, Wynn came to join him behind the counter. She didn't hesitate as she rang up Moira's purchase on the till. 'Twenty-two pounds, please. Would you like it gift-wrapped?'

Buzz had a sudden urge to laugh. It was as if Wynn was firmly staking her claim and stating very clearly to Moira to keep her hands off. Was he imagining all that, or was it only wishful thinking?

Moira, who appeared to have been struck dumb, handed over a twenty and a ten-pound note and watched mesmerized as Wynn counted out the change into her palm. 'It's for me, so no need for gift-wrapping.'

Wynn handed her the necklace deftly wrapped anyway in a piece of rainbow-coloured tissue paper and Moira grunted something that might have been 'thank you' as she left the shop without a backward glance. The door closed behind her with a snap.

'Is she after you?' asked Wynn.

'Whatever gave you that idea?' Buzz shrugged, hoping the effort he was making to look innocent was working, even though the corners of his mouth were determined to move into a smile.

'You were never a good liar, Buzz.'

'She's been terribly lonely since Frank died.'

'Frank died? How sad. She will feel very alone. They must have been married for a long time.'

He still couldn't read Wynn's expression. He'd never really felt the need to do anything about the fact that they were still married. After all, he'd always hoped maybe she'd come back to him. But the months had stretched to years and she'd never returned . . . until now.

* * *

Wynn's reaction to Moira had surprised her. She'd actually experienced jealousy that Moira was trying so obviously to attract Buzz's attention. What right did she have to feel jealousy? After all, it was she who had left. Back here in Borteen, it was hard to ignore her feelings for Buzz, about Skye, Skye's baby and the decision she had made to leave. A decision she now recognized as precipitous, reckless and stupid.

With a sigh, she realized that she had inherited another trait from her mother — the inability to admit she'd made a mistake. She took a deep breath and tried to formulate an explanation for Buzz about what she'd been thinking, but somehow the words wouldn't come out. After a long pause, in which she was aware of Buzz looking at her expectantly, she managed to utter a few words. 'Buzz, I know this trip to Borteen wasn't planned, but it has forced me to confront things I've buried deep inside of me for a very long time.'

'Me too, Wynn.'

His face lit up and Wynn's courage deserted her. 'I think I'll go and check on Skye.'

'Wynn, don't go.'

'I'm wondering if it's too late for us, Buzz. It's been a long time. You don't really know this Wynn, only the Wynn I used to be.'

'Same here, I guess, you know the old me. But maybe we can get to know each other again.'

'Are you sure you would want to try?'

'Absolutely — that is, if you are?'

'I'd love to think we could, but I also think I need to give you space to consider, and I have to return to Ireland soon to sort my business affairs at least.'

'Come back and spend Christmas with us.'

All of her fears seemed to rear up right then. She could see Buzz and Skye devastated because Ed was Skye's father. She could see Buzz never being able to cope with the thought of her being with Ed. She could even see Buzz falling for Moira and asking her for a divorce. And as always when faced with complications, with unwanted or negative thoughts, her first instinct was to run away.

'Can I leave it that I promise to try?' With that, she opened the shop door, leaving the bell ringing with a brightness she didn't feel at all.

* * *

Skye knew she would have to go and get, or else make, new clothes — and soon. Her jeans, even with the zip left down and a belt keeping them up, were getting too tight. Her loose blouses weren't loose anymore. Her stomach had suddenly grown and there was no longer any chance of hiding the fact that she was pregnant, even if she still wanted to, which she didn't. It was time to embrace her new identity.

She'd woken that morning with a ferocious hunger. Her mother had already showered and gone out by the looks of it. They were still sharing the twin room at the guesthouse and there was a sort of unspoken agreement that they would do so until Wynn left for Ireland.

Skye washed and dressed quickly. She edged down the narrow staircase of the guesthouse, hoping she wasn't too late for breakfast. The dining room was deserted, but the usual morning tower of small cereal boxes and some natural yoghurt was still on the buffet table, so Skye greedily grabbed three packets of muesli. As she turned to look for bowls, Adam was grinning at her over the top of his cup from the corner of the room. She felt her face redden. 'Starving,' she mumbled, wondering why she was explaining herself.

'Join me?' he asked, pointing at the empty chair opposite to him.

It was the last thing she really wanted to do right now, but how could she refuse when they were the only two people in the dining room? So, she took a deep breath and deposited her boxes of cereal and the bowl on his table. She avoided eye contact while she decanted the three pitifully small boxes of muesli into her bowl and went back to the buffet table to fetch some yoghurt. The gurgling in her stomach was getting louder, as if her baby was crying for food, so she took a handful of dates too.

'Sorry, I didn't mean to force you to sit with me. You might have wanted to be alone to think or something.'

'No, no. Tell me something interesting to distract me while I eat.'

'Um . . . urm.' Adam looked perplexed. 'Amazing that when someone says something like that to you, your mind goes completely blank.'

'Maybe I could ask you some questions — if you don't mind?'

He nodded.

'Where do you come from?'

'Inner-city London, which is why I need to escape every now and again to the seaside.'

'I've never been to London.'

'Where do you come from in Ireland?' He sipped his coffee.

'A quiet suburb of Dublin.'

'But then, you're used to big cities.'

'Yes, but I find each one has its own unique feel.'

'Very true.'

He buttered a piece of toast and she wolfed down a huge mouthful of muesli. The strange butterfly feeling in her stomach as the baby moved was disconcerting sitting here opposite to Adam. The dark hairs on his tanned arms became a source of fascination for her so that she didn't have to meet his eyes.

'Well, if you ever fancy a look around London, I'm happy for you to use our spare room. It's basically a broom cupboard but you're always welcome to it.'

She smiled at him, wiping a blob of yoghurt off her chin with a serviette. 'That's a kind offer.'

'How long are you staying in England?'

'That's open to discussion. I'm not really sure, probably until after Christmas at least.'

It was nice of Adam to offer her accommodation in London, but Skye wasn't sure he'd want her to waddle around looking very pregnant, as she soon would. His neighbours would surely have a field day gossiping about him having her to stay.

Before she knew what was happening, two big fat tears had begun to run down her cheeks.

Adam's face registered alarm, his eyes wide and his eyebrows raised. 'Hey, what did I say?'

Skye buried her face in her napkin.

When she finally controlled her tears, Adam was sitting upright and still like a statue.

'Sorry,' she said, sheepishly.

'No problem, but please tell me it wasn't something I said.'

'Absolutely not.' She didn't want to voice the fact that she was pregnant, even though Adam could surely tell by her shape. He was probably too polite to comment.

'Do you want to talk about it?'

'Not right now, but thank you for the offer.'

He studied his toast. She'd lost her appetite for the bland-tasting muesli.

'I've been trying to get in touch with someone over here, but no luck so far.'

'Don't tell me — in Birmingham?'

'Of course, you know about my escapade.'

'Your parents were frantic and we met that morning, if you remember, when you were on your way out with your backpack?'

'Oh, yes. I know that I made them very unhappy.' She blushed. 'Tell me, how would you go about finding someone over here?'

'Social media first,' he replied.

'Tried that, no trace.'

'Could they maybe be using a nickname?'

'I've tried everything I could think of . . .'

'Do you know what they do for a living?'

'At university.' She was aware Adam must have guessed it was a man, but she couldn't quite bring herself to admit that to him.

'If he or she are good at sport and represent the uni, they might be in the newsletters. I doubt the university would give out information, data protection and all that, but they'd probably pass on a letter.'

'Good idea. Thank you.'

Adam's face suddenly contorted as if he'd got something stuck in his throat. His skin began to look a little green.

'Are you okay?' Skye asked.

'I'll be fine. Just need some air. I'll see you around.' He virtually bolted from his seat and out of the room, and Skye found herself going back over their previous conversation to try to decide what had upset him. She couldn't think of anything and was rather bewildered.

CHAPTER TWELVE

Adam scuttled back to his room after the conversation with Skye. He knew she would wonder what on earth was going on, but when the panic overtook him, he couldn't face being near to anyone. Was the rest of his life to be blighted like this?

Who would have guessed that witnessing a work colleague end their life would have turned a normal twenty-two-year-old bloke into a gibbering wreck? Not all of the time, but it came in waves. Thankfully it was happening less often, but it still took him by surprise when it happened.

Lewis had worked on the next desk for nearly a year. They'd exchanged banter, had the occasional beer after work. When Lewis jumped off the balcony overlooking the office building atrium, his sudden death had been a horrible shock.

Adam had come into work early that morning and found Lewis on the edge of the balcony. As if in slow motion, Adam had begun to walk quietly towards him, but there hadn't been time to speak or for Adam to grab him, to pull him back from the edge. In fact, Adam often wondered now that if he had tried to save Lewis he might have gone over the edge too. It might actually have been kinder . . . better.

He'd imagined what it would have been like to fall from that balcony so many times and woken up from similar nightmares on numerous nights too. But the fact that Adam hadn't got there in time, hadn't reached out, had instead watched in frozen horror as the man jumped, was a source of huge, paralysing guilt.

Then Adam had screamed in a way he wasn't aware he was capable of before that moment and alerted the rest of the early morning office arrivals to what had happened. He hadn't stopped screaming for what seemed like a very long time, although in reality it couldn't have been longer than a few moments.

The memories of Lewis on the edge of the balcony and his own screams woke him at night and often appeared unexpectedly during his day to make him feel like a useless, quivering, panicking jelly, as had just happened when he was speaking to Skye.

Useless jelly about summed up how he'd felt since the incident. It had coloured his life, and while he didn't wish it to define him it was doing a good job of doing so. The seemingly trite responses of his therapist and others didn't help: *Not your fault. You can't help a determined suicide. Nothing you could have done.*

But were these platitudes true? Adam's tortured thoughts oscillated from believing them to disbelieving them in rapid succession. He'd lost weight and had permanent bags beneath his eyes from lack of sleep. Ideally he'd never have gone back to work but changing career in his mental state would have been like scaling a huge, scary mountain. He experienced fear all the time — an envelope through the door, an unknown number ringing him caused his heart rate to accelerate and sweat to pour out of him.

When redundancies had been announced at work, he'd been the first person spoken to. With a career change forced upon him, he'd decided that despite the overwhelming dread he had to embrace the change. The chance to change and to do something he'd always thought he'd like to do but hadn't been brave enough to explore when he was younger. It was the main reason why he was here in Borteen. He only needed to find enough courage to begin.

He hadn't reckoned on meeting Skye. She was the first woman he'd noticed in an age, but how silly was he? What woman would want him now, in this state? He could barely look after himself, let alone offer a relationship. He wondered how similar he felt to a soldier returning from the First or Second World War. It wasn't as if he'd done anything heroic, but he guessed the trauma of seeing your colleagues killed in battle might produce anxiety similar to his own. He'd realized just how bad things had become when there'd been a loud bang in the street one lunchtime. He'd only popped out for a sandwich to get out of the house. One minute the bang, the next he was huddled under a street bench with a young girl staring at him and her mother trying to drag the child away from what she must have thought a madman.

He knew Skye must be wondering about his hurried exit from the dining room. She obviously had her own demons, because since she'd been back at the guesthouse after her trip to Birmingham, she'd looked constantly distracted. Their easy banter from before she went missing didn't seem to qualify him for anything much more than a small smile when they passed each other in the guesthouse, which is why he'd been pleased that she'd sat down and had breakfast with him, even if it was a little reluctantly. He hoped that she didn't think he'd left because he'd suddenly realized as she shifted her position on her chair that she was pregnant.

* * *

When he found her crying later the same day in the communal lounge at the guesthouse, he just pulled up a chair and sat with her. He recognized from his own situation that another person couldn't necessarily do anything if you were in a bad place, but the sheer presence of another human being was often helpful, as long as they didn't try to fix you, because no one actually could.

When she eventually stopped crying and tried to wipe her face on the back of her hands, he supplied a stray serviette and a tentative smile.

'Is there anything I can do to help?' he asked.

'Not really. I appear to have got myself into a terrible pickle.'

'Would it be good to talk it through?'

'I'm not sure anything will help and I'd be embarrassed to tell you what a fool I've been.' She looked down, pink tingeing her cheeks.

'Try me. I've had my own fair share of misadventure and making horrendously bad decisions.'

Skye fell quiet and he thought he'd maybe gone too far. Then she raised her head and stared straight at him. He saw her take a deep breath.

'How about this: pregnant. No sign of the dad. Probably won't be interested anyway. In a different country to where you were born to meet a father you've never ever seen before. Being followed to England by your mother. And both parents putting a brave face on it but you know they're really disappointed after discovering the truth about your secret and why you really came to Borteen. Then being told the man you thought was your dad, who you'd really started to like a lot, might not be your dad after all. Oh, and add totally flunked exams into that mix.'

'Hmm . . .' Adam didn't quite know what else to say. 'I'm a little stunned,' he stuttered.

Skye began to sob again. 'See, you think I'm terrible too.'

He realized his mistake. 'No, no, not at all. It's just that I can't believe you're still standing with all of that on your shoulders . . . it's more than most people could cope with.'

'It is rather a lot . . . I guess.'

'So, you're entitled to some tears, I think, before you pull yourself round and decide how to cope with all this.'

'Your take on it?'

'Pregnant? It'll be wonderful. A lot of women bring up children on their own. If the guy isn't interested, it's his loss.'

'My mother brought me up alone. She left Borteen before she had me.'

'Exams can be retaken, or maybe they weren't the right exams in the first place.'

'True. I think you might actually have something there.'

'As for your true father . . . sometimes the father figure in your life isn't the man you're connected to by blood.'

Goodness, he must have learned something from his therapist after all, at least about analysing problems. Skye was looking thoughtful.

'Again, maybe you've hit the nail on the head. I've always missed having a father figure in my life and now I've found Buzz.'

'I don't know him well, obviously, but he seems well suited for the role.'

'He does, doesn't he? It's not all bad. I've found my job at the café and I'm making tentative steps towards starting my own business.'

'That sounds great. My reason for being in Borteen isn't far different actually.'

'Now I'm confused.'

'Looking for a career change after a life-changing experience.' He told her briefly about his redundancy and the death of his colleague, but he spared her too much detail.

'What an awful shock.'

'Oh, yes! I've had therapy for my nightmares and the panic that sometimes overwhelms me. That's why I left the dining room quickly earlier — nothing that you said or did — it just gets me now and then without warning.'

'Oh, Adam, how terrible. My problems are nothing compared to that.'

Skye had become so wrapped up in his story that she seemed to have calmed down about her own situation.

'Now, that's not true. We all have challenges in our lives, I think. They're all different, but nonetheless real and important to each of us.'

'And do you know what you want to do going forward?'

'Yes and no. Possibly, I guess. My mother has arranged for me to see one of her old friends here in Borteen to discuss it. I've been taking a pause, a sort of holiday, to get myself ready to face it, to try to get myself into a better state of mind. I'll let you know how my meeting goes, if you like.'

Skye crossed her fingers and wished him luck. She wiped away the tears, now almost dried on her cheeks, and smiled at him. At last, he believed they were maybe back to where they had been before she went away and had even formed a fledgling friendship. It surprised him that it was so important, that he valued her opinion of him so much after knowing her for such a short time.

'I'm going to be staying on here with Buzz for a while.'

Skye told him then about the attic room above the crystal shop, the ancient but lovely sewing machine and her new venture altering and making clothes. Adam found himself uplifted by the animation in her face and fell even more under her spell.

'I'm so pleased that it's working out for you.'

'I still can't believe it actually. I'm upset that I might not be Buzz's daughter, but as you said, maybe that doesn't matter that much after all.' She frowned.

'Will you do tests to find out?'

'Buzz is looking into it.'

'Can I ask how it made you feel growing up without your father?'

'I guess I always felt as if there was something missing in my life. Having said that, in my class at school there were plenty kids with only one parent for a variety of reasons, but it didn't lessen the impact of feeling that maybe there was something wrong with me and, I suppose, the thought I was somehow missing out.'

'I was so lucky growing up with both of my parents.'

'I was lucky too. My mother was like my best friend when I was younger and that's what made it even more difficult to push her to talk about my father and jeopardize our relationship.'

'I can see that but it will all work out, I'm sure.'

'I think it will for you too. You said earlier that maybe I failed exams because they weren't the right ones, maybe your career wasn't the right one either. Time to move on to new things for both of us.'

He laughed. 'Thanks, Skye. I do believe you might have something there. I've been making things far too complicated in my head. I'll get on with meeting Mum's friend and explore possibilities. Feels somehow less daunting after sharing it all with you.'

They both laughed at the same time.

'I look forward to hearing how you get on. How exciting!'

'We must report back to each other regularly to keep us on track.'

'I'd like that.'

Adam realized that a new inner glow had ignited and that he almost basked in Skye's smile. He knew that he wanted to make her happy if he could so that she would smile at him even more.

'Now, off you go and have that meeting with your mother's friend. You can do it. I believe in you.'

Adam gulped, but knew it was time for him to be brave. After all, there was no point being here in Borteen if he didn't do more than run on the beach.

CHAPTER THIRTEEN

'Buzz? Sorry, I still don't know quite what to call you.' Skye pulled a face.

'Buzz is fine, don't worry about it.'

'Well, anyway, now I'm staying with you, at least until after Christmas, maybe you should fill me in about these Borteen Christmas events that Christine keeps hinting at. She says the beach café is the centre of most of them.'

'Well, I guess she's right in a way. Let me see, we have the Borteen town Christmas tree dressing first. Good job it's not last year, because I was Santa.'

Skye laughed. '*You* were Santa?'

'Yes, we older residents take it in turns to dress up and hand out the Christmas decorations to the children to put onto the tree.'

'So, who's Santa this year?'

'It's Lally Kensington, the landlord of the Ship Inn, the pub I took you to. Although he's not very keen on the role.'

'Lally Kensington? Is he the man who comes into the café a lot? The one I think is sweet on Christine?'

'Maybe. He lost his wife a few years ago. He's only just getting back on his feet, but I can see he might be well suited to Christine.' Buzz looked thoughtful. 'Yes, that would do very nicely.'

'So, everyone decorates the Christmas tree?'

'Yes, the children get to put decorations on first and then the adults. We collect donations for charity. There's a band, and the town choir sing carols. Christine puts on the refreshments.'

'Sounds fun. So, what else?'

'We have a Santa fun run, a Christmas fair, carols around the Christmas tree. I do a labyrinth on the beach, as I do every few weeks to raise money for the homeless. And we organize a Christmas party for the homeless staying in the hostel in Sowden.'

'How come you're so keen on supporting that particular charity?'

'There was a very real possibility, a little while before I came to Borteen and met your mother, that I might have ended up living on the streets myself. My support for the charity is a recognition that my life could have worked out very differently, so it's important to me.'

'We all have our own stories, don't we? Moments in our existence when things can change our lives completely. A bit like that old film Mum likes — *Sliding Doors*.'

'Yes. It's interesting to think what would happen if we turned another way, took different jobs, met different people, became another version of ourselves.'

'It's making my head hurt thinking about it,' laughed Skye. 'I look forward to being part of these Christmas events in Borteen. It's quite exciting. I only wish Mum was staying too, because part of me will feel terribly guilty that I'm not with her in Dublin for Christmas.'

Buzz ruffled the pile of tissue paper on the shop counter. 'You should know that I've asked her to stay. I'm aware that a lot of time has passed, a lot of things have been revealed, but I'd still like the chance to try again with her.'

'Really? That's wonderful.'

'Yes, but she said she's not sure it's a good idea after all this time apart, and until we know about . . .'

He didn't have to say what he meant — until they knew Skye's real parentage. His face looked so forlorn that it upset her.

'That's sad, because watching the two of you together, the chemistry is undeniable.'

'Well, if it was up to me alone, I would take her back in a heartbeat. You know, I realized the other day that we're still actually married.'

'Really? Wow.'

'There was never any divorce or legal recognition of our parting. Do you think maybe you could have a word with Wynn about staying on in Borteen or at least coming back for Christmas?'

Skye shook her finger in front of him. 'Now, that's naughty — emotional blackmail — but I'll see what I can do.' She winked.

* * *

Buzz was sitting on a bench in the Borteen churchyard thinking over his earlier conversation with Skye. It was his favourite memorial bench, even though he had never known the person whom the bench commemorated. He found the churchyard a quiet, contemplative place to sit, particularly when the tourist season was in full swing. Despite their differing belief systems, Reverend Hopkins often joined Buzz on the bench and their debates about the philosophy of life were some of the most interesting conversations Buzz had shared.

Buzz believed in the immortality of the soul, in past lives and therefore reincarnation, in live and let live as peacefully as possible. Reverend Hopkins was open to listening to his theories, but with his theological degree and training to be a Church of England vicar, he had his own set of beliefs. Buzz believed in psychic abilities and signs from the universe, Reverend Hopkins believed in the will of God. Secretly, Buzz didn't think they were actually that far apart. They'd known each other long enough for Buzz to call the friendly vicar Nigel and for the two men to tease each other about their ideologies.

It was a chilly day with a stiff breeze directly off the sea. Sitting among the graves, Buzz hoicked the collar of his fleece a little higher and shivered.

'Hello, Buzz.'

The familiar voice of Nigel Hopkins made Buzz smile and he nodded in greeting.

'You're looking very thoughtful today,' said Nigel.

'A lot been going on in my life since I last saw you.'

'Oh, yes? Do tell . . .'

Before he could say any more, Buzz caught sight of movement on the churchyard path and a familiar figure came into view. 'Good morning, Adam,' he called.

'Good morning, Buzz.' Adam nodded at Nigel.

'Nigel, this is Adam, he's staying at Rose Court.'

'Ah, I've been expecting Adam to come and see me. Have you been out exploring the area, young man?' asked Nigel with his habitual welcoming tone.

'I can come back another time if it's more convenient,' said Adam.

Buzz got to his feet immediately. 'No need, I ought to get back and open up the shop anyway, so I'll leave you two to it.' He moved away from the bench and Adam sat down where he had been sitting moments before. Buzz looked back at the two men and had a feeling pass over him that they had a lot to discuss.

Buzz walked along the promenade, enjoying the sound of the waves crashing onto the beach.

He arrived back at Crazy Crystals to find Skye and Wynn standing outside of the door with Skye's things in their arms.

'You'd forgotten Skye is moving in this morning hadn't you?' said Wynn.

'No, no, I just lost track of time, that's all. Terribly sorry.' He opened the door as fast as he could and led the way inside. 'I'll get you a key, Skye, and then you can come and go as you please.'

Wynn seemed flustered and Buzz wondered what on earth was going through her head. She'd said she was pleased that Skye was staying in Borteen with Buzz, but now it had come to it, she appeared almost jealous. With the realization that Skye had said she would only move into the flat when Wynn was heading home to Dublin, he felt his spirits drop that his wife would soon be gone once more. Would he ever see her again? Or would this imminent parting be their last goodbye?

He carried Skye's rucksack upstairs. 'Let's have a drink together before Skye unpacks. There's something I want to share with you both.'

When they all had steaming herbal teas in front of them, Buzz presented Skye with a small box. She stared at him quizzically as she opened it and found it to be a DNA test.

Wynn looked alarmed and her eyes widened as Buzz gave her an identical box.

'I looked into it and this test should prove if we are father and daughter. Also, I was thinking about what you said Skye about wanting to know more about your genetic heritage, especially with the baby on the way, and I thought that if we all sent off our DNA samples together, we could maybe compile a family tree for your daughter.'

'How exciting.' Skye rapidly read the instructions on the back of the box and disappeared to the bathroom to prepare her saliva test.

Buzz was certain that Wynn would pounce as soon as Skye left the room.

'What are you doing?' she said in a stern whisper.

'At least we'll know one way or the other.'

'But what if the test proves you're not Skye's father?' she said in an even quieter, more urgent whisper.

'I don't think we can hide from this any longer. I figure we'll cross that bridge when and if we have to. If it identifies a parent–child relationship between us, we'll at least be able to relax and forget about my brother, and, if not, we'll have to think again.'

Wynn sighed loudly. 'You're right as always. At least this way we'll finally have answers, rather than continuing to wonder about the truth. I'm just scared, I suppose.'

Skye appeared back in the room brandishing her sample. 'How long does it take for the results to come back?'

'It says four to eight weeks.'

'I can't wait, because then I'll know if you're my real dad. But I wanted to say that whatever the test proves, you will always be a special person to me, Buzz, because you have totally accepted me as me.'

Buzz welcomed the hug Skye gave to him and was too choked with emotion to speak.

Buzz and Wynn exchanged a look.

Wynn appeared to come to a decision, ripped opened her own package and went to the bathroom to complete her test too. Buzz had already packaged his up ready to post with the other two.

It felt scary, as it had the potential to rip his new little family apart, but exciting all at the same time if he could be proved as Skye's father after all.

* * *

As soon as Adam sat down on the bench in the churchyard, it was as if the weather knew the importance of this meeting for him, because the wind picked up and whistled around the bench before Adam even managed to say anything, and even if he had, he was unlikely to be heard.

'Come on, let's take refuge in the church,' said Reverend Hopkins, standing up and heading towards the building before waiting for a reply.

Adam followed the man along the path and it was all he could do to continue walking behind him rather than running the other way. The enormity of the reason he'd really come to Borteen hit him full force and he began to feel very sick.

He trailed behind Nigel Hopkins into the church and was enveloped with the familiar smells of incense, dust, old wood stain and polish that he associated with ecclesiastical buildings. He breathed in the atmosphere and silently asked for divine courage for his future.

Borteen church was a product of the Victorian era, like so many of England's churches. The stained-glass windows depicted parables from the Bible, the pews were wooden and no doubt uncomfortable. Adam could already see that Borteen's churchgoers had laboured long and hard over the tapestry kneelers to be used for prayers.

Reverend Hopkins stopped for a moment in front of the altar and said a silent prayer with his head bowed. He seemed almost astounded when he noticed that Adam did exactly the same thing. The action produced a querying raise of the man's eyebrow, which Adam ignored for now.

'Well, Marion told me briefly that you had recently had a very difficult time, Adam. She said that she was worried about you and asked if I'd meet with you as an independent person, a sounding board. How is it that I can help you, young man?'

'Mum says that you're easy to talk to and helped her put some things in perspective in the past. I'm actually keen to become a vicar myself, or at least study theology, and I would appreciate your advice.'

Nigel Hopkins looked surprised. 'Now then, of all the things I imagined you might want to discuss, Adam, I will freely admit that wasn't one of them.'

'So, Mum didn't say then? It's taken even me by surprise, I'll be totally honest. The thought has been running around in my head for a very long time, but so far I've managed to resist it. It's recently become almost a need, which is why I now have to explore the possibility further. Mum suggested I come here as you are, so to speak, in the business already.'

'Right, this is going to be an interesting time, I can tell.' Nigel smiled. 'Let's sit down and start from the beginning. It's rather chilly in the church this morning. I suddenly find myself in need of tea and a warm room. Let's go to the vicarage — we'll be more comfortable there and I can concentrate on your story and why you feel you have a calling to the Church.'

They walked as quickly as they could through the stormy churchyard and reached the porch of the vicarage.

'Now, let's get out of this cold air and put the kettle on.'

'A cup of tea would be wonderful,' said Adam, breathing slowly and steadily to try to stem the panic that threatened to rise again in anticipation of discussing what had happened to him. The urge to run away grew.

The pair were soon settled in the warm vicarage kitchen. Adam looked around curiously. There didn't seem to be any sign of a female influence in this room. Nigel busied himself filling the kettle, getting some biscuits out of an ancient tin on the worksurface. It wasn't until he had placed two mugs of tea and the plate of biscuits on the table that he sat down and spoke to Adam again.

'Did your mum explain our connection?'

'She said you lodged with her family when you were both students in London.'

'Yes, it was many years ago, but we still exchange Christmas cards. Marion is lovely.'

Adam wondered then if Reverend Hopkins had been attracted to his mother back then. Nigel looked indeed as if he was remembering something from the past. He shook himself and concentrated back on Adam.

'So, why do you think Marion thought I could help you?'

'I've had a bit of a rough time lately. Mum thought some sea air and quiet contemplation might do me good, and she mentioned you when I said that I was thinking of this drastic change of career. I've often wondered about the Church, but I went in other directions, into the business world, but the death of a colleague has made me re-examine my beliefs big time . . . my self-worth even, and most definitely my future.'

'Goodness, it does sound as if you've been through the mill.'

Adam experienced another flash of discomfort and pinched his leg to try to stop it developing into full-blown panic.

'They call it PTSD these days. As I said, I've had a terribly strange year. My work colleague threw himself off a balcony right in front of me.'

Nigel put his hand to his forehead. 'Oh, Adam, how dreadful. I can see that experience would have you questioning life . . . the world . . . everything.'

'It made me realize that I have to start to live authentically right now. None of us know how long we have on this planet and I've been living a life that doesn't feel quite right, quite like my own, for a while.'

'You've had an awakening, an epiphany?'

Adam laughed. 'Yes, I guess I have.' He took a sip of his tea, which was weak and far too milky for his taste. He tried to disguise his negative reaction to the drink. 'Lewis dying like that made me question my beliefs, but ultimately strengthened the feeling that I want to do something worthwhile with my life.'

He wondered how much his mother had already told Nigel, but guessed the man would want to hear his own view of things, not just his mother's.

'I was also made redundant and then my dad died shortly afterwards too.'

'I'm so sorry about your father. Poor Marion.'

Nigel pushed back his chair, startling Adam and making him jump. The vicar went across the kitchen to rummage in a drawer. He came back with a large bar of dark chocolate. 'We need a treat,' he said and proceeded to break it into chunks on the biscuit plate. The action at least made Adam smile. They both munched quietly for a moment.

Adam was experiencing a strange mix of emotions. He rather liked this guy, liked his thoughtful, bachelor-type way of being. Why had he imagined it would be any other way? His mother wouldn't have sent him to see just anyone.

'Do I get the impression that your mother doesn't want you to consider the Church?'

'No, she asked me to forget going to university to study theology and, in the end, I gave in and did finance instead, became a city accountant in one of those cut-and-thrust businesses where there's no time to breathe, let alone be yourself. It's easy to be carried along and let time pass, but when Lewis jumped from that balcony it seemed such a complete waste . . .' Adam put down his cup and rubbed at his face. He realized from the turmoil inside caused by talking about the tragedy that he was far from over what had happened . . . maybe never would be.

'I have to ask, is this desire to join the Church now just a knee-jerk reaction to events rather than a "calling"?'

'I don't honestly know. My mother thinks it is, which is why she sent me to you.'

'Fresh pot of tea, I think,' Nigel murmured.

Adam had noticed the rather splendid wooden nativity outside of the church. Had he chosen the wrong time of year to come here? The Christmas season was bound to be a busy time for a vicar.

CHAPTER FOURTEEN

Skye absolutely loved the attic room above the crystal shop. Buzz had supplied her with an ancient vacuum cleaner, dusters and polish and told her she could rearrange things just as she liked. Then he gave her a stern warning about not lifting heavy things. He even gave her a box, so that he could take away anything she didn't want in the room.

She hadn't brought many belongings with her to England, of course, but she took great pleasure in arranging the small collection of shells, stones and sea glass she had amassed since being in Borteen along the tiny shelf on the wall. Her clothes fitted easily into the small wardrobe. She put her rucksack under the bed, once she'd vacuumed the floor.

The sewing machine was the focal point of the room and Skye hoped it would soon be the focal point of her income too. She found herself humming a favourite tune, 'Daisies' by Katy Perry, and realized that she was happier than she had been in a very long time. Christine had promised her some additional shifts at the café, so all was looking good.

She was still troubled that her mother would be leaving to return to Ireland very soon, she still hadn't found Declan and she still didn't actually know who her dad was. But, Skye reflected, it wasn't as if her mother was going to be too far away and there were always video calls and social media to enable them to keep track of each other. She wasn't hopeful of a positive outcome to finding Declan and she was enjoying being with Buzz regardless — it wasn't as if she'd known her dad for all these years, and as Adam had said, your father figure wasn't always connected by blood.

She'd secretly hoped that Wynn would stay in Borteen. Whatever she'd done years ago and however secretive she'd been, Skye knew that her mother had always tried her best for her daughter. There was no point falling out with her over the past, even though initially Skye had been upset yet again.

She even hoped that maybe Wynn could get back together with Buzz. Her mother deserved some happiness, although she recognized that a lot of water had gone under the bridge since the pair had been a married couple, living here in this very building and running the shop together.

However, despite her mother's revelation about her fling, her reasons for leaving Borteen and keeping Skye's existence secret, there was no denying the chemistry that still existed between Wynn and Buzz, and that knowledge made the continuation of them living apart seem tragic to Skye — a complete waste of what could be a good relationship.

Buzz seemed very forgiving and still had a twinkle in his eye when he looked at Wynn. Maybe it was better that her mother was leaving for a while. It gave them all a chance to reflect. It wasn't lost on Skye that when under pressure, she herself had acted in exactly the same way as Wynn — she'd run away.

Her mind pondered whether she could ever engineer the proper reunion of her parents and if she would speak to Wynn about coming back to Borteen at Christmas or leave that to fate. She decided that if anything was capable of reuniting them, then the new life growing in her womb would maybe stand a better chance of achieving that than anyone or anything else. She giggled as the baby, almost having heard all of her thoughts, moved around inside of her in what seemed like an agreement to her plan.

'Yes, little one, we'll get Grandma and Grandad back together, won't we?' Here she crossed her fingers that Buzz would be proved by the DNA test to be her father.

She glanced at her phone and decided it was time to change and get ready for her shift at the beach café. She wondered if she'd see Adam today. She'd been trying to deny the crush she was developing, but he'd been so kind when she'd been upset, and it was nice to have someone her own age to talk to in Borteen.

She almost apologized to her baby that she was thinking of a man other than her father, but then, was it a bad thing to be moving on? The guilt wouldn't go away that she would be placing her daughter in exactly the same life situation in which she'd grown up herself — fatherless — unless she found Declan and told him he would be a parent in the new year.

She didn't wish the heartache of not knowing your father on anyone else, let alone her own flesh and blood, so she knew she would have to continue the search for a man she wasn't sure she even wanted to speak to again.

How could anything with Declan ever work? He would be a distant parent at best. Her daughter would grow up with separated parents, she was absolutely sure, but was it better to know your heritage, your origins, or not? She didn't really know the answer to that question and the dilemma began to give her a headache.

It was nice to be settled into the attic room, but weird in the same way as she didn't know Buzz that well as yet. All of the anger she thought she would feel, had wanted to express when she was on the way over to Borteen, had gone. She didn't fully understand what had happened between her parents before she was even born, but Buzz was a good guy and she was pleased to discover that she liked him so very much.

She looked out at the small patch of sky she could see through the attic window for a clue as to whether she would get wet on her walk to work. The sky was blue and clear, but the air was very cold today.

As she left the shop, having said thank you yet again to Buzz and, a new thing, given him a hug before she made her way to the café. She liked the way his face lit up whenever she showed him any affection.

Walking the short distance down Borteen high street, she realized she was looking for Adam. There was a lot of activity on the promenade. A large Christmas tree was being hoisted into place. Skye stopped by the sea wall to watch and to scan the beach, again for Adam, who might be on his morning run.

It was hard somehow to go to work so close to the beautiful expanse of sand but not have time to set foot upon it. She walked into the café, picking up a couple of used trays as she went towards the kitchen area. Christine was icing cakes in a manner that suggested she wasn't best pleased.

'What's up?' asked Skye.

'Is it that obvious?' said Christine through gritted teeth.

Skye laughed. 'Something about the way you're swirling that icing onto those poor cakes says, "I'm angry, but trying not to show it and I need to get this done, so I'm working through my anger," or something like that.'

Christine threw down her icing bag. 'No hiding things from you, young lady. You must have your father's psychic powers.'

'Come on then . . . what's wrong?'

'Oh, nothing!'

Skye laughed. 'Pull the other one!'

'It's the Christmas tree dressing event on Saturday. You saw them putting the tree up outside?'

'Yes, it's huge. Buzz told me that the children put the decorations on it and that there's a band and a choir too. He also said that he was Santa last year, which made me smile.'

'I'd forgotten that. It's blummin' Lally Kensington as Santa this year.'

'Do I take it that "blummin' Lally Kensington" has upset you?'

'No. Yes. Oh, I don't know.' Christine flopped down on a chair. 'I'm only being silly.'

'Look, Christine, I've only been in Borteen five minutes and already I've cottoned on to the fact that you and Lally Kensington have the hots for each other.'

Christine sat up straight. 'Really? Is it quite that obvious?'

Skye nodded and Christine put her hands over her face. Skye didn't like to point out right now that she'd squashed a blob of icing onto her nose.

'Oh, but I'm not sure he feels the same way. Why would he choose me when he's surrounded by all those lovely barmaids every day?'

'From what I've seen, he thinks a lot of you.'

'Don't encourage me, girl.'

'Well someone has to, otherwise this situation will still be going on next Christmas.' Skye wondered at the same time whether she would even be in Borteen by this time next year.

'I don't think he's really over his wife's death.'

'I doubt you ever get over something like that, do you? I suppose you have to learn to live with it while still trying to make a new life for yourself. If you start a relationship with him, you'd have to be aware of that, I'm afraid.'

'I really don't know what to think, but when you get to my age as a singleton, it stands to reason that anyone you meet will have some past life.'

'At the end of the day, what have you got to lose?'

Christine turned a stricken face to Skye. 'Actually, a really good friend. It's what's stopped me pursuing this before, not wanting to lose that valuable friendship with Lally. We tease each other something rotten and have a good laugh too. It could be pretty awkward for both of us and for the other Borteen residents if we fell out in any way.'

'But who says that will happen? You might be a match made in heaven.'

Christine didn't manage to reply, because at that very moment the man in question, Lally Kensington, came through the café door and Christine went as red as the icing she'd been piping onto the cakes.

Skye made a quick gesture to tell Christine she had icing on her face and diverted Lally's attention. 'Mr Kensington, what can I get for you this fine morning?'

'An Americano, a croissant and a word with the delightful Christine, please.'

'To be sure. Please take a seat by the delightful Christine—' she winked — 'and I'll get your order.'

Thankfully, Christine looked to have cleaned her face and composed herself by the time he sat down.

'Can I get you a drink too, Christine?' asked Skye.

'You know, I've been working so hard since I got in this morning, I think I'll have a skinny cappuccino, please.'

'Coming right up.'

It was at times like these that Skye was pleased she'd had a Saturday job for a while in a local café in Dublin. As a result, she knew how to make all of the different types of coffees served here in Christine's café without her boss having to explain anything to her. At least it was something she felt good at.

She glanced over to where Christine and Lally were talking earnestly. Christine really did need her head examining if she thought that the man didn't fancy her, his obvious attraction shone out of him as he spoke.

Skye took their drinks over to the table, plus Lally's breakfast, and made to scurry off.

'Are you looking forward to the Borteen Christmas tree dressing, young lady?' asked Lally.

'I'm not quite sure what to expect, to be honest, never having been to one before.'

'I could listen to your lilting accent all day.' He smiled. 'One thing I think we do really well in Borteen is Christmas.'

'I love it too, but these days I feel so responsible for all of the refreshments,' said Christine pulling a less than flattering face.

'You, my dear Christine, are the kingpin of the Borteen Christmas, or should that be the *queenpin*? I shall be making a point of visiting you in my Santa outfit on Saturday to collect some cake.' He winked at Christine and Skye made an excuse to retreat to the café kitchen to leave them alone together, all the time hoping that this pair could perhaps go beyond their reservations and make each other happy.

* * *

Skye's ankles were swollen by the time she had finished her shift and her back ached dreadfully. Reluctant to say anything about it to Christine, she'd soldiered on and gritted her teeth, but when she got back to the crystal shop, she could see that Buzz was a little worried about her.

'Do you think you should be working such long shifts?'

'I'll be fine. I love working at the café.' She quickly changed the subject. 'I watched them putting up the huge Christmas tree on the promenade this morning.'

Buzz grimaced. 'Nice try, young lady. You need to rest this evening — feet up, I insist. And yes, it's the kickstart of the Borteen Christmas events on Saturday, the day after tomorrow even, when everyone gets together to decorate the town tree.'

'Sounds fun, but am I right in saying you don't really go in for a religious Christmas?'

'Just because I don't hold the same belief system as some doesn't mean I don't see the great value in events that bring the community together with positive intent, and this is one of those events. It's usually good fun.'

'Can we go together?'

'I look forward to it.'

'Sounds like Mum will have left by then.'

Buzz's face fell. 'Yes, and that's a pity.'

'You still love her, don't you, despite everything?' Skye put a hand out to touch his arm.

'Always have and always will, I think. I'm a one-woman man. Mate for life and all that. I've had plenty of time over the years to decide how to react, no matter what she might say, if I ever saw her again, and I decided I could forgive almost anything.'

'Even what actually happened?'

'I was shocked, I can't deny that. But when I'm close to Wynn, I just want to stay there.'

'The sad thing is, I believe that Mum really loves you too!'

Buzz shrugged. 'I've asked her to stay more than once now, but she has her business in Ireland and can't leave it indefinitely.'

Skye wanted to say more but was now wilting from exhaustion and knew she had to be sensible and go to lie down on her bed for a while.

Buzz seemed to read her mind or else the tiredness on her face. He turned the key in the lock, changed the shop sign to 'Closed' and pulled the blind down over the door. 'Come on, you. Time for a cup of tea, feet up on the sofa. He briefly hugged her and it was good to lean against his warmth.

'I think you'll need to push me up the stairs from behind. I'm so exhausted.'

'Come on, let's get you settled and those legs up.'

That evening they were going to the wine bar and bistro at the end of the road for a farewell dinner with Wynn. Skye tried to battle down her emotions and enjoy this evening with her mother, determined not to spend it in sadness and tears.

When Buzz insisted on paying for the meal, Skye finally took the opportunity to ask her mother if she would consider coming back to Bortcen for Christmas when he went to settle the bill.

'I need to sort out a few things and I won't promise absolutely just now, but I will promise to try and return soon.' Wynn smiled wistfully, and it gladdened her heart.

CHAPTER FIFTEEN

Adam and Nigel Hopkins were meeting for lunch at the Ship Inn. After their initial meeting they had agreed to take the time to get to know one another and discuss Adam's situation.

They had both been amused when the barmaid had asked Nigel if Adam was his nephew. This was the third time in as many days that the two had met up.

'Adam, it seems silly for you to be paying for a room at the guesthouse when I have a whole huge vicarage to myself. Would you perhaps consider coming to stay with me for a while?'

A spark of uncertainty flickered in Adam's stomach, but he had to admit that the suggestion made perfect sense. 'That would be great. I mean, my whole reason for coming here was to find out more about what you do, so staying with you would let me do that more easily, I suppose.'

'I'll admit that I'm approaching a very busy time of my year, but then if you want to get into "the business", so to speak, then at least you can see what happens day to day.'

'I would so appreciate your insights and guidance. Mum keeps ringing me to ask how I'm getting on. I've assured her I'm going to take my time before making any decisions.'

'She's your mother, she's bound to be worried, given what you've been through.'

'Yes, I forget that she saw me at my lowest ebb. I think it frightened her . . . a lot.'

'If Marion's still as lovely as she was, she'll want the best for you. I'm honoured that she trusted me to guide and counsel you.' Nigel's eyes had taken on a dreamy faraway look and Adam wondered yet again if the man had been sweet on his mother all those years ago.

'Well, if you're absolutely sure about having me to stay, I'll go and get my things and settle my bill.'

'I'm looking forward to having a house guest very much.' Nigel Hopkins reached out a hand and laid it for a moment on Adam's arm. It was only a small gesture, but Adam found he was suddenly emotional.

He walked out of the pub and took great big gulps of cool air as the familiar panic threatened to invade again. But Nigel might be able to help him with his future direction. This was a new era, and Adam knew he had to embrace it.

He walked along the promenade in a daze. The tide was high, pounding against the sea wall. Adam took a few moments to watch and listen, the spray wetting his face and hair.

When he got back to the guesthouse he bumped straight into Skye coming through the hall with a strange expression on her face.

'Hey, whatever's the matter?'

She flung herself against his chest. 'Mum's leaving today. I really thought I'd be able to persuade her to stay, but no.'

At that moment Buzz and Wynn came down the staircase. Buzz carrying a case and Wynn with a coat over her arm. Adam was embarrassingly aware that he had his arms around their pregnant daughter and that Skye had her head on his chest. He spoke quickly to tackle his embarrassment. 'Skye's upset because you're leaving, Mrs erm . . .' He realized he didn't know Skye's mother's name or if she referred to herself as Mrs.

'You can call me Wynn,' said Skye's mother. 'And it's hard to leave, but I have to, I'm afraid . . . for now at least.'

'I'll go and get the car,' said Buzz.

'I've ordered a taxi, there's no need.'

Adam saw Buzz's face fall. Skye moved away from him too. 'Mum! We were going to take you to the airport.'

'No, love, it would be too hard, too much emotion to deal with. I can't do it, so I'm just going to leave you both now. Love you.' Wynn hugged her daughter very briefly, kissed a bewildered-looking Buzz on the cheek, grabbed her case from his hand and left the guesthouse.

As the door shut behind her mother, Skye turned back into Adam's chest and sobbed loudly. Buzz flopped onto the uncomfortable-looking wooden chair in the hallway and stared at the ceiling. Adam didn't really know what to do, so he just folded his arms around Skye and prayed for deliverance.

When Buzz recovered himself and stood up, he said, 'Come on, Skye, let's go home.'

Skye shuddered in Adam's arms and mumbled a thank you. Then she and Buzz were gone too. Adam went upstairs to pack his things, feeling sorry for Skye and lamenting the fact that every situation couldn't have a happy ending.

* * *

Buzz was stunned that Wynn had left just like that too, although he had no idea how he would have got through the journey to the airport and the inevitable goodbyes when they got there. This way was cleaner but much more of a shock.

He was concerned about how Skye was feeling about her mother returning to Dublin. It seemed almost inevitable that Skye would follow her mother back to Ireland at some point, so he made up his mind to relish every moment he could in her company. He was aware of the niggling doubt about her parentage in the back of his mind, but he accepted that Skye was the nearest thing to a child of his own he would ever have, so be she his daughter or his niece, it didn't seem to matter much.

He'd never felt lonely before, alone maybe, but Wynn and Skye being in his life had made him appreciate what he had been missing all of these years and no amount of spiritual practice, meditations or Reiki treatments could make up for that. He kept reminding himself that he believed in life lessons, life pathways, soul groups, karma and destiny. Regrets and hindsight were useless. These thoughts were most likely another challenge to his beliefs, and he had to get through this phase and emerge stronger and more resolute.

* * *

Wynn sat in the back of the taxi and sobbed. It was all she had been able to do to walk past Skye and Buzz with a gruff tone in her voice and escape from the guesthouse. Was she right? Should she be leaving them now? She had business affairs to sort out, but she had a few ideas about how to do that. Maybe she could return to Borteen for Christmas at the very least. Skye and Buzz were the only family she had and Christmas would be very bleak on her own.

She had now come to terms with the fact that she couldn't change the past. It was clear that she had made the wrong decision all those years ago when she had left and then realized that she was pregnant. All the guilty chatter in her mind would serve no purpose, but somehow as the taxi got closer to the airport and she mopped at her tear-stained face, this return to Dublin seemed pointless and empty. It wasn't what she wanted at all.

What in reality had she got back in Ireland? A shop, some stock, a few bits and pieces that when she looked at them in the cold light of day didn't really amount to much. Skye was her greatest achievement and somehow she'd managed to fail even her, otherwise her daughter wouldn't be repeating the same pattern of being pregnant and a solo parent. Maybe Buzz would do a better job of looking after Skye than she had. He was a good man.

The hollow feeling wouldn't go away. The questions of doubt nagged at her and she tried to decide whose voice was speaking them in her head. She concluded that it was her own mother's voice, as if she was revisiting from the grave to point out Wynn's errors and shortcomings, exactly as she had when she'd been alive. She almost yelled aloud to her mother, *I was only repeating the patterns you taught to me! You always ran away instead of facing things!*

She checked in her bag at the airline desk and went to the departure lounge, ignoring all the glossy shops. Wynn had no need for material possessions. The only thing she really valued was the wedding ring Buzz had given to her, which for many years now she had worn on a chain around her neck, nestled between her breasts. She felt so awful today, she didn't feel she deserved to keep even that precious possession.

What now? Which way to turn? Wynn didn't really have anyone to share her dilemmas and fears with. She had friends in Ireland, but again in a cold light, were they friends or just acquaintances? She zoned out and went through the motions of getting home in as detached a way as she could manage. Inside she felt hollow and knew she had to make better choices for her future.

CHAPTER SIXTEEN

The next time Skye saw Adam, he was running on the beach on Saturday morning. The tide was well out, so he was a long way down the sand and Skye wasn't sure he would see her wave. Somehow, though, he did notice her and he altered his course to run up towards the sea wall.

She took in his slim build, probably a bit too slender — was he eating enough? He wore leggings and a rainproof neon yellow top, with his phone suspended in a clear case on his upper arm.

'How are you today?' he shouted up to her.

He jogged on the spot as he spoke and she realized that he must be quite fit. She was pretty sure she'd be stuttering and gasping after running up the beach and totally incapable of holding any conversation, even before she was pregnant. Adam vaulted the beach steps and began performing some calf stretches.

'I'm sorry about yesterday. I was so embarrassing, crying all over you.' She knew she was red-faced, and not from the cold wind.

'It's okay, honestly. You were understandably upset and I was worried about you.' He straightened up and smiled at her.

'It's really horrid, Mum going back to Dublin, but I have to come to terms with it.'

'Will you go back to Ireland now too?'

She tried to decide from his expression whether he'd be sad if she did go, but as he bent down to stretch again, it was difficult to decide. 'Not in the near future. Buzz has given me the room above the shop and I seem to have fallen into my two jobs almost by accident — the café and clothing alterations venture — so I'll hang around in Borteen for now. It's just that I'm not sure what's best to do for my baby. I mean, should she be here in Borteen or with her grandma in Dublin? It's a virtually impossible choice, to be honest. It bends my mind and screws up my head the more I think about it.'

'I'm sure it does. I don't envy you the decision, but I suppose you have to think about what feels right for you yourself at this point. Your baby is a girl then?'

'Yes, a girl.' She smiled and experienced that familiar wave of disbelief that she could be growing a baby.

He stopped stretching and faced her properly. 'Wow, a daughter. Did it make it feel more real when you found out it's a girl?'

'Most definitely. If I felt protective before, I feel ultra protective now. It made her a real person. A person who'll need a name — yet another dilemma.' She laughed.

'Exciting though, it means you get to decide her identity almost.'

'And that's scary in itself, such a responsibility. I mean, can you imagine what it was like for me, growing up in an ethnic crystal shop and having the name Skye? Ammunition for bullies or what?'

'Were you bullied?'

'Durr . . . yes. Why do you think I'm reluctant to go back now I've got a swollen pregnancy belly on top of everything else? They'd have a field day. I can imagine Daria camping out outside the shop to heckle every time I came out of the door.'

'Oh dear. I can see why you think naming your daughter is a big issue.'

'Buzz says I'll know her name the first time I look deeply into her eyes. I do hope so.' She smiled deliberately, aware that Adam might be a bit stunned by her outburst of feelings.

'Have you got time for a herbal tea by any chance?' asked Adam.

'I'm actually on my way to work at the café.' She was delighted he'd asked though.

'I won't delay you any longer then. I'll finish my run and pop in for my breakfast.'

'See you very soon in that case.'

He saluted and jogged back down the beach steps and away across the sand. Skye stood and watched him for a moment with a sudden longing deep inside of her. Why couldn't life be simple? Still, it didn't hurt to dream.

When she arrived, the café was very quiet. Christine was putting the finishing touches to rows of mince pies, iced gingerbread men and slices of Christmas cake.

'Wow, that's a lot of cake.'

'For this evening's Christmas tree event,' Christine commented.

'They look absolutely amazing.'

'It's very quiet so far this morning, people are probably saving themselves for later. Why don't you make me a latte and whatever you want, and we'll have a naughty relaxed sit down with our choice from this little lot?'

'Sounds wonderful.' Skye was saying the words but secretly thinking that she didn't want to sit down with Christine in case Adam came in, but she did as she was asked and made the drinks for them.

Christine rubbed the back of her calves. 'I've been standing up too long.'

'You do work incredibly hard.'

'You've noticed? Take my advice, try to find a career where you don't have to work beyond a reasonable working day.'

'Sounds like good advice, but life isn't always that simple, is it?'

'I shouldn't grumble, because it's good for business, but sometimes I feel as if the success of Borteen's whole Christmas rests upon my shoulders. It's always the same at this time of year, because with the café being right next to the end of the promenade where most of the town's Christmas events take place, it's the logical focus for refreshments.'

'Well, I'm here now. You can put me to work to help out.'

'It's really great having you here, Skye. You're so enthusiastic.'

Christine looked about to make another comment, but her face changed as the café door opened and Christine the confidante and life coach morphed into Christine the café owner in a split second. They both stood and Skye picked up her mug.

'Someone looks like he needs a refreshing drink,' Christine said aloud.

Adam smiled, but did Skye imagine that his look was directed at her and not at Christine? She experienced a strange feeling, or was the baby on the move again? Could Adam possibly be attracted to her? She immediately dismissed the ridiculous thought. She was pregnant and on her own; some would call it 'in trouble'. Why would a guy like Adam, good-looking and confident, be tempted by her at all?

As she looked at him, his face blurred in front of her. Skye's world tipped on its axis as, light-headed, she stumbled and her empty mug rolled across the floor.

'Skye?' He reached her before Christine did, supporting her with his strong arms and guiding her back into the chair.

'Sorry, I just went a little faint for a moment. I must have stood up too quickly.'

She saw Christine exchange a meaningful look with Adam.

'You never had one of the Christmas pastries, did you, Skye? I'll get one for each of you and whatever drink you'd like, Adam?'

'A glass of cold water and an Americano, please.'

'Now, you keep a close eye on our Skye. She's gone very pale.'

Adam pulled a chair close up to hers and stared intently at her face. 'Is it the baby? Do I need to get you home? To the doctor? To the hospital?'

She smiled at his concerned look, despite her own worries. 'Stop panicking, Adam. I went light-headed, but I don't think anything is wrong, probably a blood pressure thing like I've had before. I'll mention it at my next check-up.'

'Be sure, though. You can't take any chances.'

She almost laughed at his overly serious expression.

Christine came back with drinks and cakes. 'How's the patient?'

'She's at least got some colour back in her cheeks,' said Adam.

'I'm fine. Stop fussing, you two.'

'It's only because we care,' said Adam, and the colour definitely increased then on Skye's cheeks.

Christine grinned at her. 'Lucky girl, having a handsome young man watching out for you.'

Skye drank the herbal tea and had half a gingerbread man from the plate, even though her stomach was still rolling a bit. She excused herself to go to the ladies. She still felt wobbly but there was no way she was going to give Adam or Christine the satisfaction of knowing that's how she was feeling if she could avoid it.

As she returned to the table, Christine and Adam were discussing the historic development of Borteen. Skye cleared away the empty cups and plates and went to put them into the dishwasher. When she got back to the counter, an elderly couple were examining the cake display. Skye took their order, fervently hoping she wouldn't embarrass herself by being sick on the floor in front of them.

When Christine and Adam had finished their conversation, Adam stood up and came over to Skye.

'What time do you finish your shift?'

'Four o'clock.'

'Can I come and walk you home?'

Skye was suddenly a little irritated by his protectiveness. 'There really is no need.'

'I wasn't thinking of you this time, sorry. There was something I wanted to share with you about what's been happening with me.' He looked rather hurt.

'Oh! Sorry! I didn't realize. Your meeting, by any chance?' He nodded.

'Yes, of course, I'll see you at four. I look forward to hearing your news.' She smiled and briefly touched his arm in apology.

'Right, I'll be off. I badly need a shower after my run.'

She watched him go, wondering again about his motivations, his expectations and what had been happening to him in Borteen that he wanted to share.

Skye went to join Christine in the kitchen. Her boss was grinning as she put the finishing touches to the rows of mince pies, gingerbread men and Christmas cake slices for that evening.

'Who's made a conquest then?' said Christine, winking at her.

Skye tried to look innocent, but she knew what her boss meant. She tried to make light of it. 'He's only a friend. After all, who'd be interested in a girl this pregnant with someone else's baby?'

'Well, I rather think Adam is besotted with you, regardless of your *condition*.'

Skye thought maybe Christine was right, but she was still hesitant to believe it wholeheartedly.

Christine passed her a broken leg from one of the gingerbread men. 'Can I be serious for a second, Skye?' She waited until Skye was giving her full attention. 'Don't end up alone like me, and having said that don't end up with the wrong guy either. It's all too easy to settle for less than you deserve in this life.'

'It's so easy to say, but less easy to achieve. I thought Declan was the right guy before he showed his nasty side and

123

went off with someone else. Adam is lovely, but I still don't know him very well . . . yet.'

Christine wasn't a moaner, wasn't even a person subject to depression or anger, it seemed, but underneath the chilled-out, capable, chatty café owner, she did seem actually rather lonely. She'd told Skye before that her parents had long since gone to Borteen's churchyard, she had no siblings and had never had any children, owing to the fact that she'd never found the right man to share her life. The café appeared to do well, but it was hard work and often required long hours cooking, cleaning, preparing on repeat. Some days, like today, Skye knew it must be endless and almost thankless.

Not long after Adam left, there was another visitor. The man was wearing a Santa outfit, complete with a white bushy beard of cotton wool. Skye did a double take but then remembered Lally Kensington was Santa this year, or at least she thought it was him underneath the outfit.

He ignored Skye and spoke directly to Christine.

'Now then, Christine, I've a proposal for you.'

Christine blushed like a schoolgirl. 'Now, is that you underneath that beard, Lally Kensington?' she asked, playing along.

'Sure is. I'm just giving the outfit a test run to see if it's comfortable and to make sure no bits fall off, before I wear it for real tonight. Thought I might give you a sneak peek too.'

'Well, you make a mighty fine Santa.'

Did Skye imagine that the bit of Lally's face she could see coloured red at Christine's compliment?

Lally appeared to suddenly notice what Christine had been doing when he came in. 'Oh, yummy, are those delicious-looking cakes for this evening?'

'They are indeed. It's taken me a couple of days to get them ready.'

'Can I have one now, do you think? Only, by the time I'm finished with Santa duties this evening there won't be any left.'

'I could keep some back for when you're done, if you like?'

'Now there's a tempting offer, an assignation with an attractive woman later this evening.'

'Are you flirting with me, Mr Kensington?'

'Might be,' he laughed, and Skye was amused to see Christine blushing again.

Skye stood back to allow the two to talk. She tidied the pile of serviettes for the umpteenth time.

'Anyway, you came in to ask me something, didn't you?' said Christine.

'Oh yes. See, I got completely distracted by you and your cakes.'

'By the cakes anyway,' laughed Christine.

'Buzz has asked if I'd help him with something and I immediately thought of you.' Lally glanced at Skye and she pricked up her ears at the mention of Buzz.

'You know he supports his homeless charity?' continued Lally.

'Yes, he does events to raise money for it, including his regular "Walk the Labyrinth" thing on the beach.'

Lally nodded. 'Well, he wants to give some of the homeless people a Christmas party again, but last year's venue isn't available as it's closed for refurbishment and I wondered if there was any chance we could maybe host it in the café this year?'

'I'm not sure, depends how many homeless people we're talking about and what exactly my involvement would be.'

'Let's get together with Buzz early next week to discuss it, shall we? Now, is there any chance of a piece of that gorgeous-looking cake?'

'Oh, go on then.' Christine parcelled up a piece of cake in a serviette and got a kiss on the cheek from Santa as a thank you. 'I'll keep you a mince pie for later.' She was giggling as Lally left.

'Now who's made a conquest?' said Skye, cheekily repeating Christine's words back to her.

'Don't you dare. You know what I said earlier about Lally being a valued friend.'

'Need to take things very slowly then,' said Skye.

'Yes indeed. But I will admit, I wouldn't say no to getting a bit more friendly with Santa.'

'I'm looking forward to this evening, but probably not as much as you are.' Skye smiled back.

The two women laughed together again. Christine went back to putting the finishing touches to the cakes for that evening and Skye went out to the tables to take the orders of two couples who had just come into the café.

CHAPTER SEVENTEEN

Adam didn't know quite what to make of Skye's reaction to his worries about her health and his request to walk her home. She had obviously misconstrued his intentions, or had she? He could never have imagined himself being so attracted to a girl pregnant with someone else's baby. But . . . he was. It was certainly Skye who he thought about when he woke in the night, Skye he wanted to tell about the developments in his life, Skye he hoped would at least become his friend. And, he realized, he'd begun to think of her in idle moments rather than always feeling panicky. Surely that was a good sign.

After the little Skye had said about being bullied in Ireland and being abandoned by the father of her baby, she must be very cautious about the intentions of others.

But he decided that he just had to go with his gut feelings. Hadn't he vowed to be true to himself and not to hesitate again? Once more, the memory of Lewis launching over the balustrade and falling to his death hit him hard in the stomach. He took some deep shuddering breaths to avert the threatening panic. He had to start using this horrid cameo of life as a positive reminder, rather than something that floored him every time. He started to run hard back towards the vicarage. Skye didn't even know he was living there yet. He couldn't quite believe it himself either.

The vicarage was a vast Victorian house, built at a time when a vicar was more than likely to have a large family. Adam had been given the choice between three bedrooms — a twin room whose windows looked towards the steep wooded hill behind the building, a single room with childish wallpaper, or a double room with heavy oak furniture and a view of the sea.

'I can guess which one you'll choose,' said Nigel Hopkins. 'But I thought I ought to show you the options in any case.'

Adam had begun to feel a little doubtful when he'd been shown the other bedrooms, but when he'd gone to the window of this room, he smiled at the view. There was something magical about being close to the sea, and to have this outlook every day would be perfect.

'You do realize you might be stuck with me? I can't think of a more wonderful scene to wake up to in the morning, or any time of day actually. Yes, you might be stuck with me here, but you might not see me, I'll be too busy looking out of this window.'

Nigel laughed. 'I've got a similar view on the floor above. It's the best thing about this draughty old place. I hope you've bought plenty of jumpers with you, because you'll no doubt need them.'

'A small price to pay . . . Talking of which, we need to agree the terms of me staying here. I expect to be contributing and not living here for free.'

'I'm sure we can sort all of that out, Adam. For now, and forgive me for saying this, I think you are a wounded soul in need of sanctuary and I am more than happy to provide that as we get to know each other. I live modestly. I hate cooking, so if you have any culinary skills they will be more than welcome.'

'I'm a dab hand at omelettes,' said Adam with a smile.

'Deal. I look forward to many different varieties of omelette in my future.'

Nigel left Adam to settle in. Adam loved the room already and knew it would be a great place for contemplation.

When he collected her from the café as arranged at four, Adam asked Skye if she was going to the Christmas tree dressing.

'Buzz said we could go together. He says it's usually a good, fun evening.'

'That's what Reverend Hopkins said too.' Adam would have actually preferred to go to the event with Skye, but maybe he would bump into her there anyway.

Skye stopped walking. 'Is that who you came to Borteen to see?'

'That's what I wanted to tell you about.'

'I'm sorry, Adam. I've been so focussed on myself. This sounds like a big deal for you, tell me, tell me . . .'

She danced away and back towards him and Adam knew in that moment that he did indeed fancy this girl with her sparkling eyes and long, swinging plaits.

He told her about his discussions with Nigel Hopkins about the past and his future direction. 'Another similarity between us — I've found somewhere other than the guest-house to live too. I've moved into the vicarage.'

'Wow! That's great. I do hope you find some answers there.' Skye flung her arms around him and squeezed. Adam pulled her to him and didn't want to let go. He let his cheek rest against hers for a few seconds and then released her. The warmth of her skin on his lingered for a few tantalizing moments, but would live in his memory for much longer.

* * *

Buzz knew it was a good job that he now had Skye to consider, for if not, he doubted that he would be even thinking of going to the Borteen Christmas tree dressing. In truth, if Skye wasn't living at the house, he would probably still be keening and rocking in the shop storeroom, grieving for the loss of Wynn. He had felt hollow since she had left Borteen again.

He didn't think anything or anyone could ease his pain of loss, but he was determined to relish this possibly finite time with Skye. He had never imagined that he would ever have a family, and now he had the promise of one so tantalizingly close, he wanted to enjoy it for as long as he could.

He'd had a good day in the shop. A newly qualified crystal therapist had been in to ask for Buzz's help in choosing her healing crystals and a long-standing customer had been in to do her early Christmas shopping. Buzz was looking forward to talking about this with Skye when she got back, so he happened to be looking out of the shop window for her and caught sight of her flinging her arms around Adam in the street.

Buzz's reaction surprised him. Instead of feeling pleased, he was resentful. He had wanted Skye to himself for at least a few precious weeks. There was also the worry that Adam might be yet another man who could take advantage and potentially hurt her.

He watched the pair making their goodbyes and retreated back behind the shop counter quickly so that Skye wouldn't know that she'd been observed.

When she came in, however, he had other things on his mind. Skye didn't look at all well, and as she lurched through the doorway, she clutched her stomach and doubled over.

'Skye!' All other thoughts fled as he rushed over to her.

The shop door opened at that very moment.

'Skye!' Adam rushed in. He looked at Buzz. 'She hasn't been feeling too good all day. I'll get my car.' He rushed out of the door again.

Buzz helped Skye to sit down on the chair by the door. She was ashen, with a haunted look in her eyes.

'I'm scared . . . my baby.'

'I know, love. Stay strong.'

Very soon, there was a beep outside. Buzz glanced out and put his arm under Skye's arm to support her.

'Come on, let's get to Sowden hospital so they can check you over.'

'I want to see the Christmas tree lights switched on,' wailed Skye.

'Don't worry about that now.'

Buzz manoeuvred Skye out of the door and locked it behind him. Adam was parked half on the pavement on double yellow lines. He leaped out of the car now and opened the back door.

'Thank you for this,' said Buzz, as he rushed around to the other side of the car.

'You're going to have to tell me where to go,' said Adam.

Buzz shut the door and fastened the seatbelt around Skye. 'Okay, let's get going. Straight up the high street, please, Adam.'

Buzz fastened his own seatbelt as Adam indicated and turned the car back onto the road, and all the time Buzz could see he kept a protective eye on Skye in the rear-view mirror. Adam really cared about her too. The young man was driving carefully and steadily, but often took a glance in his mirror to check on his passenger.

It seemed to take an absolute age to travel across Pink Moor above Borteen and over to Sowden. Skye rested her head back and gripped Buzz's hand tightly, with her other hand held over her stomach.

'You know, when I first found out I was pregnant, I was scared. I didn't know what to do, couldn't imagine how I could possibly cope with being a mother, even wished I wasn't actually carrying her at times. But now I'm terrified that I might actually be losing my daughter, just when I've got used to the idea of being a single parent with all that that entails. Just when I've got used to the idea of being a mother.'

'Try to think positively until we know any different.' Buzz hoped his faith would be rewarded.

Adam didn't speak for the whole hair-raising journey. He glanced in his mirror often, although Buzz doubted that he could actually see Skye as it was now dark.

When they arrived at Sowden General Hospital, Adam took them as close to the Accident and Emergency entrance as he could, before stopping and leaping out to help Buzz get Skye onto her feet.

'I'll find you, once I've managed to park,' he gasped. Buzz glanced behind as they made their way tortuously towards the entrance and Adam was still standing next to his car watching them, as if he expected to have to rush over and carry Skye inside.

The administrator on the check-in desk had obviously been trained to spot patients with the greatest need and she soon summoned a nurse to speak to Skye. Without much preamble, she was whisked off in a wheelchair, so by the time Adam arrived in the reception area the only thing the two men could do was to drink the dreadful-tasting tea from the vending machine and wait for news.

Buzz and Adam sat in silence for a while. Buzz tried all of the quick relaxation methods he could remember but somehow this tension wouldn't let go.

'I hope you don't mind me asking, sir, but do you know anything about the father of Skye's baby?'

'I'm Buzz, no need for the *sir*. No, not a lot at all, just a name — Declan — and a possible connection to Birmingham University.'

'Hmm. Difficult one.'

'Might all be immaterial if . . .' Buzz rubbed a hand over his face and didn't finish the sentence.

'I think Skye would find that really hard now that she's started to bond with her daughter. She was even thinking about what to call the little girl.'

'She's obviously confided quite a lot in you. Thank you for being her friend.'

'She's a lovely person.'

'Your paths were meant to cross for some reason.'

'I think I'd agree with that.'

They fell silent again and Buzz wondered how long he could bear sitting here without any news about Skye and her baby.

CHAPTER EIGHTEEN

Skye was even more alarmed after the nurse in the A&E reception took one look at her and whisked her away down the endless corridors in a wheelchair. Up until that point, she'd tried to be brave for Buzz and indeed Adam's sakes. Now she let the tears fall silently down her cheeks.

'Let's have a look at this baby, shall we?' The nurse in the maternity ward asked Skye to reveal her tummy and slathered cold gel on her skin. Skye held her breath. She didn't know quite what she was expecting to see, but there was her daughter on the screen in seconds. The machine picked up the baby's strong, pulsing heartbeat and Skye let out the breath she had been holding in with a great whoosh of relief.

'Well, baby seems fine. I suspect you've had a dip in blood pressure or blood sugar.'

'It's happened before . . . I think I just panicked when I felt so bad. And this time I had a few sharp pains.'

'It's understandable to be unsure, when you've never been through pregnancy before.' She pushed buttons on the keyboard of her computer. 'Ah yes, I can see from your notes now. Has anyone spoken to you about Braxton Hicks contractions?'

'Is that what they were? Practice contractions for the labour?'

'You've obviously heard of them then. Yes, I suspect that's what you had.'

Skye sighed in relief and the nurse patted her arm. She took her blood pressure, which was now fine.

'I'll get the nurse to give you some further advice on how to handle this and then I think you can be on your way home.' She smiled and patted Skye's arm.

'Thank you so much.' Skye was relieved but felt a little silly too. Glancing at her phone screen, as she didn't ever wear a watch, she realized how late it had got and sighed, in frustration this time.

'We missed the big Christmas tree dressing,' lamented Skye, when she re-joined Buzz and Adam in the reception area.

'More important to get you checked out,' said Buzz, his arm protectively around her shoulders on the way back to the car.

'If you feel well enough tomorrow, we can go for a walk past the Christmas tree together,' promised Adam.

'I'll be free. I sent Christine a message to say I couldn't do my shift tomorrow.'

'That's wise. Even though this scare turned out to be nothing to be concerned about, you need to take it easy for a while,' said Buzz.

'Part of the problem is that I've never been pregnant before, so don't really know how I should or shouldn't be feeling.'

'I know, darling, and I'm not exactly an expert on pregnancy either.'

'Nor me,' added Adam.

'I want to FaceTime Mum when we get back.'

'That would be a good idea.'

Skye enjoyed the relieved squeeze that Buzz gave to her hand and Adam didn't seem to be able to keep his eyes off her.

Adam dropped them off on the double yellow lines out-side of the shop, promising to check on Skye the next day. Buzz thanked him profusely for his help.

Skye had strange mixed feelings, because she actually wished that Adam was coming into the flat too. She had quite enjoyed having the two protective, caring men looking out for her. Buzz made her feel cherished, but Adam made her feel . . . how did Adam make her feel?

* * *

Wynn's face was tight and anxious when they spoke to her on the video call. Buzz looked with curiosity at what little he could see of Wynn's surroundings in the background. Her living room looked dark, filled with heavy old furniture. He could see a picture of Skye on a shelf, and despite the tradi-tional furnishings there was a huge mandala dot-painted on the wall. Wynn had a purple-dyed feather woven into the end of her long plait today.

Buzz's heart and stomach turned over — he still loved Wynn and he couldn't help it. How was that even possible after the betrayal, the running away, keeping Skye a secret, the passage of so much time? Inside, he was like a young man again, breathless with overwhelming emotions, his eyes shin-ing with excitement and anticipation. He could still remem-ber the elation when he'd realized that Wynn felt the same way about him. He'd been so happy back then that he could almost have flown from Borteen cliffs.

Wynn was busy questioning Skye about her hospital visit and the reasons for it, staring at her as closely as was possible on a phone screen. The concern in her face made the furrows in her brow seem even deeper. She eventually relaxed back when Skye explained that they thought the baby had settled in an awkward place and that Skye's blood pressure had dipped as a result, coupled with the practice contractions. For the time being, they'd asked her to make sure she was never alone so that help could be summoned quickly if something happened again.

'You know, Wynn, you could always join us for Christmas . . . You'd be very welcome,' interrupted Buzz.

'And where would I sleep?'

There was challenge in Wynn's eyes. Buzz wanted to scream "in my bed" but he schooled his face. 'I have a fold-up bed. We can put it in Skye's room, then you can keep an eye on her even at night.'

Skye punched him on the arm at that point.

However, Wynn's next words took him by surprise.

'I've been busy making arrangements for the shop. And it is Christmas after all. I think I would feel much happier keeping an eye on Skye than wondering what was happening from a distance. As long as you're sure I'm okay to stay. Women see different things to men.'

'Of course you can stay, and *cheeky*!' A glimmer of excitement ignited inside Buzz. Wynn was coming back, for he was convinced that her daughter would take priority over her shop and even her livelihood. But was he deluding himself that he could win her back over the Christmas period? Now the challenge was on.

CHAPTER NINETEEN

Adam appeared at the shop door dead on nine the next morning when Buzz opened the blinds.

'How is Skye today?' He was red-cheeked from the cold and muffled up in a scarf, hat and big coat.

'She says she slept well and she seems fine this morning. Colour in her cheeks and she ate a hearty breakfast. She's in the shower right now, but come in and wait. I'm sure she'll be pleased to see you.'

Adam came into the shop and began to look around. Buzz could see his eyes taking in some of the more unusual stock, and his head snapped up when the door to the living quarters opened a little while later. The young man's expression gave Buzz absolutely no doubt that he was totally smitten with Skye. He didn't know enough about this person to be sure if he approved or not. As a man, he wanted to tell Adam to proceed with caution because his heart was well and truly in danger.

Then he turned to look at his daughter and the way she was smiling, with her eyes full of light. Maybe Adam would be lucky in love after all.

'How are you feeling today?' asked Adam.

'Much, much better, thank you, and I . . . *we* must thank you for your help yesterday.'

'I didn't do anything really. Are you up for a little walk? It's cold, mind. You'll have to wrap up well. You wanted to see the Christmas tree and I would like to have a look too.'

'I feel almost as if I have two dads at the moment,' laughed Skye. 'But that's actually rather nice. I'll get my coat.' She disappeared through the door to the flat again.

'Don't take her too far, Adam. I'm still worried about her, you know.'

'Me too and no, I won't. Just thought she'd like to see the tree decorated and lit up. And I pulled a few strings.' He produced a couple of decorations from his pocket, but as Skye returned he quickly put them back out of her sight.

'Have fun,' said Buzz, as he watched them go.

* * *

Adam was aware that Buzz had wanted to say much more to him than he had. He was understandably concerned about a man showing an interest in Skye, especially as she was vulnerable and pregnant, and Adam was not the father of her baby. Adam had wanted to reassure him that his intentions were completely honourable — that wasn't quite the right word but it said what he meant. It was actually very difficult to find the right words to express what he wanted to say and how he felt about Skye.

He wanted to wrap her in cotton wool to keep her safe, but he knew she would react badly to him smothering her with his concerns, so he settled for offering her his arm for support as they walked the short distance down the high street to the promenade. Up ahead of them, the huge Borteen Christmas tree glittered with shimmering lights against the sea wall.

'Wow. Doesn't it look lovely?' exclaimed Skye.

The light in her eyes made Adam do a double take. Skye was beautiful.

'I was so sad that you missed the event last night, so I got us these.' Adam took the two Christmas decorations from his pocket.

Skye whooped with obvious delight. She took one of the baubles and skipped the short distance to the tree. Adam joined her and they reached as high as they could to place their ornaments on neighbouring branches. They stood back to look at the other decorations.

Adam could hear music coming from below them on the beach. Skye towed him to the steps and they went to investigate the sound.

At the top of the beach there was a concrete platform and on it a band had set up their instruments — a full drum kit, guitars and a singer. A small crowd had gathered to listen. There was a sign saying the band were rehearsing for a gig that evening.

Before he knew it, Adam, not usually a keen dancer, was swaying in time to the music with Skye holding both his hands. She laughed as if she hadn't a care in the world.

'You really do feel better today?' he asked warily.

'Yes, and I think having the confirmation from the hospital that what I experienced was common and nothing to worry about has made me relax more.'

'It really is an amazing thing — being able to grow a baby.'

'I guess so. I still can't quite believe I'm doing it. Can I ask you something, Adam?'

'Fire away.'

'Hypothetical question, of course, but say we had met under normal circumstances — that is, boy meets girl at a concert — do you think we'd have fancied each other?'

Adam gulped and felt his cheeks colour. 'From my part, most definitely, but why do you think it would be any different now?'

He watched Skye gulp this time.

'You can't possibly fancy me, given . . . ?' She pointed at her stomach.

The music started up again, so in answer he twirled her around and she leaned on him when she'd circled. 'You're lovely, Skye. Very different to anyone I've ever dated before — to be truthful, I haven't actually dated many girls, but . . .'

'The big but is that I'm expecting another man's child. Doesn't that bother you?'

'Your child is a part of you, so no, I don't think it does. I've actually thought about this question quite a lot since I met you. Look, I'll even help you find her father, if that's what you truly want.'

'You'd do that . . . really?'

'Although I will say that I'd only do it for one reason: I feel as if you need closure with him before you can move on . . . maybe with someone else.' He knew his face had a silly grin plastered over it as he pointed to himself.

'The big thing is that I don't really know what closure with Declan would mean. I have to be totally honest with you, Adam.'

'But if you don't at least see him and tell him about the baby, I think you'll always wonder and never be free to be with someone else wholeheartedly.'

'So, what if you help me find Declan and he wants me and the baby back?'

'I'll have to take that chance, won't I? I'd rather you knew that you actually wanted to be with me and not him, rather than always wondering, always having that unknown between us.'

'You're worrying me now.' Skye scuffed at the sand with her boot.

'Why's that?'

'You're being too nice, Adam. Too reasonable almost.'

'And if I said I wanted you to be my girlfriend and forbade you to ever contact Declan? Then what would that make me?'

'You're right, of course.' She reached up a hand and touched his cheek gently.

'Let's go to the café, its time you had a sit down anyway. I'd like you to tell me everything you know about Declan and then on Monday morning, I'll travel to Birmingham and try to find him.'

'You really would do that?'

'I've just said I would.'

He held Skye's arm carefully as they went back up the beach steps, mindful that Buzz would want him to be extra careful with her. Adam couldn't quite believe what he'd just said to Skye. He'd in effect asked her to be his girl, baby or no baby.

* * *

Skye was astounded that Adam was willing to go to search for Declan for her and yet she knew it made sense. Everything he'd said about closure was correct. And yet she found herself scared, terrified even. Declan was such a different type of man to Adam. How would a meeting between the two of them go?

After thinking about it, she pulled him away from the route to the beach café and up the high street instead to the posher bistro café, Simply Latte, beyond Buzz's shop. She didn't really want Christine knowing what they were up to, or being able to overhear the conversation. And however much Skye had come to love Christine as a boss and friend, she knew that the café owner listened in to as many conversations as she could.

Adam appeared initially surprised at her choice of venue, but it didn't seem to take him long to cotton on to why she had headed for an alternative café.

It seemed odd being in this café and comparing it to the one where she worked. The atmosphere was very different. The little beach café was homely, this one was smarter and the prices reflected that too.

When they were settled, Skye with a herbal tea and Adam a coffee, Adam took a small notebook from his coat pocket. It was all Skye could do not to bolt, as just the fact that he intended to write down some details was scary.

'So, tell me about Declan. Surname?'

A blush made her face hot. 'Coles.'

'Right.' Adam couldn't help quirking an eyebrow at her tone. 'Subject of his degree at university maybe?'

'I think he said some form of engineering.'

'You do realize if you don't open up a little, it's going to be virtually impossible to find him, don't you?'

'I fear your opinion of me might take a nosedive.'

'No chance. I've done some pretty stupid things in my past too, so don't worry about it. Let's just try to get this done, shall we?'

'Okay.' She knew her voice sounded small and uncertain.

'Safer ground, maybe? What does he look like?'

This was easier. Skye took out her phone and showed Adam a selfie of herself and Declan. A foot taller than her, dark hair scruffily long, bushy eyebrows. Adam was scribbling notes. 'Could you send me that photo?'

'Sure.'

'Where was it taken?'

'On Grafton Street in Dublin. We'd just been singing the song by Ed Sheeran on the Luas tram, so I took a photo of us together. We'd only recently become an item and everything seemed new, shiny and hopeful.'

They exchanged mobile numbers and Skye sent the photo of her and Declan over to him.

'Has he got an accent?'

'Irish. Southern Irish actually, he's originally from Cork.'

'Any other clues — tattoos maybe?'

'He's got one on his wrist of a clock.'

'That's more hopeful. People will remember something like that.' Without probably realizing it, Adam was rubbing at his wrist.

'Do you have tats?' asked Skye.

'No, I haven't got any. My mother hates them, so I've never dared.'

Skye knew she was blushing again and it seemed as if her own tattoo was alive, throbbing, getting ready to reveal itself to Adam. Thankfully he didn't ask and it wasn't visible when she was wearing winter clothing.

'How old is Declan?'

'Twenty. He delayed going to uni for a couple of years because his mum was ill.'

'Did she get better?'

'No, she died unfortunately.'

'So sad. Anything else you can think of that would help me find him?'

'Not really.' She toyed with the spoon, before looking up at Adam. 'I don't really know him very well at all, do I?'

'Not my place to judge.'

'You must think me so awful.'

'Far from it, Skye. I guess you were besotted with Declan for whatever reason at the time you were together. All we need to know is if he wants to be part of his child's life, and yours, or not. I promise to do my best to find the answer to your question.'

'I don't honestly know what to wish for. For my baby's sake, I guess I have to try to find Declan, or rather, I hope you'll be able to. But I can't help thinking that trying to find him could be a great big mistake.'

CHAPTER TWENTY

A few days later, Skye was back working at the beach café. Christine insisted on her having regular breaks now that she knew about the problems with her blood pressure. Christine had even put a bar stool behind the counter so that Skye could sit down when she was taking orders if she had the need.

Skye felt a nuisance for needing the concession, but was grateful for the consideration and support. When she caught sight of Adam outside on the promenade, her heart sped up, but annoyingly he didn't come into the café. Maybe he didn't realize she was working. He walked off up the high street, and Skye wondered if he might be heading to Buzz's shop and she could miss seeing him.

* * *

Adam was indeed on the way to see Buzz and he was fully aware that Skye was working. He'd caught sight of her behind the counter at the café and then deliberately ducked away. He didn't want her to see him yet . . . if ever again.

The shop doorbell's strident tone always took him by surprise. Buzz darted quickly out from the door that led to the living quarters. Adam self-consciously pulled the hood of his coat closer around his face.

'Hello, Adam.' At least Buzz's tone was bright and welcoming. 'Skye's working at the café today if you want to see her.'

'I know, I saw her in the café as I came past. I actually wanted to see you first, before I tell her about what happened when I went to Birmingham to find Declan.'

'Oh, yes?' Buzz's voice was full of curiosity.

Adam pointedly pushed back the hood which he'd been using up to that point to shield his face.

Buzz gasped in shock, and he darted around the shop counter to have a closer look at Adam. 'Goodness, what on earth has happened to you?'

Adam put his hand up to his eye and winced at the jarring pain that seared through his eyelid. 'I went in search of Skye's Declan. She knows that I was intending to go to Birmingham to try and find him. We sat down together and made a note of things that might help to locate him the other day. She gave me a photo of them together too.'

'Sorry, I'm a little confused now. So, you went to Birmingham alone? And did you find him?'

Adam pointed at his face. 'Yes, I found him. It was his distinctive tattoo that helped me to track him down eventually — as I suspected, people remember things like that. I got a lead; I followed it up and I found him.'

Adam paused, pulling his hood down more fully. 'Then I approached him in all innocence and tried to speak to him, only in a friendly way, you understand. He was suspicious right away, of course, seemed to think I was a debt collector or something. Then when I mentioned Skye and Dublin, he got extremely angry. I don't believe I've ever seen anyone so incandescent with rage. He told me to "bugger off". I tried to be reasonable, placating, calm. I told him Skye had been trying to find him to tell him about something important. He said he wasn't interested in anything she would have to say, never wanted to see her again. He didn't say "her", but I won't dignify the name he used by repeating it. Sorry, sorry, that sort of came out in a great big dump of information.'

'And he hit you?'

'Afraid so. I stupidly persisted in trying to talk to the man. I should probably have backed off when I realized he was getting angry, tried another time. When I mentioned the baby, he floored me. He called me a liar and other things while I was on the floor a bit dazed, again I won't repeat them. Then he threatened me with even more violence if either I or Skye ever came after him again, left me on the ground and stormed off. Last thing I saw of him, he was putting his arm around a girl dressed like a goth with a very short skirt.'

'Whoa. That's absolutely awful, Adam. I'm so sorry it happened. You were only trying to help. Did you call the police? Report the assault?'

'I didn't really think it would achieve anything. I knew enough by then to know that I didn't want any more to do with Declan. One thing I am really sure of is that Skye is better off without the thug. I can't imagine what she ever saw in him in the first place really.'

'What a horrid thing to happen.' Buzz pulled Adam to face him so he could have a better look at his injuries, which thankfully appeared to be only superficial.

'I wanted to speak to you before Skye, because I feel it's extremely important that she doesn't try to see or contact Declan, particularly on her own. Who knows what he would do if she challenged him, especially about the baby. She should forget all about him and the notion that he might somehow want to be part of his child's life. You could never leave a child safely with a man with a temper like that, or I couldn't anyway.' Adam was aware he'd kept talking, probably saying too much.

'Adam, I'm so sorry this has happened.' Buzz moved to hug him and Adam was so surprised he didn't resist the brief embrace. Buzz released him and made him stand under one of the shop spotlights to take a closer look at his eye again. 'Only bruising, thankfully, but he could have broken something so easily.'

'It sure hurts. I don't know how much Skye has shared with you about my own story?' Adam looked at Buzz and could tell by his puzzled expression that he didn't know anything at all. 'Now isn't the time to tell you everything, but suffice it to say I'm living at the vicarage at the moment. Reverend Hopkins was outraged when I came back with this shiner. I couldn't decide if he was mad about Declan's behaviour, or me looking like this when I'm living with him, or both.' Adam tried to laugh, but it hurt his eye again and he winced instead.

'I look forward to hearing your own story another time and your link to my friend, Nigel, but I can see why you wanted to tell me about your trip to Birmingham first. I feel terribly responsible somehow, even if I didn't know what you had planned, and I'm absolutely sure that Skye will be completely mortified.'

'I didn't think it fair to show her the mess my face is in when she was at work.'

'Probably wise. Shall I get us some mugs of strong tea while we wait for her to come home?'

'Sure. I'm not exactly wanting to be seen around the town looking like this. I don't know many people in Borteen yet, and I don't really want to be remembered as the guy with the black eye.'

'Sit yourself down on one of the stools behind the counter. I won't be long. I suppose if a customer comes in you'd better put your hood back up or dive into the storeroom?' Buzz shrugged helplessly.

Adam sat behind the counter, taking in Buzz's strange, eclectic shop. Some well-thumbed cards lay next to the till. Adam thought they were tarot cards and made a note to ask Reverend Hopkins for his opinion on such things. He was also curious about the vastly differing paths taken by human beings. What had led Buzz to be in Borteen, running a shop like this and having a belief system that was seemingly so different from his own? He hadn't yet asked Nigel Hopkins how he himself had ended up in Borteen either.

The sign above the shop door lintel outside of Crazy Crystals read 'Witches Welcome'. Inside the shop was mostly dark, the first impression being the strange smell of incense. One wall had cabinets full of crystals and strange objects incorporating crystals that Adam couldn't even guess at their use or purpose. The other side of the shop had rails of colourful ethnic clothing, crinkly skirts and woollen coats. The rest of the wall space was covered with bags, pictures and mirrors. Shelves were packed with carved wooden dolphins, jewellery, bells and incense burners. What looked to Adam remarkably like bric-a-brac was piled in boxes on the floor.

He had an irrational fear of a customer coming in while Buzz was making the drinks, but no one did. Buzz came back balancing a tray and presented him with a purple mug with a pentangle on the side of it. The tea was thankfully normal English breakfast tea, nice and strong with not too much milk.

Buzz settled himself on the other stool. 'Skye finishes her shift soon and you can get the difficult bit over with.'

'Even though I feel like bolting when you say that, I suppose it makes sense. Otherwise, she'll think I'm avoiding her, but even so I'm worried about her reaction to my face.'

'You do know she's going to be extremely upset, don't you?'

Adam nodded.

The shop door chime sounded and a customer came in, hailing Buzz in a friendly manner and heading to the cabinet of crystals. Adam shrank back and pulled up his hood once more.

As he sat in the shadows of the shop, he wondered where this episode would leave him and Skye. He'd only tried to help her and it had backfired spectacularly. Well, that wasn't strictly true, he'd actually been curious about Declan for himself and needed to know if the guy intended to be a father to his baby or not, whether he was interested in Skye at all.

Adam had realized on his way back from Birmingham that he wanted Skye for himself. He wanted to protect her, wanted to support her, wanted her to support him too. He would love her baby; he was sure of that. However, he knew he would have to tread softly, as maybe Skye would be upset that Declan didn't want anything to do with her or his child, despite what she had said about not being sure.

Adam himself was certain. He wanted Skye and her daughter to be part of his new life, but would she feel the same about him?

CHAPTER TWENTY-ONE

Skye burst through the shop door a little while later.

'Did Adam come to see you?' she asked breathlessly.

Adam had pulled his hood up and shrunk back again as the door opened and the dreaded door chime sounded yet again. His heart began to thud.

'Yes, he's here waiting for you, Skye. Have your ears been burning? We've been talking about you,' laughed Buzz.

Adam could tell he was trying to keep his voice calm and soothing as he went out into the shop area.

'All good, I hope? Hi, Adam.' Her face registered confusion that Adam didn't come out to greet her as Buzz had. Buzz put his hands on her arms, forcing her to look at him.

'Now, we don't want you to get upset . . .'

'About what exactly?' Skye's tone was wary.

'You'd better show her, Adam. But Skye, please take a deep breath.'

'What are you two on about?' said Skye with a decidedly worried expression on her face.

Adam walked around the counter, his hood still hiding most of his face. He stopped where she could see him and pulled the hood back. His heart was beating loudly in his ears.

Skye squealed.

'Your poor face. Did you have an accident?'

Adam watched her face go through a variety of expressions and emotions, until shock took over. 'Not Declan? Please don't tell me Declan did this.' The name Declan was said in a faint, bewildered tone.

Adam nodded. 'I'm afraid so. I went to Birmingham as promised.'

Skye launched herself against him, holding him tightly around his waist and sobbing into his chest. He met Buzz's eyes over the top of her head. Buzz gestured that he was going to leave them to it, and he turned the key in the lock of the shop door so that no one would come in, put the 'Closed' sign up, pulled the blind and disappeared through the door to the flat.

Adam ran his hand down Skye's thick plait. It reached all the way down her back and was finished at the end with beads. He loved the feel of it.

'I'm so sorry. I should have gone to find him myself and not let you go for me.' She breathed the words against his chest.

'Given how he reacted when I did find him, I'm rather glad you didn't go by yourself.'

She moved away and reached up her hand to cup his injured cheek. He couldn't help but wince as the skin was so tender. 'Did you tell him about the baby?'

'He didn't believe me, insisted I was lying. Told me never to contact him again and sent the same message to you, I'm afraid. Then he punched me.'

'Declan always was quick to anger.'

Adam held her forearm. 'He's not hurt you before?'

She looked down, suddenly sheepish. 'A few pinches, and he bruised my arm once when he squeezed it. He was angry with me.'

'Oh, Skye. Please don't go near that man ever again.'

'He seems to have made it abundantly clear that he doesn't want to know me anymore, or his baby.'

'Let me take care of you instead.' The words erupted from his mouth before he could stop them coming out. What happened to taking things slowly?

'Do you realize what you've just said?'

'Yes. I want us to be together. I care about you. I want to stand by you, Skye. I'll be the father of your baby. You can even put my name on the birth certificate if you like.' There, now he'd said it, expressed the thoughts that had been going around and around in his head on the train back from Birmingham. 'Marry me.'

'I could not let you do that, Adam. No!'

She'd pulled away and the gap between them suddenly felt vast, cold, empty and uncertain.

'Whyever not?'

'You hardly know me, Adam. And I'm pretty certain that our backgrounds, maybe even our belief systems, are vastly different.'

'I don't think any of that would matter if we were willing to work at it. I think I'm in love with you.'

She picked up on his words. '*Think* you're in love with me?'

'*Know* I'm in love with you!'

'Adam, I hoped that we were becoming good friends . . . genuine, valuable friends. I'm still reeling from finding out Declan wasn't for me, from being pregnant, from hopefully meeting my father for the first time, from living in a different country and away from my mother. I can't commit to you on just a whim. I believe it's even more important now that I find a way to support myself and my baby on my own, without a man, without relying on anyone completely.'

'That plan sounds very . . . lonely.'

'That's as may be, but it's how it has to be. I'm sorry if I led you to believe any differently . . .'

Adam was alarmed that tears had appeared in his eyes. 'I'm sorry I made assumptions. I've stepped over a line. I think I'd better go now, before I embarrass myself any further. Say goodbye to Buzz for me.'

He turned and walked away, pulling his hood over his damaged face as he fumbled with the key in the lock and stumbled out through the door onto the thankfully quiet high street.

Walking briskly towards the beach, Adam wondered how he could have got things so spectacularly wrong. But then, he'd gone against his own advice. Instead of taking things slowly and gently, hadn't he rather suggested that Skye needed rescuing and that he was the man to save her? It all seemed mistimed and misconceived with hindsight.

He'd blundered in without really thinking about what was going through her mind, about what was important to her, and instead he'd presented himself as some sort of selfless hero or knight in shining armour. He realized belatedly that he'd been a complete idiot and he feared he'd destroyed what had been developing into a deep, comfortable friendship and maybe, given time, much more. He'd misread the signs, opened his mouth too soon, again tried to rescue someone, and it looked like he'd lost everything.

When he reached the sand, he broke into a run. Not that exhausting himself helped in the slightest, but at least it went some way to dispelling the tension in his muscles.

His energy spent and tears of loss drying on his face, he walked slowly back to the vicarage to decide his next move. Time perhaps to go home to his mother, tell her what he'd been discussing with Nigel Hopkins, try to let his physical wounds heal and his emotional ones too. Maybe he wouldn't be staying in Borteen until Christmas after all.

* * *

When Adam had gone, Skye stood still in the middle of the shop for a long while completely stunned. What had she done? Had she just turned her back on something wonderful? Would she live to regret her words, her independent stand? She knew in her heart of hearts that Adam was one of life's good guys and she appeared to pick the baddies as a rule.

He'd made everything sound so simple to fix that it had inflamed her determination, anger even. He seemed to think he could whisk her up, protect her, marry her and give her baby his name. That they could all then live happily ever after like a fairy tale.

It all sounded so tempting with hindsight, but was that really the solution? She could see problems ahead, because they came from different backgrounds. Her upbringing had been unconventional, alternative some would say, with her mother talking about runes, moon cycles and the ancient festival days. And even though she hadn't grown up with her father, here she crossed her fingers yet again. Buzz ran Crazy Crystals, made labyrinths on the beach and gave tarot readings. She got side-tracked for a second thinking that she should maybe ask Buzz to do a reading for her.

The fact was that Adam might find all of that difficult. She generally kept it quiet when she was dating a guy, because in truth, she hadn't really established if this was just her mother's way of thinking, and now her father's, or actually her own too. She did suspect she was nearer to her mother, and Buzz's, ideology than anything she would find at the vicarage with Adam.

Her school life had been spent celebrating Christian festivals, of course, singing hymns and carols, because that was how it was at a conventional school, but she knew it was time to examine her own soul and work out exactly who she was going forward, if for no other reason than she would soon be a parent herself and have to decide how to educate her own daughter in what to believe, how to be in the world.

Her steps seemed heavy as she mounted the stairs to the flat. She could see Buzz reading a book in the lounge, but she couldn't face him yet. She tried to go quietly past in the hallway and up to her room, but he heard her footsteps, of course.

'All okay?'

'Not really, but could we talk about it later? I need a shower and a little nap.' She didn't wait for an answer, just scooted past and on up the stairs to the sanctuary of her attic room.

* * *

Buzz got the distinct impression that things were not okay at all with Adam and Skye and he couldn't help feeling rather sad. He put the sandwich he'd made for Skye back into the fridge, after debating whether to call up to her that it was there and deciding against it. He went back down to the shop, taking with him the cheese and pickle sandwich he'd made for his tea.

The shop had a distinctly strange atmosphere. Adam and Skye must have argued. He lit the sage smudge stick he habitually kept behind the counter and wafted it about to cleanse the energy of the space, drawing the familiar outlines of ancient symbols in the air and watching the smoke curl away to the ceiling.

He'd only taken one bite of his sandwich when the door chime sounded and, to his surprise, Nigel Hopkins burst in. Buzz had an odd reaction to Nigel being here in his space. They were long-standing acquaintances, even friends, but it was almost as if the headmaster had come to call. They usually met in neutral territory, the pub, the café or the churchyard, not in each other's very different lairs.

'Reverend, nice to see you here.'

Nigel Hopkins smiled. 'Smells like a church, Buzz.'

Buzz laughed. Maybe they weren't as different as he imagined. 'What can I do for you?'

'Need to talk to you about Adam.' Nigel was clearly agitated, shifting from foot to foot.

'Ah. I did wonder if it might be to do with him.'

'He's packing to leave.'

'What?'

'Seems he's done what he came here to do — that is, meet me, pick my brains a little — and now he's going. Wouldn't have anything to do with your daughter, would

155

it? This change of heart seems very sudden. I thought he was staying in Borteen until Christmas. I was actually looking forward to it.' Nigel ran a hand over his face and Buzz suspected he was emotional.

'I haven't managed to speak to Skye properly yet, but I believe something happened when Adam came to tell her about his trip to Birmingham.'

'The trip to Birmingham on some errand for Skye that resulted in him getting beaten up?'

'Yes. So awful. I couldn't believe it.'

'I didn't react well to his face looking like that. I'm ashamed to say I should have listened rather than reacting. I didn't handle it well at all.'

'Don't be angry with yourself. I was rather shocked at his appearance too.'

'Can you let me know what Skye says, please, Buzz? I don't know how to play this. Unfamiliar territory.'

'I can see that. Of course I will. I'll speak to her as soon as I can and get back to you.'

Nigel looked so downhearted; Buzz couldn't help feeling sorry for him. He didn't know the full story of why Adam had ended up living at the vicarage, but Nigel Hopkins was obviously upset that he was not staying on for longer.

It seemed important to get Skye's side of the story as soon as he could, so once again he shut up the shop — he appeared to be doing this much too often lately — and went to see if she was still in her room.

'There's no need to lurk outside, come in, I'm awake,' she said.

Buzz pushed the door open cautiously.

'Sorry, I thought you might be napping.'

Skye was curled up on the bed, her pregnancy bump seeming more pronounced than ever today.

Buzz went over to sit on the chair by the desk. 'I just wanted to make sure that you're okay.'

'I'm fine, but I may have upset Adam badly and it feels rather mean since he put himself out to go to Birmingham

156

for me and got beaten up for his trouble. I didn't even offer to pay for his train ticket, I realize now.'

'Don't worry about the train fare, I'll deal with that. It's just, I could do with knowing a little more about what happened between the two of you. Nigel Hopkins is troubled because Adam's apparently packing and intending to leave Borteen.'

'No!' Skye sat bolt upright.

'Can you give me a clue as to why, so that I can tell Nigel?'

'A difference of opinion, that's all, but I didn't think he'd just go. Having said that, it's probably for the best in the end.' She lay back down.

Buzz was at a loss about how to get Skye to reveal more. 'When Adam was here this afternoon, what he was saying . . . Skye, he cares a lot about you, has your best interests at heart, I believe.'

'Thinks he knows what's best for me, more like.' Skye had a hard set to her lips he'd never seen before when she finished speaking.

'Ahh . . . So, he didn't bank on you having a mind of your own, is my guess.'

'Something like that.' She was now studying the pattern on the duvet cover.

'Do you want to go and see him? Ask him not to go, maybe? Sort things out?'

'No. I think it's probably better if he goes and moves on with his life.'

'Are you absolutely sure about that?'

'Yes, I'm sure . . . I'm fine. Just a little tired today. I might get a sandwich and then do some sewing.'

'Well, with that I can help you — your sandwich is already made and in the fridge waiting for you.'

She got up and came to plant a brief kiss on his forehead. 'Thank you, and I'm sorry if all this has upset your friend.'

'I promised to update him, so if you're certain you're all right and don't need me, I'll head over there now to speak to him.'

'Sure, I'll see you later.'

She scrubbed at her face and there was moisture in her eyes, but he didn't dare comment on that, not yet anyway.

'You do know that everything will work out exactly how it is meant to, don't you?'

She looked straight into his eyes. 'You sound so like my mother. I do know that really. It's just that when you go through crappy stuff like this it's sometimes difficult to believe it for a while.'

'Plenty crappy stuff about, I'm afraid.' Buzz deliberately used Skye's terminology for life's ups and downs.

CHAPTER TWENTY-TWO

Buzz found it amusing that in all the years Nigel and he had been friends, sharing philosophical arguments in the church-yard, pub and café, Nigel had never been to his shop until today, and now he was about to knock on the vicarage door for the first time too.

He looked with curiosity at the old Victorian build-ing, which must have been built not long after the church. There was no sign of Adam's car in the driveway, which Buzz thought ominous. Had he already left?

There didn't appear to be a doorbell, so Buzz banged the huge brass knocker in the shape of a cross. Through the panes of glass at the sides of the door, Buzz could see Nigel coming down the hall looking as if the weight of the world was on his shoulders.

'Buzz, thanks for coming over. I fear it might be too late. Adam's already gone.'

'Oh dear. Did he say any more about why he was leaving?'

Nigel ushered Buzz into the house and down the hallway to a comfortable lounge with battered leather chairs flanking the fireplace, where a real fire was burning and spreading warmth into the room.

'You know, I've never been inside the vicarage before? It's a lovely building and really homely.'

'I do feel very lucky to live here, it's just ridiculously huge for one person.'

'It must make it even harder after sharing the house with Adam for a short while. How did that come about, by the way?'

'It's a long story, probably better kept for another time. He said that he needed to go back to London to see his mother, but I don't believe he was telling me the complete truth because his departure was so sudden. It was surely more than a coincidence that he left shortly after talking to Skye about Birmingham and getting that shiner of a black eye — another topic he refused to discuss properly.'

'I think you're probably right about his meeting with Skye. She was terribly upset after their conversation in the shop. She seemed to be suggesting that Adam believed he knew what was right for her and her baby. His certainty that he knew best obviously annoyed her because she said she was old enough to make up her own mind without a man interfering.'

Nigel frowned. 'I can see Skye's point of view, although I do believe that Adam genuinely cares for her.'

'On that, I think we can agree, and ironically, I think Skye thinks very highly of Adam too. With what little I know about Adam's recent experiences, maybe he wants to try to rescue someone he sees as a soul in trouble, but he probably didn't count on Skye being such an independent woman.'

'What a mix-up. How can two people who could be so happy together, or at least very good friends, make each other so upset?'

'Hmm, it happens all the time. Look at my wife and I, we've been apart for eighteen-plus years and yet I think we're as attracted to each other as when we first met.'

'That's so sad. Myself, I never found love — well, not since a brief flirtation in my youth . . .' Nigel paused and looked over at Buzz.

Buzz could tell by Nigel's face that he regretted his words almost as soon as they were out of his mouth.

'Your secret is safe with me.' Buzz jolted as a realization dawned on him. 'Don't tell me . . . something to do with Adam, by any chance?'

Nigel nodded, his face a picture of misery. 'Yes, Adam's mum. I was besotted with her at one point, but she chose Adam's dad. I even told her to choose Adam's dad, so hey-ho.' He studied his shoelace. 'It was such an honour that Marion suggested me to help her son when he was at a low ebb.'

'It seems to me that all of these conundrums require the passage of time before they can be settled.' Buzz didn't add that his inner knowing was leading him to that conclusion.

'Yes, you're more than likely right. Leaving well alone often leads to the greatest healing and resolution.'

'However, I don't want you hiding away here in the vicarage and feeling alone. I don't think we've ever exchanged mobile numbers, but I believe we should now, so that we can keep in touch about the kids. And if you need a chat over a pint or a coffee, you can call or text me.'

'That's kind, Buzz. I appreciate it. I'm going to be busy with Christmas things soon anyway. The time of year will be a distraction.' Nigel went to rummage on a messy table and searched out an ancient-looking mobile phone.

'Meanwhile, I'll subtly see if Skye will tell me any more about what went on between them. Something else must have been said to make her so angry and for Adam to go away.'

'Yes, indeed. And I have to say, his departure has made me feel rather sad and empty. I've been enjoying trying to guide him and I don't think we've quite got to the bottom of things yet.'

Buzz pulled the surprised Nigel into his shoulder for a brief man hug and three shoulder pats before he let him go.

* * *

Adam regretted his actions almost as soon as he was driving up the hill out of Borteen.

The journey proved to be a good time to examine what he'd said and done, although at times he was worried that he hadn't been concentrating sufficiently on the road to be safe.

He knew that Nigel Hopkins was really upset that he'd packed up and left without promising to return. The only concession Adam had made to his feelings had been to scribble his mobile number on a piece of paper, which he'd left prominently on the worksurface in the vicarage kitchen.

He really must ring Nigel soon to explain in more detail why he had left — after all, it wasn't Nigel's fault. The man had shown him nothing but kindness and consideration after Adam's plea for help. He'd also humoured Adam's desire to know more about the life of a vicar. Adam still hadn't decided if that was the life path he actually wanted to pursue rather than a knee-jerk reaction to what he had been through.

Then there was Skye. He couldn't help the depth of his feelings for her. He adored her and had been truthful about wanting to marry her, with or without the baby. He'd just completely cocked up and mistimed his proposal and his vow to accept her unborn daughter as his own.

Everything had seemed straightforward in his own head, but he hadn't allowed Skye sufficient time to catch up to his way of thinking. He could now see that all too clearly with hindsight, but at the time he'd gone in all guns blazing with his proclamations of what he thought was best for Skye and her offspring. He'd been a complete and utter idiot playing the hero, some sort of knight in shining armour. She was no pushover, she'd never allow a man to dictate her life, otherwise she might still be with that complete tosser Declan.

He sighed yet again. If only he'd taken things slower and sowed the seeds of a possible future together in more subtle ways. Instead, he'd blundered in and ensured that Skye brought down the shutters on any potential relationship, most likely because she believed him to be yet another man trying to control her and her life. Added to that, she now had the safety and well-being of her child to consider.

As he got closer to home, his thoughts moved to his mother and her feelings. He wondered guiltily how she'd been coping — not only had she recently lost her husband but her son had apparently abandoned her too. And with her son having been obviously damaged by the suicide of his work colleague, she would probably have feared him doing something stupid for all the time he'd been away.

Adam groaned. He was fast becoming someone who was inconsiderate to the feelings of others and he didn't like the idea one bit. That wasn't who he wanted to be at all. He had to make amends with his mother, Nigel Hopkins and most importantly with Skye.

However bad he was making himself feel on the journey, he should have known that his mum would simply be pleased to see him alive and well. As soon as he pulled into the drive-way, he saw the curtains twitch, and before he'd even got his bag out of the car, the front door was open and his mother was racing towards him with her arms outstretched. He could tell by the tightness of her embrace how relieved she was to see him. Adam's guilt intensified when they got into the house and he could see the tracks her tears had made in her make-up in the short while since he'd appeared.

'How did you get on? How have you been feeling?' Marion Belfont said, mopping at the tears with a tissue.

'I'm much brighter.'

'It's lovely to see some colour in your face.'

Adam had deliberately turned the undamaged side of his face towards her.

'And Borteen?' She looked puzzled at his stance. 'What's the town like? I've often wondered about the place.'

'I love it there . . . And Reverend Hopkins was very kind and welcoming.'

'How is Nigel?'

'He's fine.'

Marion put her hands up to her face and her skin went very white as she finally noticed his black eye, which today had tinges of yellow too. 'Adam, your face! What happened?'

'It's a story to be told over a cup of tea by the fire, I think.'

'Nothing to do with Nigel, I hope?' She ushered him through the hall.

'No, Nigel didn't hit me.'

'That's not what I meant and you know it.'

She went through to the kitchen and began to make tea for them both.

'How have you been, Mum?'

'You've been in touch most days, Adam.'

'Yes, but it's different actually being here in person.' Adam knew he had gained weight and his face more colour while he had been away. In contrast, his mother looked somehow smaller, thinner, paler and sad. Adam felt guilty again.

'Sorry I left you on your own.'

'Nonsense,' said Marion, pouring the milk into the tea. 'It is so important to me that you get your future sorted. As for me, I'm sad, of course. Your dad dying has left a big hole in my life, but I have to get on with things.'

'Understandable when you two were together for so long.'

Adam gave her a big hug and then carried the mugs through to the lounge.

His mother flopped onto one of the chairs.

'Was Nigel able to help you?'

'He's in the process of it, but I decided to come home for a little while.'

Marion's face became more animated. 'Has he got a family of his own?'

'No, he lives completely alone at the vicarage in Borteen. He's never married or had children.'

'Oh, that's so sad. He was always such a lovely man. He deserved to be happy.'

'He strikes me as a typical bachelor.'

'Did you take a photograph of him, of the two of you together?'

'No, I'm afraid I didn't. Maybe I will next time I'm in Borteen.'

Her face fell and Adam had an idea. He quickly searched for Borteen Church on his phone and sure enough there was a picture of Nigel and a short biography of the vicar. Adam passed his phone over to his mum.

She looked at the picture and sighed.

'Did you two have a thing going on back then?' asked Adam.

'Not really. He lodged with us when we were both students. He was always good as a sounding board, and when your dad and I had a few problems after we'd been dating for a while, he helped me to see both sides of it and we resolved our differences and got married. Nigel was a good friend and I always knew that he was on my side.'

Adam didn't comment that he'd got the distinct impression that Nigel had fancied his mother back then. 'He was kindness personified. He had fond memories of being a student in London. He even offered me a room at the vicarage so that we could spend more time together — more time getting to know each other.'

'So, you get on well? You like him?'

'Yes, we get on very well. I just hope I haven't scuppered all that by leaving so suddenly.'

'And why on earth did you do that?'

'I'll tell you in a minute — and about the black eye.'

Marion huffed but seemed to accept that he wasn't yet ready to talk. 'You still want to study theology, become a vicar?'

'I do need a change. What I was doing before I was made redundant was meaningless and didn't make me happy. I'm still trying to establish what I really want. But Lewis's death has sort of tarnished my desire for the cut and thrust of the business world, if I ever had that in the first place.'

'To be fair, even when you were a small child mad on building Lego, you used to build churches all of the time.'

'Really?'

'I'd say life is too short — do whatever makes your heart sing, Adam. Seriously, go for it if that is what you want.'

'There is another reason I'm reluctant to go back to being a student.'

'Which is?'

'I've met a girl. To be a vicar I'd have to start at the beginning again. In finance, I at least have a track record and can earn a living, assuming I can get another job. Can you see my dilemma?'

'If she loves you, she'll wait for you to train.'

'Yes, but it's far more complicated than that . . . she's expecting a baby.'

'Goodness, that was quick work! But hang on, unless you met her before you left, you haven't had time to meet someone and make a baby. Are you sure she's not trying to con you? Is the baby really yours?'

'The baby isn't mine! She was pregnant when I met her.'

'Oh, Adam, please be careful.'

'I know, but it's really not how you're imagining things, she's actually reluctant to get together because of her baby and I think I've totally blown things with an argument we had.'

'Why is life so blummin' complicated?'

'I've really no idea, but it always seems to be. Is it okay for me to stay for a little while, Mum?'

'Why do you need to even ask that? This is your home. I'll just see what I've got to cook for you for tea.' Marion got up and went through to the kitchen to look into the fridge.

Adam rose and went to join his mother. He leaned back against the central island.

'Right, I'll make a start. Why don't you take your things up to your room and give me your washing? I'm suddenly feeling very hungry. You can tell me more about your girl and Nigel over tea.'

166

Adam sighed. 'I don't think she'll ever be my girl now unfortunately.'

As Adam climbed the familiar stairs of home, he couldn't help but look at the family photographs lining the walls. Adam at various ages, usually with either his mum or his father. He was suddenly sad too that his dad was no longer here to hear any of his news or to offer his own counsel.

CHAPTER TWENTY-THREE

Skye was surprising even herself with the sewing machine. She was now regularly taking in mending and alterations and had started to make tote bags, little purses and make-up bags after a visit with Buzz to Busy Pins, the material shop in Sowden. Buzz had agreed she could sell her new product range in his shop, and she experienced a glow of pride every time he said that something had sold.

She had much more freedom to be herself here in Borteen. Although she was busy amassing acquaintances, no one really knew her story apart from a select few, and that thought was so liberating. No one to tease or bully her about being from a single-parent family or a teenager 'in trouble'.

She loved Buzz's dry wit and his way of looking at the world in alternative ways.

Most importantly, she was also beginning to bond with her baby. Lying back on the bed, she stroked her stomach and spoke to her bump. 'What do you think, little one? I think it's developing into a good life in Borteen and maybe you should be born here after all?' She giggled as the baby moved, as if she'd understood the question her mother had asked. 'We love Buzz, don't we? We need to find a way of persuading Grandma to join us here in Borteen too. But I know that's a big ask, because she has her shop in Dublin. I'm just sad about Adam, he was developing into such a good friend, maybe more, when I sent him away, literally sent him packing. Oh, how I wish I'd reacted differently, little one, because I think you would like Adam too.' The baby lurched in apparent agreement.

* * *

Buzz may have called himself spiritual, pagan even, but he did not expect others to share his own belief system and was not in any way judgemental of people who held other views or practised other religions. His philosophy was very much live and let live.

As he told Skye, 'Who really knows? We won't actually know the truth until we've left this life. I don't judge others, or try desperately not to anyway. Even if you look at Christianity, there are so many variations of belief and some people get hung up about that and sometimes so angry, even violent. I always say, if there was only one way to heaven, there would be one hell of a big queue.'

Skye didn't seem to be able to get her head around his extreme tolerance. He was enjoying their philosophical chats, but was disappointed that he had so far been unable to get her to tell him any more about her unfortunate disagreement with Adam.

Buzz, Lally, Nigel and Christine were meeting at the beach café to discuss the annual Christmas meal for the homeless of the Borteen and Sowden areas.

Last year's meal had been held at a community centre in Sowden, but it was closed for refurbishment. Buzz had had the idea of bringing the participants to Borteen this time, so that the often troubled individuals could have a trip to the seaside as well as a Christmas meal. Lally had asked Christine to host it at the café, but Buzz could tell that the café owner was a little bit unsure about the whole thing. He imagined that she was worried about the extent to which she and her café were expected to be involved in the organization and cooking of the meal, and Buzz knew he would need to reassure her.

He could see a clear disturbance in Christine's aura and she inevitably noticed that he was looking at her in what must look like an odd way with his eyes half-closed.

'Buzz, you've got that psychic face of yours on. Come on, tell me what you can see,' challenged Christine.

'Your energy is on the move. I can see swirling colours in your aura.'

'And what exactly is that supposed to mean, Buzz?'

'You're entering a time of change; things will look very different for you after Christmas.'

'I've no idea what you're talking about.' At that point she glanced at Lally, giving Buzz little doubt where her thoughts were centred. 'Oh well, let's hope any change, if indeed there is one, is positive,' she added.

Buzz shivered at her words, suddenly troubled, then shook his head to try to refocus on the meeting. 'The hostel in Sowden is aiming to put up twenty homeless souls from the Borteen and Sowden area for a week over the Christmas period. As you all know, I try to support them whenever I can. Maybe some of you don't know why it's so important to me, so let me explain. I suffered a bad period in my life before I came to Borteen and I very nearly ended up living on the streets myself.'

He paused to let that sink in. 'I remember my time without a home very clearly, as if it were yesterday — the worries, the fears, the temptations to be involved in petty crimes to finance mind-numbing drugs, the interminable cold. There were freedoms too, but most vividly . . . I remember the hunger pains. I know one meal won't make a vast difference in the scheme of things, but it would save the hostel from having to provide it, and I'm hoping it might be fun for those involved to come to the seaside too . . . many of them live with darkness, depression and disability for the rest of the year.'

'Well, I'm always up for helping,' said Lally. 'My brother lived on the streets for a while.'

'I feel very strongly about this too,' said Nigel Hopkins. 'In fact, I can offer the church hall for next year's event, or even this year if Christine isn't totally sure.'

'How does the Sunday evening before Christmas suit, Christine? It would be after your normal closing time, of course.'

'That sounds as if it could work,' she agreed. 'I'll say yes, with the proviso that the café is left clean and tidy to open for normal business the next day.'

'That goes without saying, and thank you.' Buzz put his hands together and bowed to Christine.

Buzz asked Nigel to stay behind after the meeting for a catch-up. He'd made a point of checking up on Nigel several times since Adam had left Borteen — Buzz had come to realize Nigel had seen the young man as a protégé or maybe even a sort of apprentice — but he was usually embroiled in the pre-Christmas events of both the church and the community and didn't appear to have much spare time for brooding.

'Have you heard from Adam?' Buzz asked.

'No. He did leave me a note of his mobile number, but as yet, I've been reluctant to disturb him as he so obviously had a lot to work out in his own mind.'

'A quick text to say you're thinking of him wouldn't hurt though, would it?'

'You think not?'

'I insist. Come on, you can't worry about someone that much, try to help them and then just leave it there — you can't give up on him. Did he tell you much about his mother?'

'From what Adam said, she's well. Her husband died recently, which led to her suggesting me when Adam needed someone independent to talk to, I think. We've always sent Christmas cards to each other, or rather I used to send one to her parents and she continued the practice when they passed. What can I say about Marion Belfont? I guess she was probably the unrequited love of my life. Sounds silly to say it, because I only lived in the Belfont household for a short while and I tried to hide my feelings about her at the time. It would have been too awkward. Then, of course, she met Adam's dad, Arthur.'

'Right now, send that text message. Do it while you're with me then you won't chicken out. And yes, I am bullying you into it. Otherwise, you'll waste time wondering about Adam.'

Nigel got his ancient mobile phone out of his pocket. It was all Buzz could do not to laugh at the sight of it, but he bit back his comments.

'What do I say?' Nigel's finger paused over the screen.

'Keep it simple. How about: *Hoping everything okay with you?*'

Nigel pursed his lips in concentration, then pushed send with a flourish and ran a hand through his hair.

Text message sent, Buzz went to order more coffees and by the time he sat back down with Nigel at the table, the man appeared stunned to have already received a reply. He passed his phone to Buzz so that he could read the response.

Hi, sorry I left so suddenly. Things resolving now. Can I be cheeky and ask to stay with you at the vicarage again, so that we can continue our discussions?

Nigel grinned. He took back the phone and replied.

'What did you say?'

'I said, *Yes, no problem*, of course. Had you better warn Skye?'

'No, I think we'll let her discover that Adam is back when he returns. I'm thinking more and more that I should just keep out of the situation. Let them work things out for themselves.'

'You're more than likely right.' Nigel began to hum 'We Wish You a Merry Christmas'.

CHAPTER TWENTY-FOUR

Buzz walked back to Crazy Crystals with a smile on his face, unable to stop humming the popular Christmas song too. He was so wrapped up in thoughts about his friend and the situation with Adam that it took him a few minutes to register that a taxi was dropping someone off outside his shop. The taxi, parked on the double yellow lines, had its hazard lights flashing as the driver unloaded a case and a huge backpack from the boot. Buzz sped up to see the owner of the luggage, his heart rate accelerating and a strange unfurling sensation in his stomach. Could it possibly be? Could it?

The taxi driver closed the boot and there stood Wynn. Buzz exhaled and hurried to greet her and take her luggage from the pavement and into the shop. Her eyes met his and she looked rather sheepish, even though she was smiling.

'Sorry to appear unannounced,' she said, after paying the driver. 'I've come for Christmas as you suggested. I do hope that's okay?'

'No problem at all, more than okay. Skye will be so pleased to see you.' *And me too*, he wanted to add.

'How's she doing?'

'Very well — blooming, in fact.'

Buzz thought he knew how Nigel had felt such a short while ago as happiness flooded through him that Wynn was back. He hummed the first few bars of the same Christmas carol in celebration.

* * *

Skye exclaimed in delight at seeing her mother, but Wynn wondered how it would work sharing the attic space that Skye was no doubt enjoying for herself.

Buzz had told Wynn that he was still perturbed about Skye and Adam, because Skye had refused to tell him exactly what had gone on between the two of them. Buzz filled her in on what little he knew about the falling-out. Adam going in search of Declan, getting walloped, coming to the shop to see Skye and then packing his bags and retreating suddenly back to his mother's house in London.

Wynn repeated a phrase to Buzz that he often quoted himself: *Time will tell, everything is working out as it should.*

Christmas events were ramping up in Borteen and Reverend Hopkins seemed to have become a regular visitor to the shop, using Buzz as a confidant. Wynn found this amusing, as she'd never imagined the two very different men as best buddies.

Wynn had been making crystal jewellery for a while and had been selling pieces online in tandem with the physical shop in Ireland. She'd somehow managed to bring all her stock and materials with her and intended to continue with the business while she was in Borteen. She'd even had a small spark of excitement about increasing her range in the web-based market. Maybe Skye could help her with the jewellery making, maybe they could have a Christmas sales stall. Surely Borteen would still have a Christmas market. She soon found, however, that Skye now had growing business interests of her own.

Buzz showed an interest in the jewellery and promised to clear a space in the shop to display it. She and Buzz were slowly beginning to talk more, albeit mainly about practical things so far. Wynn repeated her own words in her head: *Time will tell, everything is working out as it should.* There was no point trying to rush things with Buzz; they had to take the time to work out where they stood with each other once and for all. She needed to be sure of Borteen, of Buzz, of Skye even, before she declared the momentous decision she had made in Dublin.

* * *

Skye liked working for Christine at the café, but had accepted that shorter shifts were now better for this stage of her pregnancy. Sorrel at the vintage clothing shop had begun to put more business her way and was paying her a good rate for the jobs she completed. What with this and the products she was selling in Buzz's shop, she had begun to make some money for herself at last.

However, the argument she'd had with Adam hung over her like a dark cloud. She felt awful that he'd left Borteen seemingly because of her words. Part of her couldn't help feeling regretful that she hadn't simply been able to accept the solution he'd been offering her. However, knowing what she was like, a compromise would only have been possible for a short while; she would have eventually rebelled. Saying yes to Adam would almost have been as cruel as saying no.

It was annoying that the appeal of the guy himself had been increased dramatically by his willingness to rescue her from her current situation. She'd already fancied Adam, but now she thought he was truly lovely. But — and it was a big but — she'd now closed the door on that future and, it seemed, on the friendship that had been developing between them. The thought filled her with a great sadness.

She was overjoyed that her mother had come back to Borteen for Christmas, but rather resentful that for now they had to share a room, just when she'd been enjoying the unique attic space all to herself.

Also, Wynn had a strange air about her since she'd come back, almost as if she wasn't saying exactly what she meant. Skye knew that Buzz had asked Wynn to keep an eye on her and her health — plus, she was sure, to report back anything she learned about what exactly had happened with Adam.

Christmas in Borteen seemed to be gathering pace. There were more and more lights appearing, and it was impossible to go into the shops without being bombarded by the usual songs and carols. The season of good will. Skye decided to just go with the flow and see where it led.

* * *

Buzz didn't quite know what to make of Wynn's return to Borteen either. He'd asked her to come back for Christmas, of course he had. If anything had motivated her return, he was sure it was to keep an eye on her daughter and her grand-child. Wynn had shown no sign of unlocking the mystery of what had happened between Skye and Adam despite Buzz hoping she would get to the bottom of things.

Wynn was still Wynn, but distanced somehow, as if there was something else going on in the background of which Buzz was unaware. He couldn't help but be disappointed and somewhat confused. As always with people close to him, his psychic insights had not given him any useful clues.

When Buzz met Nigel in the Ship Inn on Friday evening, he was looking forward to using Reverend Hopkins as a sounding board and also curious to see if he had heard anything more from Adam.

'Any news?' asked Nigel, putting a pint of real ale in front of Buzz.

'Nothing really, except Wynn is back in Borteen.'

'Nothing *really*, what are you like?' Nigel winked. 'Oh, yes?'

'Doesn't seem to be back for me though, just for her daughter.'

'Skye's not said anything more about Adam yet?'

'Not mentioned him at all. Have you heard anything yourself?' said Buzz, wiping beer froth off his lip with his finger.

'Nothing since he asked to come back. Whatever was said appears to have settled into a permanent rift between them.' He made an appreciative sound about the taste of his beer.

'I did hope that Wynn would be able to unlock the mystery, but it's more been a case of the two girls sticking together and keeping their secrets secret. So if Wynn knows anything at all, she's not telling me.'

'How is it at home with two women after being on your own for so long?'

'Weird. I feel like the odd one out . . . outnumbered.'

'Maybe you should take off on a holiday and leave them to it.'

'You could come too. We could go fishing maybe.'

'Do you fish then?'

'No, I've never had a go at it. You?'

They both laughed and then sipped their pints in contemplative silence for a while.

'I'm looking forward to seeing Adam again, but worry if returning is the right move for him, or for Skye.'

'No point in worrying, I doubt there's anything we can do, but I'll have another go at speaking to her. We really could do with knowing what happened.'

'I'd appreciate that. If nothing else, we need to be sure whether it's wise to encourage them to meet up again or to try to keep them apart.'

CHAPTER TWENTY-FIVE

Buzz chose mealtime the next evening to talk to Skye. Wynn had prepared homemade bread and soup. Buzz felt awkward broaching the subject yet again, but knew he needed to try.

'I had a pint with Reverend Hopkins yesterday evening at the Ship Inn.'

Skye looked up with alarm barely disguised on her face, her full soup spoon halfway to her mouth.

'He asked me if you'd heard anything from Adam lately?'

'Why on earth does he think I would hear anything from Adam?' Skye's tone was defensive.

Buzz put down his own spoon with a clatter he hadn't intended. It made his next words appear sharper than they were meant to be. 'Now, come on, Skye. You and Adam were getting very close before he went away. I mean, he went to Birmingham especially for you and even got thumped in the process. You two seemed to be developing into good friends and I'm still confused about what happened that day to change things, but I would really, really like to understand.'

'He decided to go to Birmingham all by himself. I didn't ask him to, he volunteered.' She'd put her spoon back into her soup bowl.

Wynn flashed him one of her looks, and Buzz tried a gentler, more conciliatory tone. 'I think Reverend Hopkins needs to be reassured that it wasn't his fault that his protégé left Borteen.'

'I didn't make him leave. I didn't send him away.' Skye had her arms crossed firmly over her bump and her face looked pinched and white.

Wynn's eyes widened in warning to Buzz.

He should have left it there, should have let the subject drop, but somehow he just couldn't. 'But something happened that day in the shop. Did he try it on, by any chance?'

Skye sighed heavily and gave Buzz a dark look. 'Oh, for goodness' sake — try it on when I'm this pregnant? I'm not going to get any peace until I tell you the full story, am I?'

Wynn put her hand on Skye's arm. 'You don't have to say anything if you don't want to . . . if you don't feel ready. Don't let Buzz pressure you. And Buzz, give it a rest. Leave the poor girl alone.'

He held up his hands in front of his face in a gesture of peace. 'No, your mother's right. I'm sorry, I was out of order. This is between you and Adam. You don't need to say anything to justify what happened. My loyalty should be with you and not Nigel Hopkins. Sorry again.'

'If you must know — Adam asked me to marry him.' Skye paused as both Buzz and Wynn took in noisy breaths.

Wynn spoke first. 'But you refused? You didn't feel the same way about him?'

A tear was tracking its way down Skye's cheek and Buzz decided not to say anything else for the moment.

'Adam's had a bad time and got into the habit of trying to rescue people — everyone. I was worried that I was just another person he was trying to help, rather than him having genuine feelings for me. And it seemed too soon in our relationship to be making such a huge commitment.' Skye wiped a tear from her cheek.

'But were you at least tempted, sweetheart?' asked Wynn quietly.

'Of course I was.' Skye pushed her soup bowl away, rested her elbows on the table and put her head into her hands. 'Adam is the nicest guy I've ever met. I found myself wishing that we'd connected when I wasn't pregnant, so we could have found out if our relationship worked in normal circumstances, without the complication of the baby, but I realize that's only a dream. I'm pregnant — fact. It isn't Adam's baby — fact. I couldn't agree to marry him right now, but unfortunately when I said no to his suggestion, his proposal, he seemed to think I was rejecting him completely, as if I had no feelings for him at all. And that's so not true. But now he's gone and there's no getting all the good bits of us back and I feel . . . I feel so sad, so wretched, so . . . broken-hearted, and yet we've only danced together once and never even so much as kissed.'

Wynn put her arm around her daughter's shaking shoulders.

Buzz had his answers at last, so why did he feel even worse now than when he hadn't known exactly what had happened?

Wynn handed Skye a wad of tissues from the box Buzz kept on the side shelf.

Skye looked totally miserable and suddenly very young and vulnerable.

Buzz gulped back his own emotion. 'Skye, I'm so sorry and I'll stop going on about this now, but I feel it's important to know whether you will give me permission to tell Nigel Hopkins what happened between you and Adam. I promise I won't if you really don't want me to.'

'I'm all right with you telling him about the proposal, but please, please don't tell him how I really feel about it all, just that I refused and that Adam took it badly. I wouldn't want my true feelings to get back to Adam, I'd be so embarrassed.'

'All right, thank you for that. I promise to be careful what I say. I'm sorry all this has upset you so much. Sorry that Adam's suggestion backfired spectacularly and drove the two of you apart. Actually, I find it so very sad, because from what I could see, you two were good for each other.'

'Sad about sums it up.' Skye pushed back her chair. 'I'm not hungry. Sorry about the soup, Mum. I'm going to have a lie-down.'

Wynn looked thoroughly angry now that Skye had left the room. She glared at Buzz.

He felt contrite for, in effect, bullying the truth out of Skye, but also at the same time triumphant that he'd solved the mystery at last and would have something enlightening to say to Nigel.

Maybe he should volunteer to go and see Adam himself to try to sort out the unfortunate situation. He could ask Nigel for the address.

Wynn was looking at him without blinking.

He hung his head. 'I know I went too far. I was getting frustrated with not knowing what happened, but it's no excuse.'

'Well, when Skye's calmed down, I think you need to apologize properly.'

'I promise. I'll cook a special meal, Skye's favourite macaroni cheese maybe, and beg her to forgive me.'

'That sounds like a good idea. Now, while we're having confession time, I've got one of my own.'

Buzz held his breath, wondering what she would say.

'I needed to go back to Dublin to sort out the shop. The truth is that when I was there on my own I realized all I cared about was over here in Borteen now — my daughter, my granddaughter and you . . .'

'Oh, Wynn.'

Wynn silenced him by raising her hand.

'Anyway, I sorted the shop and jumped on the plane over here.'

'Thank goodness for that,' said Buzz.

'I'll tell Skye myself when I'm ready. But I just wanted to say that as I have this awful tendency to run away, and yes, I realize I've done exactly that more than once. I want to take things really slowly here and learn what's possible for me and, if you're up for it, for us too.'

'Let's enjoy Christmas, enjoy being together with Skye. There really isn't a rush and as we said before we need to take time to get to know each other again.'

'I'm so happy to hear that, Buzz. Right now, I think I need to go and be with Skye. Can we talk again soon?'

'Happily! Go and check on Skye, I want to visit Nigel anyway.'

* * *

Buzz sat on the memorial bench in the churchyard next to Nigel Hopkins and looked closely at how the church sat in the landscape at the end of Borteen's seafront promenade. He'd just told Nigel what he'd learned about the reasons for Adam's sudden departure.

'I guess I have to take heart from the fact that it wasn't anything that I said or did,' said Nigel. 'Adam must have been extraordinarily embarrassed that he'd completely mis-read the situation with Skye and been too hasty.'

'She's upset, obviously, to have lost a friend,' added Buzz, 'but I think she knew that she couldn't just waltz into a marriage and, in effect, take on a substitute father for her baby, however kindly and genuinely the offers were meant.'

'Adam should maybe have taken things a little more slowly and built up to his proposal. And Skye is right, since his work colleague's suicide, Adam has tried to rescue as many souls as he can. No wonder she was unsure.'

'I do so wish he'd been patient. They seem such a good match and I firmly believe it could actually work . . .'

The two men sat in quiet contemplation for a few moments before Buzz spoke again. 'Has Adam said any more about returning to Borteen?'

'Not yet. He did send me a text saying that his mother wasn't very well at the moment, so I guess he'll stay with her until she's better.'

'So, time will tell for Adam and Skye.'

'I'll send up a few prayers for a happy resolution for them both.'

They returned to silence for a short while and then the pair strolled along the promenade. Buzz watched Lally exchanging banter with his staff outside of the Ship Inn and wondered yet again about his relationship with Christine at the café.

'I'm still raising money for the homeless, so I'll do a labyrinth on the beach several times every week from now until Christmas.'

'I must come and have a go at walking one of your labyrinths. I've always fancied a go.'

'I'd be glad to welcome you. Talking of ancient symbols, I was looking at the church and wondering what was there before it was built.'

'Would you like to see the crypt some time? There are some strange structures beneath the church, suggesting something older, maybe even ancient . . . some other building was indeed there before.'

'I'd love to. Have you ever heard of ley lines?'

'Heard of them but don't really know too much about the concept.'

'Don't get me started or we'll be here all day, but I'll just say for now that a ley goes straight through your church. One goes straight up Borteen high street too.'

'And what does that mean, exactly?'

'It means that the church is on an energy line in the landscape and forms an energy point. I'll see if I can draw it all on a map for you to explain it properly.'

'Sounds like a subject for another philosophical discussion in the pub. I look forward to it.'

The men said their goodbyes and Nigel turned back towards the church. Buzz headed to the corner store to buy some things for their evening meal. He wondered if a relationship between Skye and Adam was doomed before it had even properly begun, or was there still hope?

CHAPTER TWENTY-SIX

Although there was no doubt that Skye was enjoying most aspects of her new life, in some ways she still felt strangely detached. Maybe she was scared that this wasn't actually real and could stop at any point.

She loved Buzz already regardless of whether he was proved to be her father or not. She worked at the café and had come to love Christine almost as a second mum, as she was so accepting of Skye and the pair had such fun working in the café together. She was doing more and more alterations for Sorrel at Polka Dot Paradise and Sorrel had introduced her to Suzy Meadows from the Cancer Research charity shop, who was surprisingly the drummer in the rock band Adam and Skye had danced to on the beach.

Suzy had asked Skye to make new costumes for the band members. It was for a Christmas concert on the beach stage, so a lot of work in a short time. The brief for the costumes was black, allowing for ease of movement and with detachable Christmas elements. It was actually quite exciting to be designing things from scratch and Skye promised some sketches and prices as quickly as she could.

When Skye admitted that she was worried she might not be able to make the band costumes to a high enough standard, Suzy told her that a good-enough job was fine and that she was sure Skye would make something a million times better than she could ever produce herself.

Suzy seemed on short acquaintance to be such a refreshing person. Skye couldn't believe how unconventional she was, and proud of it, from her asymmetrically cut hair, her dozens of earrings and tattoos, to her distinct way of dressing. She appeared to have a way of cutting through the crap most people got hung up on in life.

'You don't play an instrument, do you?' asked Suzy.

Skye laughed and professed a proficiency to play the triangle in percussion lessons at school.

All in all, it was starting to look like a sustainable way of life in Borteen. So why did she so often feel like running away again? She really couldn't understand her own thinking sometimes.

If only Adam had not proposed that day. Her life would have been good with him as a best friend, someone to confide in. And, who knew, things might have developed for them as a couple given time. But she was aware that life was rarely perfect — look at Buzz and Wynn. True love happened for a few. Happy lives happened for a few. Most people had ups and downs, good times and bad. She needed to cultivate being grateful for the positive things she did have.

Wynn and Skye were making jewellery at the kitchen table. Skye was trying to perfect a technique of wrapping a crystal in silver wire that she'd watched a video about on YouTube.

'Do you miss Dublin?' asked Wynn suddenly.

Skye looked over at her mother. 'Sometimes. I miss how easy it is to get around on the Luas trams and the buses. I miss wandering around the streets and looking in the shops, even if I couldn't afford to buy things in most of them. I loved the scarves and food in my favourite shop, Avoca. I miss the big book shops and the huge department stores. It was easy to meet up with friends in the centre of Dublin too.'

Wynn sighed. 'The knitting shops are great in Ireland as well.'

'I haven't seen you knitting for a while.'

'Maybe I should make some clothes for the baby.'

'Nothing too old-fashioned though, please.' Skye winked.

Wynn play-cuffed her ear. 'Cheeky. But in all seriousness, are you going to dress your daughter in pink?'

'Rainbow colours, I think. We're hardly a conventional family after all, are we?'

'No. Conventional is definitely not a word you would use to describe any member of this family.'

Skye and Wynn spent a companionable afternoon making jewellery, and by the end of it, Skye was pleased with the pendants she'd produced. Wynn promised to list them in her online shop to see how popular they were.

Skye loved helping Buzz lay out his labyrinth on the beach too. There was something meditational about rhythmically digging in the sand, but also the intention of connecting to ancient energies with the shapes required to make the walking path.

Today, when they'd laid out the labyrinth, Skye walked it slowly, concentrating deliberately just on the next footstep, and she saw Buzz smiling at her because she supposed the peace she had begun to feel as she walked was evident on her face.

'That's better,' commented Buzz. 'You look troubled at times, so it's nice to see your face completely relaxed.'

She gave him a brief hug.

Some of Buzz's regulars began to appear to put their donations into the bucket. Curious newbies looked over the sea wall and Skye beckoned to them and explained about the labyrinth.

She smiled across at Buzz and realized she was enjoying herself. The day was cold, but bright and clear. The tide was well out, the beach was huge and the smell of the seaside made her feel relaxed and rather sleepy. She stood staring out towards the sea. There was a runner, alternately running and skipping near to the waves. His actions made Skye laugh. He reminded her of a playful puppy. As he began to run up the beach, she thought her eyes were deceiving her — but no, it was Adam. He was back!

How to react? She hadn't got long to decide what to do. What to say? Did she run? Hide? Stand her ground?

Adam seemed to have made a decision about exactly how to play their first meeting after . . . after their misunderstanding. He hailed Buzz and smiled before running straight up to Skye as if nothing untoward had ever happened. Her cheeks glowed hot when he stopped in front of her.

'Looking well, Skye. I'm back in Borteen for a while and I'd like to say that I'd be very very happy if we could turn back time to when we were good friends. I'll understand if you don't want to, of course.'

Skye took a deep breath before answering. 'I'd like that very very much too. I miss my special friend, Adam.'

'Well, that's settled then. Friends?'

She was a little bewildered but pleased as he high-fived her, smiled and ran on up the steps to the promenade and out of sight.

Skye sighed contentedly and hugged the donation bucket with relief and joy.

'Adam's back,' she said unnecessarily to Buzz. He laughed and came over to hug her tightly.

When she'd got over the surprise of Adam's appearance, she began to shake the donations bucket more enthusiastically than she had all morning and was even tempted to sing, but then that might make people avoid the labyrinth, she giggled to herself.

As the tide came in and it was time to abandon the labyrinth to the waves, the donations bucket was satisfyingly full and Skye's spirits were soaring. She couldn't wait to tell her mother what had happened and that Adam, her special friend, was back.

'Come on, let's get you warmed up and count the donations,' said Buzz. 'It looks as if we've done rather well. Might even be a record collection — all down to you, of course.'

Skye was aware of feeling somehow lighter on the way up the high street. She couldn't wait to see Adam again now that he was back in Borteen and they had broken the ice.

* * *

Adam was ludicrously pleased with himself. He'd managed to get the first meeting with Skye over without any trauma, maybe resulting from him rehearsing it so many times in his head. Best of all, she'd looked pleased to see him, if rather surprised. It really couldn't have gone any better. He hadn't given Skye any opportunity to avoid him. Goodness knows what he would have done if she'd said they couldn't return to the friendship stage of their relationship. He suspected he might have cried.

Buzz had rung him for a chat the week before. Adam knew that his mother was relieved about the call because Adam had been restless since he'd returned home and Adam was sure she'd feared him returning to the deep depression he'd descended into after Lewis's death. If he was totally honest with himself, Adam had actually feared the same sort of outcome.

It hadn't taken much for Buzz to convince him to return to Borteen. After all, Adam knew deep down that he'd been too precipitant in asking Skye to marry him. He'd regretted it as soon as the words were out of his mouth and he'd watched the expression on Skye's lovely face change. Maybe now they could start again. They were at least friends and that was a good start.

CHAPTER TWENTY-SEVEN

It was the day of the Santa fun run. Skye and Buzz, along with most of the rest of the population of Borteen, gathered along the high street and on the promenade to watch the antics of the runners in their obligatory Santa outfits.

Skye knew that Adam was running in the event as Nigel Hopkins had told Buzz he was. The road had been closed by the police especially for the occasion. As the starting claxon sounded, she could see a sea of red-suited Santas tearing down Borteen high street towards them. Even though it was only for fun, she could see that an Adam-shaped Santa was in front of the runners and felt very proud. She cheered and waved along with the rest of the spectators.

Adam saluted her as he ran past, pausing to collect his winner's medal before continuing onwards with most of the runners down the beach steps and across the beach to the surf. It was a tradition to jump into the sea after the race.

The next time Skye saw Adam he was dripping wet and shivering, his teeth chattering uncontrollably as he returned from the sea to the promenade.

'The water was freezing,' he commented.

Skye wished that Buzz had enlightened her about the ending to the race. If he had, she might have brought a towel with her to wrap around her friend.

* * *

Buzz watched Skye, her pregnancy now bloomingly evident whatever she wore, and maybe more so because she no longer felt that she had to hide it. He was so delighted that she and Adam had made friends again. Skye would undoubtedly need friends when the baby was born.

Although Buzz was happy to be here with Skye watching the event, he was a little concerned about Wynn's behaviour. She hadn't wanted to accompany them today and now he thought about it, she didn't go out of the flat much at all.

She spent all of her time making jewellery for her Etsy shop. As he puzzled over the way she had been acting, he had a thought — was Wynn short of money? Maybe her reluctance to come out with them was so that she wasn't tempted to spend unnecessarily. Suddenly her behaviour had taken on a completely new meaning. But how did he broach such an issue without upsetting Wynn?

Skye was saying something to him, but he hadn't caught her words as he was so wrapped up in his thoughts. 'Buzz, quickly. Can I have your coat?'

He saw then that Adam wasn't looking too well. Rather than take off his own coat he dashed over to the nearby St John's Ambulance station and alerted them to a patient in need.

'I do wish the runners wouldn't insist on jumping in the sea at this time of year, but they do it every time,' said the man on duty, grabbing a foil blanket and rushing over to Skye and Adam.

* * *

Adam was soon sitting on the steps of the ambulance wrapped in the warming blanket and he wasn't the only runner who needed one. Skye made sure Adam was recovering and then suggested that she went to find Reverend Hopkins.

'There's no need, really. You can walk up and down with me until I get warm.'

'And what am I going to do if you collapse, eh? I can hardly carry you, can I? You gave me such a fright, you noggin.'

Adam's smile was wide and sunny at her words despite the pallor of his cheeks.

If anything had convinced Skye that she had feelings beyond just friendship for Adam, then this event had done it. She'd experienced a whole range of emotions this morning and it wasn't even ten o'clock. She'd been proud at seeing him running and being one of the fastest. She'd been overjoyed that he'd singled her out for a salute. She'd laughed at him jumping into the surf, worried when he was so cold and then been terrified that he might die of a heart attack or something, and all before she'd had the chance to tell him she really did care.

Now she felt like a fussing mother hen, as she pulled the warming blanket higher around his shoulders as they walked along the promenade to warm him up. She wanted to make sure he was safe and thankfully they bumped into Reverend Hopkins.

Reluctantly, Skye told them she had to go to work, so when she'd updated Nigel about what had happened, she left the pair sitting on a bench and walked home to change into her café uniform.

* * *

When Buzz got back to Crazy Crystals, Wynn was still sitting exactly where he'd left her — at the kitchen table with her jewellery-making equipment all around her. But she looked very thoughtful.

Buzz couldn't keep quiet any longer. 'Wynn, what's going on?'

Wynn was fixing hooks onto a row of brightly coloured wooden earrings. 'Whatever do you mean?'

'You're acting strangely.'

'Am I?' She looked up with a startled expression on her face as if she'd been caught out.

'You're working on those earrings as if your life depends upon it. Are you short of cash or something? You would tell me if you needed help, wouldn't you? And you're hardly speaking to me.'

Wynn carried on working and Buzz thought she was going to ignore his probing questions. However, she seemed to suddenly make a decision and pushed the earrings aside. They settled in an untidy heap. 'I have a couple of things I'm debating with myself and they're starting to eat away at me.'

'You know you can tell me anything, and besides, you really don't think anything can be a bigger surprise than finding out about Skye, do you?'

'Before I forget, and I promise I'm not trying to change the subject, but did you ever get any psychic insights about Skye in the past? Did you suspect anything or have confusing signs, perhaps? I'm genuinely curious.'

'I was only thinking about that yesterday and in short, yes. I obviously wasn't clear about the context and I think I thought a couple of times that I was just connecting with you across the ether, but now I know about Skye, I realize it could have been her I made the connection with. All I have been really sure about all of these long years was that you were still alive and not in the spirit world. However, it's difficult to get insights, as you know, when you're too emotionally close to an issue or a person.'

Wynn put her hands over her face and wiped away a tear. 'I used to check in on you too. To try to find out if you were okay.'

'I've not been okay since you left, Wynn — more like in survival mode, not totally whole.'

'It's been the same for me. I was a complete fool.'

Buzz grasped her hands and pulled her to her feet, and they stood looking deeply into each other's eyes for a long while. Somehow it didn't feel the right moment to close the gap between them, but Buzz sensed that the gap itself could easily get smaller. 'So, your confusions?'

'One, I still can't believe that you're not terribly angry with me, that you haven't shouted and raged about me leaving you alone without any explanation all of those years ago.'

'Wynn, do you think I've not been through all of the emotions possible in those years on my own? I used to stand on the clifftop and scream sometimes. I tried to think of all of the reasons you would possibly go, hated myself, hated you too.'

'I'm such a terrible person, so awful that I could make you feel like that — that I was so wrapped up in my own stuff that I left you with no explanation, no communication. That I ran away, just as my mother used to do when I was young, rather than facing things, accepting the consequences. It's no excuse, of course, to say I was repeating patterns learned from Mum and I am so, so sorry, Buzz. If I said sorry every day of my life, it still wouldn't be enough times. And, if I were in your shoes, I've no idea if I would even be able to stand having me here in your home right now. I know people describe you as calm but there is calm and then calm.'

'I've questioned myself, of course I have, run through every scenario, every reaction, every permutation, every emotion. I didn't want to react in an aggressive or angry way when you returned, because even after all of my ranting on the cliffs for all of these years, I know deep down that I'm meant to be with you.'

'Are you sure though, Buzz? A lot of water has gone under the bridge in Borteen and Dublin after all.'

Wynn broke away, went back to sit at the table, as if she couldn't cope with his answer. She began to sort the tumbled earrings into pairs.

'I am sure, but are you running away again?'

She looked up startled. 'It seems to be my natural pattern to run, but I've promised myself, and I promise you now too, that I will not leave Borteen until we resolve things between us one way or another — unless of course that results in you asking me to go.'

'And I promise you we'll take the time for each other and see what we have left of our relationship after all these years. I'm hoping that we may be pleasantly surprised.'

'Me too, Buzz, me too.'

Buzz sat down next to her and began to help her to untangle the earrings. 'You know there's a Christmas market in a couple of weeks' time — we could book a stall and you could sell your earrings and Skye can sell the things she's been making too.'

'That might be fun. We did a Christmas fair the first year we came to Borteen, do you remember?'

'We did, didn't we? Goodness, we were so young back then.'

'Young and foolish, I was.'

'Young and hopeful. Idealistic maybe.' He resisted the urge to put a hand on her shoulder.

'We were all of those things.'

'And now? What are we now? Is there something else you aren't telling me?' He stared at her as she sat beside him and she finally met his eyes.

'Ah, yes, about that . . . dilemma two. I've tried not to mention this before as I didn't want to rush you in any way, didn't want to put pressure on you, when after all it's completely my fault that we are in this situation. I'm still convinced that you'll struggle to ever trust me completely again.'

'Go on.'

'I think it might be better if I find somewhere more permanent to live, maybe in Borteen, but definitely a place Skye can call home. Somewhere she can look after her baby.'

'What about your shop in Dublin?' Despite feeling momentarily puzzled, Buzz thought he'd had a premonition about that before she said anything more.

'Well now, when I went back to Dublin, I couldn't settle at all. I came to the conclusion that I would never be happy away from my daughter and granddaughter, so when I got an unexpectedly generous offer from Katrin who has been looking after the shop, I saw it as a sign, accepted it and agreed to sell the lot — the shop, the business and the living space.'

Wynn was so obviously apprehensive about Buzz's reaction. She screwed up her eyes so that she couldn't see his face. Buzz forced himself to think, rather than just give in to his gut reaction, which was to run around the room yelling with joy. But then Wynn hadn't mentioned him in the decision process for selling her property in Dublin, or her future here in Borteen. She hadn't mentioned him at all. So maybe his joy was misguided.

'You haven't said anything.' Her tone was now distinctly wary.

'It sounds like completely the right decision for you, Skye and the baby.'

'That's it? That's all you have to say? You're being Mr Detached and Calm again.'

'Does it actually matter what I think? After all, you didn't mention me.'

'Yes, of course it matters.'

It was a bald statement, but he experienced a leap of . . . of what exactly? Hope, he concluded. 'I think that it makes perfect sense for you to be near to your daughter, especially when your granddaughter arrives, and if you had a proposition to enable that to happen, it seems that fate has played a hand and I can see why you took the offer, jumped at it even. Does Skye know what you've done yet?'

'No, I haven't found the right time to tell her.'

'And you don't think she'll want to go back to Dublin to have the baby?'

'Actually, she says she wants to start over, somewhere people won't gossip about her because she's pregnant or a single mother.'

'I can understand she might feel like that.'

'You've been concerned because I've been frantically making jewellery?'

'Yes, but mainly because I was worried that it meant you were getting short of funds and were embarrassed to say anything, or that you'd changed your mind about us trying again.' He picked up a stray earring and examined it more closely.

'I've been making the jewellery mainly to give myself a purpose. Despite feeling it was the right decision, I've been quite rudderless since agreeing to sell the shop. It all happened so suddenly that I think I could possibly be in some sort of shock.' She began to gather up her things, as if she thought the conversation at an end.

'And what about us, Wynn?'

'As we said earlier, we need to take it slowly to find out if there is an "us" anymore. But I can say with my hand on my heart that I would like there to be. I'm completely to blame for this situation and I think if I were you I would never trust me again, but I would like us to try. After all, I still love you.'

'I don't think the universe is finished with our story quite yet.'

'And that's yet another shock too after all this time.'

'You know that you're welcome to live here in the flat as long as you like, although I recognize that it's not ideal sharing a room with Skye. If you want to stay in Borteen, would you like me to put the word out for somewhere for you to rent?'

'Yes, I think that might be best. And, if we truly are going to give *us* another go, you're going to have to romance me, and living on top of one another like this might not help that at all.'

'You'll need to romance me too, of course!' Buzz winked.

'Deal. I'd be more than happy to. I realize what a fool I've been and I'd like the chance to make up for that. But I'm scared, Buzz.'

'What are you scared about?'

'That we have a hiccup in our plans to get to know each other and I head for the hills . . . run off again.'

'What about if we agree a code word?'

'Code word?'

'A word or phrase we say if we think we ever need to pause and rethink at any time. Something that might stop you running too.'

'Sounds like a good idea.'

Buzz planted a kiss on her forehead just as Skye came into the room. Buzz was pretty sure if she hadn't arrived right then that he and Wynn would have attempted a proper kiss to seal the bargain they'd just made.

'How's Adam?' asked Buzz, aware that he was disappointed not to start romancing Wynn straight away.

'By the time we met Nigel, he was fine. I left them on the promenade and came back to get ready for work.'

Skye went into the kitchen area to grab a banana.

'Hey, Skye, you might soon have to choose which parent to live with,' said Wynn.

'What do you mean?'

'I'm looking for somewhere to rent in Borteen.'

'Really? How wonderful!' It was Skye's turn to kiss her mother and do a jig round the room. 'What about Dublin then?'

'I've sold the shop.'

'Wow! You could knock me over with a feather.'

'Are you upset?'

'Not at all, especially if it means we can all be together.'

'Buzz and I want to take a little time to get to know each other again and I think it might be easier if I had my own place . . . for now.'

'Christine lets out properties. She owns quite a few houses and flats in Borteen, most are holiday lets, but I think some aren't suitable for that. Shall I ask her about it?'

'Yes, please.'

'Exciting! Can't wait to hear more. Got to dash though, my shift starts soon. See you both later.'

'I've got it,' announced Wynn.

'Got what?' asked Buzz, confused.

'Our code word.'

'Go on then.'

'Well, I figure it has to be something we could say in public, so how about "Second Amethyst"?'

197

Buzz laughed out loud. 'The name the shop was supposed to have. I was even having the sign painted until you said it should be Crazy Crystals instead.'

The name was a nod to their early relationship when everything was right in their world.

'Perfect!' they said at exactly the same time and both of them dissolved into giggles, which probably did more to release the tension between them than anything else.

CHAPTER TWENTY-EIGHT

Skye walked down the road smiling about seeing Buzz kissing her mother. And her mother had sold up in Dublin too. But how did she feel about her mum being part of her new start in England? How did she choose where to live, especially when the baby came along, if there was truly a choice between her mother and Buzz? Could they be completely reconciled and living in the same place by then?

The questions were flying around her head so much, she didn't realize until she nearly bumped into him that someone was blocking the pavement in front of her.

'There you are. Thought I'd have to search round this pesky seaside place forever to find you.'

'Declan?' It was all Skye could do to keep her balance. The shock of seeing her former boyfriend and the father of her baby here in Borteen was immense.

Before she realized what he was going to do, Declan reached out his hand to touch her pregnancy bump.

'So, you are preggers. Is it really mine? Really my baby?' His tone was unmistakably sarcastic.

'Well, ruling out some sort of miracle, yes, seeing as I've never slept with anyone else in my life.'

Anger was simmering and rising to the boil. She had the urge to beat her fists against his chest, to scream and shout. Why had she ever believed that Declan was the man of her dreams, with his surly expression and disdainfully curling lip? Why had she been so foolish as to trust her virginity to him, to get so carried away that she forgot all about the condom they were supposed to be using? She'd been a complete and utter naive idiot, although she reminded herself that her daughter was now so much a part of her that she couldn't imagine not being pregnant and she was so looking forward to meeting her.

'Why are you here, Declan? You told my friend Adam very clearly that you didn't want anything to do with me or *my* baby.' She brushed his hand off her stomach and just about resisted running away.

'Wanted to be clear about your intentions, Skye. I mean, you hear so many stories about men being pursued for lots of money after a girl's got herself pregnant deliberately.'

'What! I think you'd better go.'

'As I said, I'm not going anywhere until I know your intentions.'

'Well, if you truly want to find out what Skye intends, I think it might be better if you go somewhere to sit down and talk rationally, rather than yelling like a fishwife in the street.' The voice was unmistakably Adam's and had a steely edge to it. Skye was relieved she was no longer on her own with Declan, who today seemed extra scary.

'Ah, lover boy. Want another thumping?' Declan's snarl was back.

Adam was still wearing his Santa outfit and holding his warming blanket, false beard and red hat in his hands. In other circumstances the scenario might even have been funny.

Skye didn't want to give the two men cause to fight. 'I need to get to work. If you follow me, Declan, I'll get you a coffee, and if it's quiet we can talk.'

'Do you want me to come too?' Adam's tone was now more unsure.

'It's probably best if you don't, but thank you so much for supporting me, Adam. You are truly a good friend. And I really don't want to get sacked for causing a brawl at the café, do I?'

'Well, you have my mobile number if you need back-up. I'll hang around here for a while until I know everything's okay.' Adam turned on his heel and left before Skye could say anything more. Her instinct was to go too, but Declan was the father of her baby and she had to speak to him.

Skye was very reluctant to take Declan to work, but didn't see that she had much of a choice. At least Christine was aware of the situation and would make sure that she and her baby were safe. She led the way down the pavement at a brisk pace and Declan trailed sullenly behind her all the way to the café.

* * *

Adam found it almost impossible to walk away and leave Skye on her own with Declan. He was greatly concerned about her safety and hadn't hesitated to speak up when he saw the pair together, but he knew that he was only likely to inflame the situation by sticking around and it would hardly help his friendship with Skye when she'd asked him to go.

Instead, he walked the length of the promenade, clutching his phone tightly in his hand, just in case Skye rang him to ask for help.

He cursed himself that he'd mentioned Borteen when he'd met Declan in Birmingham before things had turned ugly. It was his fault that the man had found Skye again.

The urge to protect Skye only cemented the fact that his feelings hadn't changed towards her at all. He cared deeply about her, and even though it seemed highly unlikely, he prayed now that she wouldn't be reunited with the father of her child.

* * *

Skye was shaking when she opened the door to the café. Christine looked up and then glanced pointedly at Declan as the café wasn't yet open.

'Hi, Christine, is it okay if I give Declan a coffee before we open, please?'

'Suppose so . . . ah, *Declan*, Declan?' Understanding dawned across Christine's face.

'Yes. *The* Declan.'

Skye led the sulky Declan into the empty café and pointed at a table. There was little hope she could have a private conversation with him here, but then maybe Christine's presence would stop any discussion getting out of control.

She went to hang up her coat in the storeroom and took her apron from the hook. Christine followed her into the small space.

'You okay? Do I need to get back-up? Tell your parents?' she whispered urgently.

'Hopefully not. He seems to want reassurance that I won't be demanding money from him for the baby. Do you think you could you listen in, just in case?'

Christine pulled her into a brief hug. 'Be brave, girl. I'm here if you need me. Might be worth recording the conversation though? I'll keep my ears open and my rolling pin to hand.'

That last comment made Skye smile. She tied the strings of her apron behind her, realizing all at the same time that she was getting more rounded so there was less string to tie than before.

'What can I get you to drink?' she asked Declan, just as if she were taking a normal customer's order.

'Don't think I want a drink,' he muttered.

'Suit yourself.' Skye didn't sit down. She could see Christine rearranging pastries at the counter.

'Look, Skye, if that really is my baby in there—' Declan pointed at her stomach — 'then tell me, why the hell didn't you get rid of it before it was too late?'

'She's part of me. I could never have "got rid" of her. I would never have recovered from doing that. I feared that I had lost her several times and that's made her even more precious to me. I've realized that I want her more than anything. I just thought you should know about her, your daughter.'

'A girl?' A strange expression passed over his face, but then in an instant the snarl was back. 'Well, I'm stating right here and now that I don't want anything to do with this — ever, do you hear? Do you understand? You're on your own if you choose to have the brat, and don't think you can get any money out of me, because I won't pay a bean.'

He stood up and Skye stepped quickly backwards, suddenly fearful he might hit her.

'That's me told. As I said, I just thought you might want to know that you were going to have a daughter.'

'Well, I don't want to know. As far as I'm concerned, that in there is your little bastard and nothing to do with me. I'm off now. Have a good life and please don't give the brat my name or contact details . . . never ever.' He pushed the chair back under the table, causing a horrible scraping noise.

Before he got to the door, however, Skye had moved fast to grab the rolling pin out of Christine's hand and barred the way.

Declan's face was a picture.

'You going to hit me with that?'

'Don't tempt me. You're not leaving here until I've had my say.' She raised the rolling pin.

Declan took two steps backwards.

'My purpose in contacting you was a genuine one, to see if you were interested in being part of your daughter's life. I was giving you a choice, Declan. Now I'm not. You keep well away from us. If I ever see you anywhere near here I'll report you for your attack on Adam and back it up with information about the times you've been physically abusive to me too. As for money, I'm not aware that I've ever mentioned being after your money, but I think you'll find that given a few simple DNA tests any court in the land would say you were liable for maintenance — maybe I'll consider that one, so don't think you can relax just yet. I'd suggest too that you're more careful and considerate in your relationships in future. As for my opinion of you, Declan Coles, you're a sad bully and I'm so glad I've finally seen you for what you are.' She lowered the rolling pin and stepped to one side. 'Now go, and good riddance.'

Declan virtually ran out of the door and Skye sank into a chair as Christine began to applaud.

'Well done, girl. I'm so proud of you.'

The café door opened again and Skye instinctively raised the rolling pin to defend herself.

Adam burst through the door, concern written all over his face.

'Sorry, sorry, I know you told me to keep out of it, but I just had to make sure that you're okay, Skye.'

'I'm fine, thank you. Christine had her rolling pin at the ready.'

Christine came around the counter and took the rolling pin from Skye's hands. 'Horrid man. I'm glad he's gone. Nothing would have given me greater pleasure than to brain him with this, but Skye very nearly did the job instead. I think you should take him to court and claim child maintenance anyway.'

'A subject for another time maybe, but for now I'm relieved he's gone.'

Adam sighed loudly. 'I agree. Thank goodness he left and I saw him heading up the high street before I came in.' He sat in a chair near to Skye and stretched a hand over the table towards her.

She really wanted to hold his hand. Really wanted to feel his comforting arms around her, but hadn't they agreed they were to be just friends?

'I think that's enough drama for one day and we haven't even opened the café door yet,' said Christine. 'Are you staying in Borteen for Christmas, Adam?' Her gaze was on Skye even though she was talking to Adam, and Skye guessed that her face was ashen.

'I need to go home again, otherwise my mother will be all on her own.'

Skye felt her spirits dip even further, but why? She'd refused Adam. Refused to let him rescue her. Had she been wrong? It would have made life so much simpler if she'd just given in, but was that worse still? Would she just have been settling for something comfortable and safe? Far better to build a strong friendship from here and see where it led.

'Thanks for looking out for Skye, young man. You can have the first coffee of the day on the house. Skye, are you sure you're all right? You've gone very pale. You'd better have a green tea.'

'It's only shock setting in about seeing Declan and being so full of anger, but I guess I have the closure I wanted; he wants nothing more to do with me or *my* baby.' As far as Skye was concerned, the baby was now hers completely.

Adam finally touched her hand and she looked into his eyes for long enough for his unspoken message of support to warm her heart.

CHAPTER TWENTY-NINE

Skye and Wynn's Christmas market stall was situated almost directly outside of Crazy Crystals. The high street was quiet as they set up their display, one side for Wynn's crystal jewellery and the other for Skye's fabric makes. Skye couldn't help but glow with pride as she viewed her products, most of them her own designs, arranged on the table. Her mother's jewellery was spectacular and shone beneath the spotlights Buzz had managed to rig up above them using an extension lead plugged into a socket from a first-floor window.

At five thirty, piped Christmas music began to emanate from the promenade and Wynn and Skye danced around — to keep warm more than anything else. By six there was an influx of people milling around the stalls and Skye was delighted to make her first sale of a tiny coin purse to Maeve, who ran a gift shop in Borteen.

From the point of making the first sale, trade was brisk and Skye began to think she hadn't made enough things to sell. She had to stop the ridiculous notion of fetching the sewing machine and making things on the go. Instead, she made sure she had one of each type of item displayed and began to take orders on a pad of paper supplied by Buzz.

'Your makes are going down so well.'

'Mum's jewellery is selling fast too.'

Buzz stood between the two women, and when there was a lull in trade, Wynn turned to him. 'I made something special for you.'

'For Christmas?' he asked.

'I thought you could have it early.' From her pocket she produced a thin plait of brown leather strands with a single but rather spectacularly coloured amber bead in the centre.

Wynn handed it to Buzz and he examined the item closely. 'Beautiful piece of amber.'

'It reminded me of the flecks in your eyes and I knew it was yours as soon as I saw it.'

Buzz undid the fastener and placed the necklet around his neck. It fitted snuggly with the amber bead designed to sit in the hollow at the base of his throat.

Skye could tell that Wynn was pleased, especially when Buzz examined what it looked like in the mirror she had on the stall.

'Am I allowed to give you a kiss to say thank you?' he asked.

Skye couldn't help but watch in fascination as her parents embraced and their lips met. She knew her suspicions about them still wanting each other were sound, and her mother appeared to have softened somehow.

It seemed almost fated that when she turned back to face the stall because she'd caught a glimpse of someone approaching, it turned out to be Adam.

'Adam, good evening. What's the rest of the market like?' she said.

It was Buzz that answered from near her shoulder. 'Why don't you go and take a look with Adam? I can look after your side of the stall, and yes, I think I'm perfectly capable of taking orders if anyone asks.'

Skye felt a bit put on the spot and she feared that Adam would too. However, he was far too much of a gentleman to say anything, and smiled and offered his arm to her. They headed down towards the promenade together, Skye not daring to speak as yet, but noticing that he took care to protect her from any jostling by the other shoppers. It made her feel ridiculously happy that he cared enough to do this — unless, of course, he just feared Buzz's wrath if she got hurt.

They skirted the huge Christmas tree. Skye tried to spot the decorations they had placed on the branches earlier in the month. They walked along the promenade where the path between the stalls was wider. On one side were food stalls, selling everything from hot dogs to popcorn to doughnuts to candyfloss. On the other side there were all sorts of gift stalls.

'Would you like a coffee? Oh, I forgot, you don't do coffee, right?'

'I wonder if anyone's serving green tea?'

'I'll find out. Stay here.'

He left her on a bench and made his way through the crowd. He emerged back out of the throng a little while later with two takeaway cups.

'Success — green tea. I had one too.'

He sat down next to her on the bench and Skye used the cup to warm her hands.

'Thank you. I thought you were going home for Christmas?'

'I'm staying with Reverend Hopkins until Christmas Eve and then I'm back home with my mother for a week. Nigel has promised to show me what his job entails from now until Christmas, so that I can make up my mind whether it's what I want for my future. The jury is out at the moment. Nigel has helped me to see that I was perhaps looking for a refuge in the Church, but I've resolved that regardless of what I do, I have to have a job that means something to me in future. I may even work for a charity. Think I'm done with the pursuit of material wealth for the sake of it. Sorry, that came out in a long burble.'

'It sounds great and I agree. As long as I'm happy and have enough money for me and my daughter to live in reasonable comfort, I'll be content.'

'And will you stay in Borteen longer term?'

'As you said yourself — the jury is out on that one. It certainly looks as if my mother and Buzz will be here, so I guess it's logical when I might need support with my baby going forward.'

'Did I imagine seeing your parents kissing earlier?'

'No, you didn't imagine it. I fully expect them to get back together when they both stop being so silly about it.'

'Fantastic,' said Adam, sipping his green tea with a dubious expression.

They walked to the end of the promenade and back clutching the takeaway cups.

'I'd like to buy something from you and a piece of jewellery from Wynn for my mother's Christmas presents.'

'Mum has some lovely pieces of jewellery.'

'Come on then, you can help me to choose.' Adam took her empty cup and put it with his own, she suspected still half-full, in a recycling bin. He offered her his arm again and she took it happily.

'How was your green tea?'

'An acquired taste, I think. I'll try chamomile next.'

Skye smiled up at him.

'Let's get my Christmas shopping done.'

'I don't know what your mum likes though. What colours does she wear?'

'Now that's easy. Navy-blue trousers and cardigans with bright-coloured tops underneath.' He laughed and she was pleased that they seemed to be easy with each other again.

She helped him to pick out a make-up bag, a coin purse and a labradorite pendant from their stall and then he said goodnight. She was sad that he'd gone and it was all she could do not to run after him and haul him back to her side.

It soon came time to clear away the stall. Buzz had put a one-pot meal in the oven earlier on — his vegetable curry was fragrant and the naan breads and rice very welcome after an evening of standing at the stall.

Skye tried to hide her puffy ankles, but Wynn, with a mother's eyes, couldn't help but notice, and made her put her feet up as she and Buzz cleared up together. Skye was aware of their friendly banter as they worked at the sink.

'We make a good team, us three,' said Buzz, warming his hands on a cup of herbal tea a little later.

'You know, sometimes I wish we were like other families and had hot chocolate and cakes,' said Skye frowning.

Buzz and Wynn both laughed and Wynn commented, 'Are you getting strange pregnancy cravings?'

'Is that really a thing?'

'Oh, yes,' said Wynn. 'When I was expecting you, I went mad on lentil and bacon — yes bacon — soup.'

'I thought you'd always been veggie!' exclaimed Skye.

'Not always! And if you speak to most vegetarians, I think you'll find if they miss anything from their old diet it's often bacon.'

'Really?'

'I'll confirm that,' agreed Buzz.

'Anyway, I went mad on lentil and bacon soup when I was carrying you. Was even known to cry when I couldn't get any.'

'So, you think I could be craving hot chocolate and cake?'

'I think it can sometimes mean a mother is lacking something in her diet,' mused Buzz. 'Wynn's bacon was probably a need for protein and yours suggests a need for glucose or fructose.'

'I had a friend who wanted to eat coal, so goodness knows what she was lacking. I had another who ate beetroot in vinegar constantly and was irrationally scared that meant the baby might have a huge beetroot-coloured birthmark,' said Wynn.

'Strange process, pregnancy. I'm glad I've never had to go through it,' said Buzz with a serious face that had Skye and Wynn giggling uncontrollably.

As she made her preparations to go to bed, Skye remembered something she had to say to her mum. 'Christine has had some thoughts about rentals for you in Borteen if you still want to go ahead. She said we could do some viewings early tomorrow if that would suit you?'

'Sounds exciting,' said Wynn, and Skye knew that she didn't imagine the crestfallen look on Buzz's face.

CHAPTER THIRTY

Christine had suggested two possible options for Wynn's accommodation in Borteen, and Skye went with her mother to view the properties. One was a flat with a sea view but right on the corner of the high street and likely to be noisy at night in the holiday season. The other was at the other end of the high street, almost at the top of the hill, and even before they got up to the door, Wynn was looking excited. Skye knew this one was right, despite feeling out of breath after the steep walk.

The row of whitewashed cottages must have been some of the oldest buildings in Borteen. There was no parking, but the tiny front garden had rose bushes, now bare, but with the promise of flowers after the winter. There were basically only two small rooms downstairs, plus a lean-to kitchen, with a yard beyond and two bedrooms with a tiny shower room. It was available to rent fully furnished. Everything was old like the building, but clean and so to her mother's taste it was untrue.

Christine was laughing when Skye and Wynn came down the stairs from the bedrooms. 'From your faces, do I take it I've got a new tenant for Garden Cottage?'

'If the price is right.' Skye could see that Wynn had closed her eyes and crossed her fingers behind her back.

* * *

Wynn moved into Garden Cottage the next day. Buzz had terribly mixed feelings. It seemed on one hand as if his wife was leaving him yet again, but on the other at least she wasn't going far and he knew that if they were going to fulfil their promise of romancing each other, they needed space to do that. Rekindling their relationship wasn't something they could rush, and Buzz believed that it was worth taking the time to get it right. They had a second chance for happiness and Buzz really didn't want to spend his twilight years alone. The dream was now to be with Wynn.

'You've never been to Dublin, have you?'

'No,' he said warily.

'I have to take a small van over to get the rest of my stuff. I was thinking you might like to come with me.'

'Question is, when?'

'I was thinking in the new year.'

'Sounds like fun.'

'So, maybe you need to concentrate on "romancing" me before then, so we can have even more fun.' Wynn winked and Buzz was afraid he would blush.

'Dinner tonight, seven?'

'Ooh, where are we going?'

'Give a guy a break. I haven't quite worked that out yet,' he laughed.

'I only meant, do I need to dress casually or posh?'

'Make it posh.' He winked.

Buzz walked back down the high street wondering where on earth he could take Wynn that was *posh* and, more to the point, what would he himself wear?

He met Skye coming the other way, puffing a little with the effort of walking up the hill and carrying flowers.

'For your mum?'

'A housewarming gift.' Skye smiled but Buzz could see from the rings beneath her eyes that she was tired. He'd heard the sewing machine whirring until late the previous evening.

'You know if you want to move into Garden Cottage with your mum, I'd be fine with it, don't you?'

Her face fell. 'I'm actually enjoying the attic room, if it's still all right to stay?'

Buzz felt a glow of happiness unfurl within him. 'That's perfectly fine with me.'

* * *

Skye carried on towards Garden Cottage, glancing back at Buzz as he strode down the hill towards the sea and his shop. His hair was pulled back in its usual ponytail, tied low at his neckline, and his combat trousers were topped by a khaki hunting coat, but when they'd been talking she'd caught sight of the amber necklet Wynn had given to him nestled at his throat and a glimpse of a colourful shirt beneath the coat. He was as far from a conventional father figure that you could get, but she knew instinctively that he had a good heart and that he cared about her. It was sad that she'd missed out on knowing him for so much of her life.

She still couldn't believe that Buzz and Wynn had lived apart for so many years as they seemed so suited to each other in lifestyle, activities, ways of thinking — every way, in fact.

Her mother had at last talked to her more about the reasons for her leaving Borteen. Wynn had told Skye very seriously about her tendency to run away, just like her own mother, if a situation or relationship became difficult. Wynn had stressed that she was working hard to not repeat the pattern and she was telling Skye in the hope of stopping her reacting in the same way in her life.

Wynn had gone on to explain that she couldn't believe that Buzz had given her another chance and that the two of them were taking things slowly to see if they could make a go of it.

It was difficult to be patient, but she could see signs that Wynn and Buzz were growing ever closer. Maybe Buzz could move into Garden Cottage with Wynn instead of her and she could enjoy the flat above the shop with her daughter, she mused. But was that just wishful thinking, an impossible dream?

* * *

After much angst, Buzz eventually settled for booking a table at a little Italian bistro restaurant in Sowden. He couldn't believe that at his age, his pulse was racing as he made the booking, but then he'd noted that Wynn and the thought of romancing her appeared to have been doing strange things to his heart lately. He decided to arrange for a taxi there and back so that he and Wynn could share a bottle of wine without the worry of driving.

Wynn looked lovely in a purple velvet dress, her hair caught in two loose plaits either side of her head, when he arrived at Garden Cottage to collect her. Buzz was wearing dark trousers and a colourful shirt. He'd brushed his own hair till it shone, mainly because he'd suddenly become nervous at the thought of spending the evening completely alone with Wynn and got carried away as he thought about what romancing his wife might actually involve.

It appeared that Wynn might have similar worries, as they both spent the taxi ride showing a great interest in the driver's work, and when they arrived at the restaurant the extensive menu and wine list were happy distractions too.

Buzz gulped as the waiter moved away from their table having taken their order. He'd opted for bread and olive oil with black olives to start, as had Wynn, and then he'd ordered a main of vegetable-stuffed cannelloni and Wynn vegetable lasagne. Buzz had chosen a bottle of red wine to go with their meal.

Wynn looked suddenly shy and much younger than her years as he looked at her across the table, and it made Buzz decide to come clean about his current feelings.

'We don't know how to do this yet, do we?'

'No! My heart rate increased when the waiter went away.' Wynn put her hand over her mouth in a gesture of embarrassment.

Buzz laughed. 'Mine too!' He stretched out his hand to Wynn. She clasped his fingers.

'How can we be so shy together?'

'Maybe we both need a glass of that wine.'

'I don't drink very often these days, so it'd better be a small glass.'

Wynn squeezed his fingers and then released his hand with another shy smile as the waiter reappeared with their olives and bread. The man made a show of dispensing olive oil and balsamic vinegar into little bowls and Buzz could have sworn he was flirting with Wynn despite being much younger than her.

He was just trying to smooth down his raised hackles when there was an exclamation from right behind him.

'That can't be you, can it, Wynn? After all these years! I thought you'd run away. My brother told me you'd gone, so you're the last person I expected to see here in Sowden.'

Buzz clenched his teeth — it was unmistakably the voice of his brother Ed. He turned slowly and Ed now realized, given the expression on his face, who was sitting at the table with Wynn. Ed appeared much older than the last time Buzz had seen him, but then he supposed he himself looked more lined too.

'Well, well. Long-lost sister-in-law and my long-not-seen brother — together of all things!'

Buzz decided there was nothing for it but to put a brave face on the meeting. A glance at Wynn suggested that she was terrified, and her complexion looked as white as the tablecloth.

'Evening, Ed,' Buzz said, attempting to keep the hostility out of his voice, but knowing full well that he was failing.

Wynn didn't say a word. She sat looking between the two men as if she was watching a table tennis game.

Buzz now knew, of course, that his brother had slept with Wynn all of those years ago behind his back, resulting in Buzz being alone for so many years, but Ed wasn't to know that he was aware of what had occurred or indeed the depth of hurt and emotion that the revelation had stirred. Buzz decided he would keep Ed in the dark about that secret if he could. He needed the man to go away before he thumped him. For a non-violent soul, he was surprised by the urge to punch Ed repeatedly.

Thankfully another waiter appeared right then by Ed's side with two huge carrier bags.

'Family takeaway,' said Ed, shrugging his shoulders. Before he took the bags, he produced a card from his pocket and slapped it onto the table next to Buzz. 'Just in case you've lost my contact details. You should both come round for a drink soon and fill me in on what's been happening with you both. It's been far too long — especially missed seeing you, Wynn.' He put a hand on her shoulder as he moved past to take the food bags and Buzz saw Wynn wince and shrug him off.

'Now, I'd better get this food home while it's hot. Toodle-pip.' He saluted, and Buzz realized he had no remaining brotherly feelings towards Ed at all. He had absolutely no desire to see or hear from the man ever again.

* * *

Wynn's blood was boiling. The way Ed had deliberately touched her seemed to be making a point, rubbing Buzz's nose in the fact that they had slept together, even though she was pretty sure Ed wouldn't know Buzz knew about that. Although Buzz had said that his brother had dropped hints over the years.

She had to nip this in the bud. If they ran into Ed again, which was highly likely, Ed had to know Wynn's feelings about him and his suggestions.

She folded her napkin on the table and got up. 'Excuse me for a moment, Buzz. Back in a second.'

Buzz would hopefully think she was off to the ladies, but she diverted out of the restaurant and into the car park. It was easy to spot Ed, putting his carrier bags into the back-seat footwell of a huge black four-by-four.

As he straightened, Wynn stepped out of the shadows.

'Wynn, how lovely. Can't keep away from me? Fancy a quickie in the back of the car?'

Wynn stared at him and it took all of her energy not to kick him somewhere sensitive. 'I wanted to set the story straight, Ed. Stop talking like you did just now in front of Buzz. You were a moment of idle curiosity all of those years ago. You are nothing to me. Your brother is worth a thousand of you.'

'So how come you've been away from him for so long?' he sneered.

'Shame! That night should never have happened between us and to be clear, it never will ever again. Keep well away from us, Ed. Buzz and I are giving our marriage another go and I don't want you waltzing in with your suggestive comments to drive a wedge between us.'

'And what if I told him what happened back then?' Ed was puffed up like an indignant chipmunk.

'He already knows, because I told him, so butt out if you don't want him to deck you.'

Ed seemed to deflate before her eyes. 'Buzz knows? Yikes. Right, I'm off to get this food home before it's cold. I'll steer clear of you both, don't worry; I think that's probably best now. Have a good rest of your life, Wynn.' Luckily, he jumped in the driver's seat without a backward glance and started the engine, or else Wynn was sure she would actually have delivered a well-aimed kick.

She went back into the restaurant, but as she sat at the table she could tell that the damage had already been done and the mood of the evening that showed such promise had changed completely.

Buzz couldn't look at her, and she spent most of the time studying her bread. The food tasted like cardboard. Any spark of companionship and humour had been extinguished by Ed's appearance.

The meal passed largely in silence. Wynn asked Buzz to pass the pepper and Buzz questioned if she wanted more wine, which she refused. He pushed the half-full bottle to the side of the table. They didn't order desserts. Buzz paid the bill and they went outside to find a taxi. He threw his brother's card in a nearby bin after tearing it viciously into tiny pieces.

This time there was no friendly banter with the taxi driver, only silence, which Wynn filled by going over and over in her head the time on the beach when she'd told Buzz about her infidelity with Ed. Then she wondered about the revelations of the DNA tests, the results of which should surely be due to arrive soon.

The kiss that Wynn had fondly hoped for at the beginning of the evening didn't happen, and they barely wished each other goodnight.

Buzz marched off down the high street, and as Wynn shut the door of Garden Cottage, she wondered where the disastrous evening left the tattered remnants of their marriage.

She closed the front door and leaned against it as tears began to flow. She'd known that meeting Ed sometime was a possibility, a probability even, but the reality had been much worse than she'd imagined. She shrugged off her coat and went upstairs. Pulling her case out from under the bed, she began to pile her underwear into the bottom of it.

One drawer was empty before she realized what she was doing. She sank down onto the bedside chair and began to chant. *Second amethyst, second amethyst, second amethyst.* Why hadn't she remembered to say that in the taxi tonight?

She had promised Buzz and herself not to run away again and here she was about to do just that. Wynn quickly put her underwear back in the drawer and the case back beneath the bed.

* * *

Buzz stomped down Borteen high street in a foul mood. He got to the door of Crazy Crystals and almost put his key into the lock, but he knew he was unlikely to sleep with this maelstrom of emotions swirling within him.

Instead, he put the key away and continued down the road to the beach. He sat on the beach steps and tried to be soothed by the sounds of the ocean.

Had he been too reasonable about Wynn returning, too trusting? Would he ever really be able to relax in his marriage again? Should he tell Wynn it was all over instead?

He found it very telling that neither of them had used their agreed code that evening. Did that mean that there wasn't any chance for them?

He could tell that Ed had enjoyed making Wynn squirm in the restaurant. But then he also knew that Wynn must have gone to speak to his brother when she left the table. Oh, that he could have heard that conversation. It didn't help that Wynn hadn't told him she'd been to talk to Ed when she returned after supposedly visiting the ladies for far too long.

After all of his certainty that he and Wynn were still meant to be together, doubts had now crept in. He didn't like the direction his thoughts were heading and began to repeat their code — *second amethyst, second amethyst, second amethyst*. Each repetition was more and more desperate as he tried to reignite his hopes for the future.

But, as he got up to go home, a thought occurred to him. Ed had always been jealous of his little brother, most likely because their mother doted on her youngest child. Was it possible that Ed had set out to seduce Wynn, rather than it being a chance coming-together as Wynn had implied? It didn't excuse Wynn's behaviour, of course, but it suddenly made complete sense. Ed could have decided to take something from Buzz, another one of the little revenge episodes that had happened over the years, but this one with much bigger consequences. Buzz prayed then that Skye wasn't one of those consequences.

He had to keep the faith, had to breathe again. He walked home reciting *second amethyst* with each step.

CHAPTER THIRTY-ONE

Skye had gone to bed early the previous evening. She had been excited about her parents going on a date and the potential for them reuniting properly at last, but waking the next morning to the sound of Buzz crashing about in the kitchen below, she sensed something was not quite right. Maybe her hopes of reconciliation had been premature.

Showering quickly, she was relieved she had planned a sewing day for today and was not working at the café. Christmas seemed to be approaching at a rapid rate, matched only by the rate that Skye's bump was expanding. She couldn't believe she had begun to waddle, and the maternity dungarees that she had made herself with material from Busy Pins, and which she'd thought would always be too big, now were the only outfit she was completely comfortable in.

She was aware that she'd soon have to discuss reducing her hours at the café with Christine yet again. Buzz wanted her to stop the café work entirely until after the birth, but she enjoyed the interaction with Christine and the fact that it was something away from the intensity of her family dynamics. Sighing at her swollen ankles, she took one more look in the mirror before going down to the kitchen to say good morning to Buzz, share breakfast and find out exactly what was going on.

Buzz appeared to be having a noisy clean-out of the saucepan drawers.

'Is everything all right?' she asked tentatively, although she could tell by Buzz's expression that something was in fact very wrong.

Instead of saying anything, Buzz dropped the saucepan he was holding back into the drawer with a crash and sank down to sit on the kitchen floor. 'I think your mother and I are doomed,' he said and put his hands over his face.

'Did you two have an argument? Do I need to bang your heads together?' She tried to keep her tone light, although inside the feelings of panic were beginning to multiply. Even the baby seemed to be holding her breath.

'We met Ed, my brother, at the restaurant.'

'Oh . . . Ed? The Ed who could be my father?'

She never got to ask any more about the meeting as at that very moment there was an enormous bang outside, followed by several other loud noises.

'What the . . .' exclaimed Buzz. He leapt to his feet. 'I'm going to find out . . . Be careful, young lady, if you venture out. We don't know what that was, but it sounded pretty bad.'

'You be careful too,' said Skye, but Buzz had already gone, taking the stairs two at a time in his hurry.

Skye couldn't see anything from the front windows, so as her curiosity was aroused she put on her coat and shoes and went to see what had happened outside. Buzz had not reappeared.

She rushed out of the shop door and then jumped backwards on the pavement as a police car with sirens blazing sped past her. She'd just relaxed again when more sirens and a fire engine came roaring down Borteen Hill, followed by another police car and an ambulance. What on earth was going on?

She felt her pulse quicken and her heart began to thud even more when she realized that the emergency service vehicles had parked up near the promenade, the huge Christmas tree with its twinkling lights seeming incongruous in the early morning light behind the more garish flashing lights of the ambulance and police cars. She quickened her pace as it became obvious that something had happened at the beach café. She didn't get much further down the road, because police officers were blocking the way and turning people back.

She retreated to the opposite pavement, her hands up to her face in shock, as she realized there was a huge lorry seemingly embedded in what was left of her place of work. As she watched in horror, flames began to rise from the building along with thick black smoke.

Suddenly, arms reached around her, making her jump, and she was crushed almost painfully against a firm chest.

'Skye, thank goodness you're okay. I thought you might be in the café.'

It was Adam, and Skye relaxed into his safe, comforting hold.

'Have you seen Christine?' she asked in a shrill voice.

'No, I'm afraid not. Do you think she'd be in the café this early?'

Skye nodded against his chest, fighting the tears that were threatening. 'Did you see what happened?' She knew her voice sounded shaky with shock as she pulled away from him slightly.

'I was running on the beach. I heard the enormous bang. It looks as if a huge lorry has come down the hill and gone straight on . . . straight into the café.'

There was quite a crowd gathering around them as more residents of Borteen became aware of the dreadful incident and came to see what had happened. A policewoman asked everyone to move back. 'The fire crew are worried of possible explosions. You all need to move further up the high street, please.'

Skye gulped. Adam put an arm around her to prevent her being jostled by the other onlookers as they moved further up the pavement.

'I can't see Christine anywhere. And Buzz went down there to see what was going on too.' Skye tried to look around again. 'Adam, I'm starting to get really scared. I have a horrible feeling. Where are Christine and Buzz?'

'Whereabouts in the café would Christine normally be at this time of day?'

'In the kitchen, I would guess.' She gulped at what that might mean.

* * *

Adam's heart rate had slowed a little after its initial acceleration. He had realized a lot of things during the last fifteen minutes. The shock and fear that had overwhelmed him when he saw the drama unfolding at the café was completely and totally wrapped up with his feelings for Skye. If he needed any confirmation that the proposal he'd made to the girl who had got completely under his skin in such a short time was still valid, this was it. He was in love with Skye, she wasn't just another lost soul he was trying to rescue as he had initially feared. The thought that something awful could have happened to her had shaken him to his very core.

'Skye, will you please go home? I promise to come and tell you when I know more.'

'But I need to be sure that Christine is all right!' wailed Skye. 'And Buzz is here somewhere too.'

'Look, getting upset or making yourself ill isn't going to help.'

'Adam, stop wrapping me in cotton wool. I'm pregnant, not dying.'

'I can't help caring about you. I've tried to rein it back. I've tried not to let it show, but I do care and I can't help it.'

Skye became very still and quiet next to him and he thought he'd maybe said too much yet again. He risked a glance sideways and she looked up into his eyes.

'Thank you. That means a lot.'

Adam let out the worried breath he had been holding in.

Out of nowhere, Buzz came across to them, asking for any news. Skye flung her arms around his neck and sobbed.

He said that he'd been watching from closer to the promenade until the police had moved him on.

People began to crowd back onto the pavements as an
ambulance drove away and up the hill just as another blue-
lit ambulance zoomed down the road towards the incident.
It was impossible to see what was going on from where they
were standing in the high street.

'We're not doing any good hanging around here. If you
won't go home to wait for news, Skye, let's walk to the end
of the promenade and along the beach,' Adam suggested.

'Great idea. I'm so full of tension — a walk might help.'
Skye turned to Buzz. 'Can you keep your eyes peeled for
Christine and text me if you hear anything, anything at all,
please?'

'We probably won't be able to see much more from the
beach though, so don't get your hopes up,' said Adam. Buzz
and he exchanged a worried look.

'It will just be a relief to do something.'

At that moment, Skye's mother appeared through
the crowd and flung herself at Buzz. She said something strange
which Adam didn't understand: 'Second amethyst.' She cupped
Buzz's face in her hands. 'I imagined you dead — the shop
blown up.' Wynn burst into tears and clung on to him.

'Come on, Adam, let's leave the olds to sort themselves
out.' Skye was smiling as she said it. 'I'll explain later,' she
whispered.

It was slow going to begin with, because so many people
had gathered along the promenade as well as at the bottom of
the high street, but as they got further along the beach road
there were less people. They made their way to the smaller
steps down to the beach at the far end of the promenade,
close to Owl Corner Crafts.

Adam went down the steps in front of Skye so that he
could help her down, but she brushed him off impatiently
and he knew that he was being overprotective yet again.

As soon as they got onto the sand, Adam realized that
this probably hadn't been a good idea after all. For one thing,

there were a lot of other people on the beach trying to see what was going on, for another, from this distance, you could see the sickening truth of what had happened. The huge articulated lorry that must have careered down the hill was firmly embedded in what little was left of the café building.

Skye turned to Adam with wide eyes and a pale face. 'Christine! Anyone in there wouldn't have stood a chance.'

'Skye, I know you don't like me to try to rescue you from things, but this time I'm insisting. Let's go to the vicarage, get warm and have a hot drink. The situation at the café won't be resolving itself any time soon. You can't do anything, neither can I. I'll ring Buzz when we're settled, so he knows where you are, and I can ask if there's news. Come on.'

He grasped her arm firmly and for once she didn't argue with him. She meekly walked alongside him, the fight seeming to have gone out of her completely.

She was very quiet and her face almost white as he settled her at the vicarage kitchen table. As quickly as he could, he placed a mug of herbal tea and two digestive biscuits in front of her.

Before he had chance to ring Buzz to update him about their whereabouts, Skye's mobile phone screen lit up and she answered the call with shaking hands. Buzz was talking so loudly that Adam could hear every word.

'They found Christine. Miraculously, she's okay. She somehow saw the lorry coming and ran into the storeroom, but then she was trapped until the firemen found her. They're taking her to hospital to be checked out, just in case.'

'Phew. Thank you for letting me know.' Skye burst into tears and Adam had to resist holding her close to him. Instead, he took the phone and told Buzz where they were, found a box of tissues and made fresh mugs of tea.

* * *

Wynn had run down Borteen Hill so fast earlier that she had nearly fallen headfirst on the pavement. The numerous emergency vehicles passing by the cottage with their blaring sirens had alerted her to the fact that something bad had happened.

After a virtually sleepless night in which she tossed and turned and replayed meeting Ed the previous evening, she had a horrible sense of dread that something might have happened to Buzz which would rob her of the opportunity to try again and make amends.

Once she had established that Buzz and Skye were safe, she thanked any deity that she could think of and waited with Buzz for news of Christine. As she stood next to Buzz waiting, she was very aware that when she had hugged him in relief earlier, he hadn't put his arms around her, and the dread machine started up again in her mind.

When things seemed calmer, she said Buzz's name and he turned to her. 'We need to talk,' she said.

'Yes, I agree,' he replied and grasped her hand to lead her away from the crowd watching the aftermath of the crash and up the street to the shop. Wynn's stomach turned over as he unlocked the door, as he didn't seem to be behaving the same towards her as before.

They were silent as Buzz led the way up to the flat. Seemingly on autopilot, he filled the kettle and set it to boil.

'Buzz?'

'Did you go and speak to Ed after he left the restaurant last night?'

It was a bald question, delivered in an alarmingly neutral tone.

'Yes,' she confessed.

'So why didn't you say, when you came back to the table?'

'I didn't want to upset you again, or churn everything up once more.'

'Really?' His tone was disbelieving and her heart sank.

'Look, Buzz, Ed and I didn't so much talk as I told Ed exactly what I thought of him and his behaviour. I also told him in no uncertain terms how things were going to be in the future, in that he was going to steer clear of us. Oh, and

I just about resisted kneeing him in the one place men don't like to be kneed.'

Buzz laughed then and she could tell he had visualized the scene.

'So, either I go now and pack, or we reset, forget about blummin' Ed and get back to our slow romancing.'

She saw Buzz sigh and the stiffness went out of his stance. '*Second amethyst*, most definitely.'

'Thank goodness for that, because one thing seeing Ed taught me was that I fancy you something rotten, and I can't believe I've wasted so many years of not being with you for one awful fumble with that man. So, *second amethyst* times a million and let's not waste any more time.'

* * *

A warm glow replaced the frostiness that had enveloped Buzz the night before. When Wynn had suggested that she leave, he knew very clearly that that was not what he wanted.

He moved to pull Wynn in for a hug.

'Tea?' he smiled.

She smiled back. 'You sure know how to romance a girl.'

'Might even manage a croissant if you're lucky,' he joked.

Just then there was a ping from his laptop, which sat on the kitchen table. Buzz had an inner knowing that he had to go and look at the email that had arrived.

'DNA results,' he announced, and watched all of the colour leach out of Wynn's face as she sank onto a chair.

Buzz ignored her and sat down to read the email and its charts and information.

When he was sure he understood the implications, he moved a chair to sit by Wynn. He took her hands and looked deeply into her terrified eyes.

'Well?' she squeaked.

'I just had the best early Christmas present ever.' He couldn't stop his huge grin. 'Skye is my daughter.'

Wynn squealed and launched herself at him.

* * *

When Skye returned home later, she found Wynn and Buzz sitting seemingly to attention in the kitchen. She wondered to begin with whether she had interrupted them mid-clinch, but then it became apparent that they were waiting for her.

'Is everything okay? You two are looking very serious. What's going on?'

'We've been waiting for you to come back home. I've had an email about the DNA tests,' said Buzz.

Skye's heart rate immediately sped up. 'Have you opened it?'

'Yes,' said Wynn, reaching out to hold Skye's hand.

Wynn and Skye had signed to give permission that their tests could be compared with that of Buzz and that the results would all be sent to Buzz.

'Come on then, tell me.'

'The report states very clearly that you and I have a father-to-daughter relationship.'

After all of the uncertainty, Skye couldn't believe that he'd said what she'd been hoping for. Buzz and Wynn got up and folded Skye into a group hug. They all had tears in their eyes.

'So, you're definitely my dad? I'm overjoyed. I couldn't have a better father.'

Buzz for once seemed unable to speak, but he hugged her tightly instead.

Skye thought she might explode with joy. She spoke to her bump, making Buzz and Wynn smile. 'See little one, you have the best grandad and grandma in the world.'

'I'm so happy,' said Buzz. 'I still can't believe it. Merry Christmas to both of you!'

* * *

When the lorry was finally towed away, there wasn't much left of the poor little beach café. Christine and Skye stood staring at the wreckage together the next day as the insurance company contractors began to board up the site.

'I'm afraid it's going to take a while to get my poor little café back up and running again,' said Christine woefully.

'I can't believe that no one was hurt, apart from the lorry driver, and thankfully he's going to be fine.'

'We were so lucky that no one was killed or badly injured. It doesn't bear thinking about if the accident had happened slightly later in the day; the café would have been full of breakfast customers. If you had been working, you'd have been there too.' Christine hugged Skye close to her, or as close as her bump would allow.

At least Skye didn't need to discuss reducing her working hours after all. Poor Christine wouldn't be trading again until well after the baby had arrived.

CHAPTER THIRTY-TWO

Some good had come out of the café tragedy, as the incident had at least broken the ice between himself and Wynn after their encounter with Ed. The DNA test results had been a game changer too.

Wynn had been spending much more time at the crystal shop and was eating most of her meals there now.

While Buzz was thankful that no one had been seriously hurt in the incident at the café and happy to hear that the lorry driver had now been released from hospital, he was troubled that the arranged venue for the homeless charity Christmas lunch had literally disappeared. He'd seen the state of what remained of the café building before the insurance company had moved in to board up the site. It seemed mean to make a fuss, as it was such a devastating blow to Christine's livelihood, but it was a problem he needed to solve, and quickly, as he couldn't face letting people down.

He spoke to Nigel Hopkins, hoping he would stand by his earlier offer.

'Use the church hall,' said Nigel instantly. 'The facilities aren't as good as those at the café, but with a bit of help, I'm sure we could make it work. And one bonus is that it's already decorated for Christmas.'

'We need another meeting of the band of helpers to discuss it, I think. I'll ask Lally when he's free.'

'What about Christine?'

'Do you really think she'll want to be involved after all that's happened?'

'I think you should at least ask her. She might be very glad of the distraction, given she has no business to run at the moment.'

'True. The accident still seems unbelievable, but then I'm so thankful there were no fatalities.'

'Yes, we could have been facing a very different Christmas in Borteen.'

It turned out that Nigel was indeed right. Christine was more than happy to help at the church hall, making a comment about idle hands not doing her any good.

Buzz's team consisted in the end of himself, Wynn, Skye, Nigel, Adam, Lally and Christine.

Christine did most of the cooking, ably assisted by Wynn. Buzz, Nigel, Adam and Lally distributed the food and drinks. Skye was having a tired day, but was very popular as someone to get conversations going on the tables.

The individuals attending the Christmas lunch from the Sowden hostel were mostly men and they all appeared to take Skye and her baby bump being there as a chance to talk about their own families, often with extreme sadness about their losses and misunderstandings from the past.

Buzz noticed how Lally and Christine seemed to have grown even closer following the café incident. He'd seen the devastation on the pub landlord's face when Christine was missing and it contrasted with Lally's ready smile for her today.

At the end of the meal, the homeless charity co-ordinator turned up to thank Buzz and the others for their generosity. He did a speech of thanks and surprised Buzz by presenting him with a top fundraiser award. Everyone in the church hall cheered and clapped enthusiastically.

Then, after months of planning and the worry of rearranging everything last minute, the lunch was seemingly over in a flash. The minibus loaded up the Christmas hostel residents and Buzz and his team waved them off before being left to clear up.

Adam offered Skye his arm to walk back to Crazy Crystals and Buzz and Wynn linked arms behind them. It was growing dark as they made their way along the promenade.

When it was wide enough, Buzz increased his pace, taking Wynn along with him as he wanted to mention something to Adam.

'Hey, Adam. You know you said you would possibly consider working for a charity in the future?'

'Yes,' said Adam with a cautious tone in his voice.

'Well, I'll float this idea and leave you to ponder it — the hostel and associated homeless charity are looking for someone to manage their finances and do some extra fundraising too. Your name popped into my head as soon as the manager mentioned it.'

'Wow, really? Can you let me have his contact details, please, so I can find out more information? That opportunity seems much more than just a coincidence.'

'Yes. I'd call it a sign, young man,' laughed Buzz.

Buzz could see Adam's smile even in the growing darkness.

CHAPTER THIRTY-THREE

Buzz was elated that Skye had been proved to be his daughter. It was like a dream and, to top that, he would soon be a grandad too.

When he and Wynn had been on one of their walks along the promenade, something they had started to do every day, he had suggested an idea that had been going around in his head.

'Wynn, I know you and I have never done things conventionally. Christmas has usually been a time of reflection for me, long walks, meditation, art, drumming, but this year I'd like to try something different.'

'Go on,' she encouraged him.

'I would like us to try a conventional Christmas.'

'What, midnight mass at the church?'

'That's not quite what I meant, more a family Christmas — a tree, presents, lights, a nice meal, games, maybe even a Christmas stocking for Skye. I know, I know, she's not a child, but I've missed out on all that.'

'I think it would be lovely to have a family day. Maybe I could stay over that night.'

'Now you're talking,' laughed Buzz and Wynn cuffed him playfully on the arm.

* * *

The band was playing on the concrete platform below the beach steps. Thankfully the weather was dry and clear, if rather cold. Skye was thrilled to see the band members wearing the outfits she had designed and made. She turned to Buzz and Wynn and couldn't keep the excitement out of her voice. 'What do you think? The costumes came out fab, didn't they? Doesn't Suzy look great in hers?'

Buzz came over to hug Skye and she delighted in the obvious pride that shone from his eyes. 'You've done so well, darling. It was a lot of work in such a short time.'

Skye loved the fact that she could finally call Buzz her dad. It somehow made her feel more settled, more complete.

Suzy Meadows normally played the drums but for this song she was the vocalist. As if she had sensed Skye's enthusiasm, at that very moment she flicked up the fringing that Skye had incorporated on her short skirt and the sequins she had sewn on glittered in the stage lights.

The music was unique to Suzy's band, but somehow timeless too. The audience consisted of people of all ages and they all seemed happy to sway along to the rhythms, enthralled by the band members, their voices and their skill at playing their instruments.

Skye positioned herself with her back against the sea wall, so she could support herself on it if she got too tired. Wynn and Buzz stood next to her, but as a new song began, she realized that her parents had moved closer to each other and were smooching with their arms entwined, staring intently into each other's eyes. It was as if something had subtly changed between them since the café accident. She'd always known that these two should still be together and it was frustrating that they refused to allow themselves to let go and give in to their true feelings.

Skye was thrilled to see them together, but at the same time, Wynn and Buzz dancing made her feel dreadfully alone. She shrank back against the sea wall and shivered. Looking around, everyone else on the beach appeared to be dancing in pairs. She contemplated leaving the event, but remembered she hadn't brought her door key to the shop with her and she didn't want to ruin the moment for Buzz and Wynn, now they finally seemed to have hooked up again, by interrupting them to ask for a key.

She knew that there was a hot chocolate stall up above the beach on the promenade and she decided a hot drink might help her to feel a little better; she'd acquired a taste for the sweet drink at the café. She was surprised to see Adam approaching from the opposite direction as she reached the stall. He had said that he wouldn't be able to come to the concert as he was packing in readiness to go home to his mother's for Christmas. She saw his face light up as he caught sight of her, but then it was as if he schooled his features and closed down his emotions. Skye was alarmed to find tears in her eyes. She had been the one to say they could only be friends, after all.

Adam pulled her to one side and put an arm across the back of her shoulders. 'What do you say to a walk further down the beach?'

He bought two cups of hot chocolate and they made their way down the beach steps. The beach was huge today with a really low tide, one of the reasons the band's performance had been set for this date. Adam and Skye didn't speak at all until they were away from the crowd, all jigging to the music in seeming unison. Further down the beach away from the people listening to the concert, it was as if they were in a world of their own.

They stood staring out to sea, sipping their drinks. As Adam finished the last of his, he whirled away. Skye shivered. He used the empty cup to make a sandcastle and Skye did the same, although it was a little awkward to bend down with her bump. Soon they were enclosed in a sandcastle circle, giggling like children.

'Shall we paddle?' he asked.

'You must be mad, it's freezing.'

'Maybe, but don't you think it might remind us we're alive?'

'Adam, I'll miss you while you're away . . .'

'I'll miss you too.' He put his arm around her shoulders and they began to walk back up the beach.

When they reached the promenade again, Adam stopped and stared out at the darkening sky. 'Shall we make moon wishes?' he asked.

'Moon wishes?'

'It's something my mum and I used to do. Make a wish on the moon.'

She could sense rather than see his smile.

'I wish for a safe delivery for my daughter.'

'I'll second that and wish that the charity job turns out to be the one for me so I can stay here in Borteen.'

They laughed and stood side by side. It was great to be back to being friends but she couldn't help but add an extra silent wish that maybe they could eventually become much more.

The baby chose that moment to wake up and kick Skye. She took it to be a sign that her daughter approved of her trying to get closer to Adam again.

'Come on, we're going to have a dance before I head home to Mum's for Christmas and I have a present for you that you must promise not to open until Christmas Day.'

* * *

Adam was very reluctant to be leaving Borteen and in particular Skye. Nigel had said it was his busiest time, so Adam shouldn't worry about leaving to share Christmas with his mother. It was surely where he was supposed to be at this time of year, but Adam could sense a sadness in his eyes.

Adam had valued his talks with Nigel and knew exactly what his mother meant about the man being a good listener. With Nigel's help, Adam had finally realized that he had been looking for some sort of refuge to take him out of the swirling emotions caused by Lewis's suicide. He was now searching for an opportunity to play to his existing strengths but make a difference too, like the job at the homeless charity. He had recognized that right now probably wasn't the time to make a huge leap into something completely different, at least not until his emotions had stabilized.

As Nigel waved him off, he asked Adam to extend an invitation to Marion Belfont to spend New Year with them at the vicarage. Adam was curious to see how his mother would react to that idea and wondered again about the paths a human life took, often full of ifs and maybes. One thing was clear for his own destiny — he would certainly be back here in Borteen in January. He had a job interview and he was determined to be in the seaside town to greet Skye's baby when she arrived in the world.

* * *

Skye had been somewhat bewildered by her parents — and she could actually now say parents with conviction — seemingly going over the top with Christmas, but it was lovely how much laughter this had caused in the flat.

They had put up lights and decorations, and presents were gathering beneath the tree. Skye went along with the theme, adding her own gifts for Buzz and Wynn.

She couldn't help being sad that Adam wasn't close by, but as promised he had slipped a small, prettily wrapped package into her hand before he left the concert. She wanted to open it but was making herself wait until Christmas Day.

Buzz explained that he felt he'd missed out on her childhood and wanted to spoil her this year. 'Next year there will be a baby in the house.' Skye was sure she didn't imagine the moisture in Buzz's eyes.

He'd also been planning a special Christmas lunch. The fridge was fit to burst with treats and the main course was a special nut and cheese roulade to be accompanied by roast vegetables.

When she woke on Christmas morning, opening her eyes to see Wynn looking at her from the camp bed installed specially so that she could spend the night at the flat, they both found that Buzz had left Christmas stockings for each of them.

They giggled as they opened them and explored the contents — an orange and some Bluetooth earbuds for Skye and an apple and a lovely decorative hair comb for Wynn.

When Wynn went to the bathroom, Skye opened her gift from Adam, holding her breath in anticipation. It turned out to be a pretty braided friendship bracelet, and as she positioned it on her wrist it seemed more precious than if it had been made of gold.

After their special lunch, the three went for a slow walk along the promenade and across the beach. It was enough to make Skye sleepy for the rest of the day, as she exchanged a few text messages with Adam.

* * *

On New Year's Day, Skye, Buzz and Wynn met up at the Ship Inn for supper with Lally, Christine, Nigel, Adam and his mother, Marion, who Nigel had invited to stay at the vicarage for a few days.

Skye was very curious about how she would get on with Adam's mum, but was pleasantly surprised that they found plenty to talk about regarding a shared passion for sewing and that Adam appeared to have told his mother all about her.

Adam had mentioned that Marion and Nigel had known each other years ago and she made a mental note to ask Adam how they were getting on together after so many years apart.

The pub was full of good cheer as most of the Borteen locals were gathered together to welcome in the new year. Skye lost count of how many people wished her well, but she was really only interested, she realized, in sitting next to Adam and feeling the warmth of his leg against hers on the bench seat as she listened to the others talking about their resolutions and dreams.

CHAPTER THIRTY-FOUR

Skye's pregnancy seemed to be zooming by and her bump was now enormous. At the beginning of February, snow came down suddenly while Wynn was at Buzz's to share an evening meal, as she now did most days.

Having looked out at the deepening snow, Wynn declared it was time for her to go. As she put on her coat to go back to Garden Cottage, Buzz had a strange expression on his face. Skye wondered if she was in the way. If she hadn't been here tonight, would Buzz have asked Wynn to stay over and not on the camp bed? As it was, he insisted on walking her mother up the high street, despite Wynn's protests that it was only a few yards and totally unnecessary.

Skye kissed her mum, rubbing her bump and deliberately not commenting about it as she had yet another painful Brackston Hicks contraction and went to get ready for an early night.

* * *

Outside of the shop door, the night air was cool and the snow had settled evenly on the road. The ludicrousness of the situation was not lost on Buzz. A man who loved his wife was walking her up the road to a cottage where she slept totally separately from her husband. He was still at a total loss about how to change the dynamics of this state of affairs and rather wished that Wynn had not rented the cottage in the first place.

Wynn's thoughts must have been travelling in a similar direction, because when they reached the gate to the small garden that separated the rented cottage from the road, she turned to Buzz, her eyes gleaming in the light of the streetlamp.

'What happened to my romancing, Mr Buzzard?'

'Erm . . . I'm finding that I'm still very out of practice and even at a loss about how to do it.'

Her face clouded for a second. 'But you haven't changed your mind have you — about us, I mean?'

'Absolutely not. If anything, I care about you more than I ever did.'

'Care about me?' She was wincing.

'Oh, all right, if I have to state it out loud — I love you, Wynn, and I was only thinking just now in my kitchen that I wish I'd never let you move out of the flat again. These "few yards", as you call them, feel like another ocean keeping us apart just as surely as the Irish Sea.'

'Well, well, so you've been thinking about it, about us?'

'Of course I have. How could I not? I've been desperately wondering how to change things to get you back in my life properly again.'

A snowflake landed on his nose and Wynn reached up to brush it away.

'How about this . . .' Wynn put her hands behind his head, worming her fingers into the greying locks above his ponytail. Her hands were hot and electrifying as they reached his scalp. He had an almost out-of-body experience, as Wynn pulled him closer and placed her lips onto his after an agonizing pause.

Buzz had just begun to relax into Wynn's embrace when a loud wolf whistle rent the air and they leapt apart. Buzz nearly slipped over on the snow-covered ground. Fred the butcher was walking past on the other side of the road with his dog. 'Get a room, you two,' he joked loudly.

Wynn laughed and waved at him. Then she spoke quietly to Buzz. 'I actually have a room.' She inclined her head towards the cottage. 'Would you like to see it?'

'Temptress! I'd love to see your "room".'

And that was it. They'd crossed an invisible line. Almost like the teenagers they'd been when they first met, they tumbled laughing into the cottage and Wynn fumbled for the light switch then yanked the curtains closed as she and Buzz couldn't get enough of each other's lips. They both reached for each other's hair ties and Wynn pulled Buzz's hair free to settle around his face and Buzz carefully unravelled her plait, delighting in the wavy length of her hair.

Wynn pulled away to look at him. 'Just want to see what you looked like with your hair down.'

'Ditto,' he replied, his hands still stroking her hair.

Then Buzz noticed the chain around her neck and pulled the wedding ring she had worn all of these years free of her blouse.

'You wear your ring?'

'I always have, even if not on my finger.'

'Would you let me put it back onto your finger?'

She reached behind her neck to release the chain and Buzz took the ring off it.

He went down on one knee and put the ring near to the tip of her index finger. 'Wynn Upton, would you please agree to be my true wife again?'

'Buzz Upton, yes.'

Buzz then gently manoeuvred the ring past her knuckles until it rested in its rightful place.

Then by mutual unspoken agreement, they were on the way up the steep cottage staircase, never letting go of each other and at one point pausing precariously at the edge of a step to kiss.

Breathless and heart pumping, Buzz finally got to the top of the stairs. Up here was in darkness, the only light coming from the front of the cottage where the streetlight shone through the bedroom window. Wynn darted away to close the curtains and put on a bedside lamp, then threw off her shoes, shrugged off her coat and reached out to grab Buzz again.

Buzz knew she was so caught up in her passion that she hadn't noticed that things had changed for him. He fervently wished that they hadn't. Here he was, at last within reach of his goal, a true reconciliation with his wife, but the pain that had begun to sear through his chest was now undeniable and all encompassing. It robbed him of speech and breath. He caught sight of a horrified look breaking out on Wynn's lovely face just before he faceplanted on the floorboards.

* * *

Wynn's passion and lust disappeared in an instant. Buzz looked very strange, his face contorting as he clutched his chest and fell to the floor. Where was her bag? Her phone? She realized in horror that it was downstairs and that Buzz was blocking the narrow doorway. She fell to her knees next to him, but then knew without doubt that he needed medical attention.

She ran to the window, yanking back the curtains again and thrust the window wide. Fred the butcher was on the opposite side of the road with his dog returning from their walk. Wynn yelled out of the window. But he didn't seem to hear her. She had a brainwave and wolf whistled. Fred turned and looked over.

'Help! It's Buzz. Can you get an ambulance? Please?'

Fred stood frozen for a second and then, juggling the dog lead, he took out his mobile phone and she could see him working the screen. Wynn breathed out heavily now she knew that help would be on its way. She pushed her feet back into her shoes, grabbed a pillow and put it under Buzz's head. He groaned so at least she knew he was still breathing . . . still alive. She gulped. Although not wanting to leave him, she knew she had to get the front door unlocked for the paramedics to get into the cottage.

Squeezing past Buzz, her heart breaking with imaginings, she trod as carefully as she could down the steep staircase with her shoelaces still untied. They didn't need the complication of her falling down the stairs too.

The door thrust wide, she saw that Fred was now outside minus his dog.

'Can I help?'

Wynn stifled a sob and ran back in. 'He's upstairs, I think he's having a heart attack. Can you tell the paramedics where to come, please?'

She didn't wait for an answer, rushing back to Buzz as she thankfully heard the sirens of an ambulance coming over the hill.

The rest of the night was a complete blur. The paramedics managed to get Buzz off the floor and checked him out. An ECG confirmed that he was indeed having some sort of heart incident and he was taken away in the ambulance destined for Sowden General Hospital. Wynn only managed to briefly squeeze his hand as he was whisked away.

She couldn't believe that less than an hour ago she had been looking at a night of reunited passion with her estranged and beloved husband and now . . . now . . . She couldn't let herself dwell on the possibility of becoming a widow, even if it had popped into her head. She wondered what to do about telling Skye, but decided to let the girl sleep in ignorance for now. Skye too was probably imagining the two of them in the throes of lovemaking. Her daughter would be mad at her, but what could she do right now except sit with Wynn in a cold hospital waiting room?

Now, how to get to the hospital? Wynn retrieved her bag and her coat and couldn't believe that Fred was outside the cottage door swinging his car keys.

'Let's get you to the hospital,' Fred said, with an almost apologetic smile. 'Thank goodness I have a four-by-four to cope with this snow.'

Wynn, overcome with his kindness, scared the poor man half to death by launching herself into his arms and sobbing against his chest as the adrenalin of the crisis began to depart and the shock took over.

'Hey, hey. Come on, let's get to Sowden. He's a tough guy, he'll be okay. Might need some tender nursing though, so good job you're here in Borteen.'

Fred insisted on staying with her in the hospital waiting room, supplying tea and chocolate bars. Wynn hadn't drunk real tea for years, but was glad of its mild stimulant properties in keeping her awake. For once, she didn't even read the label of the chocolate; she always made sure what she ate was fair trade approved, but now was not a time to be hung up on principles, now was a time to do what was necessary to survive, to pray to the universe and indeed to any god who would listen to her. She needed Buzz alive and well — he was going to be a grandfather for goodness' sake.

Fred had made the reception desk aware of where they were waiting and it was a good couple of hours later before someone came to see them.

The woman was tall, her hair straight and spiky, but her smile was genuine. 'Mrs Upton?'

'Yes,' said Wynn, nearly spilling her latest drink.

'Buzz is asking for you.'

Wynn stifled a sob. That meant he was still alive.

'If you follow me, you can see him now.'

Wynn glanced at Fred, who was looking very tired by this point.

'Don't worry, I'll wait here for you.'

'Thank you so much.'

She marvelled at how kind people were to each other most of the time. She didn't even buy things from Fred's butcher's shop, being as she was a veggie.

Buzz was as pale as the bedsheets in the A&E cubicle. He was wired up to a monitor that let out a rhythmic beep and had a drip leading into his arm. A faint smile danced over his lips when he saw her.

'Hello, you.' She didn't want to disturb anything, so she settled for stroking one of his fingers.

'Hello, yourself.'

'You gave me such a fright.'

'Gave myself one too.'

'But what have they said? Are you okay?'

'Heart attack. They need to do more tests, but the docs seem to think I'll make a good recovery, if I follow all the advice and take some pills, of course.'

'We'll do whatever we need to do.'

'Have you told Skye?'

'Not yet. I didn't see the point of giving her a sleepless night when I couldn't actually tell her much.'

'Good call, but you do know she'll be mad with you.'

'I'm prepared for that.'

The doctor came back into the cubicle and looked at the monitor. 'We are admitting you for some more tests and assessments. I'm only waiting for confirmation of a bed on the coronary ward.'

She rushed off and Wynn subsided onto the chair next to Buzz. She looked at the monitor herself and thought back to all of the episodes of *Grey's Anatomy* she'd watched on television. The heart trace seemed to be regular, but what did she really know? Watching TV drama wasn't medical training.

'Look, this is all going to take ages. Why don't you go home for some sleep?'

'I just wanted to satisfy myself that you're okay. I'll get you some pyjamas and things from the flat. Is there anything in particular you want me to bring?'

Buzz raised an eyebrow and she guessed that meant he still didn't wear pyjamas. He'd preferred a loose kaftan shift thing in the past.

'I need to tell Skye what's happened and Fred has been so kind waiting with me, but he's tired too.'

'Off you go. I'm in the right place.'

'You do realize I drank normal tea in the waiting room and ate normal chocolate? Look what you've reduced me to.' She laughed and touched his arm as she got up to leave.

'Terrible,' Buzz commented. 'And Fred will have you eating bacon before we know it.'

She pulled a face. It was a relief to be laughing with this man who meant the world to her, who had forgiven her for her transgressions, who she wanted to be with for the rest of her days. The man she had almost lost.

'You'd better get better, Mr Buzzard. I'm expecting much more romancing in my future and we have unfinished business from yesterday evening.' She laughed again as his heart monitor registered a higher pulse after her words. 'And now I'd better go before I get told off by the nurses for getting you excited.'

She planted a chaste kiss on his forehead before leaving the cubicle and making her way back to Fred, who was mightily relieved to hear her reassuring news of Buzz.

As they drove over the top of the hill and Borteen Bay and the town lay outlined in snow below them, the sun was rising and Wynn gave thanks to all of the various deities she'd prayed to in her panic when she thought she was about to lose the love of her life.

Buzz would fight back from this and Wynn intended to be there for the journey. She was never going to let go of him again. Then she realized with horror that there was an ambulance parked outside of Crazy Crystals. Skye?

CHAPTER THIRTY-FIVE

Skye had been quite relaxed about what she thought were practice labour pains she'd experienced the day before, but she woke shortly after midnight with pain searing through her belly.

She waited and tried to breathe through the pain but knew instinctively she needed help. Was Buzz back? She padded to his room, but the bed hadn't been slept in. What a night for her parents to finally get together. Then she found his abandoned mobile phone on the kitchen table. She called her mother from her own phone, but it went to voicemail several times.

Trying not to panic and wanting someone with her, she scrolled her contacts.

'ADDDDAAAMMMM!' The pain absorbed her again and it was difficult to reply to Adam's frantic enquiry about what was happening when his surprised voice answered her call.

'The baby is coming. I can't get hold of Buzz or Mum. And I'm a bit scared. It's too early.'

'I'll be there as quickly as I can. Are you able to let me in?'

'I'll go down to the shop and phone the maternity ward too.'

* * *

When he burst through the door to Crazy Crystals, stamping accumulated snow off his boots, Skye was on all fours on the shop floor tiles gasping against the pain. 'Have you called anyone?'

'You! And the maternity ward at the hospital. They said to come as soon as possible.'

Adam responded without thinking. 'Have they seen the snow?'

Skye looked distressed and he immediately regretted his words.

'Seriously, my car wouldn't make it up the hill, I'm afraid. I wonder if a taxi could.'

There was a tear in the corner of Skye's eye and he could tell she was scared.

'It's cold down here. Come on, let's get you back up to the flat while we make a decision.'

They only made it to the kitchen when she doubled over again. When the contraction passed she called the maternity ward and Adam took the phone, putting the call on loudspeaker so they could both hear what was said. He explained that he didn't think it safe to try to drive in the snowy conditions.

The woman's voice was annoyingly calm. 'I've just been told that the snow on Pink Moor is drifting and we're waiting for a snow plough to clear the roads. But we'll get an ambulance to you as quickly as we can. What is happening with Mum? It's her first pregnancy, isn't it?'

'Yes. Her first baby, and she isn't supposed to be due until the end of the month.' Adam reached out and instinctively rubbed circles on Skye's back.

'It will be ages before baby arrives then. Plenty time for the ambulance to get to you.'

'Are you sure about that?' Skye was panting against the next wave of pain.

'How far apart are your contractions?'

Adam looked at Skye. 'They seem to be coming more or less constantly now.'

Skye was nodding her agreement with clenched teeth.

'Okay. Not to worry. My name is Benita. Mum is Skye, yes? And you are?'

'Yes, Skye is having the baby and I'm her . . . friend, Adam.'

'Okay, Adam. I'll stay on the line for you both for as long as I have to. If we get cut off for whatever reason, ring back and ask for me.'

Adam felt his heart rate speed up. If the ambulance couldn't get to them and they couldn't get to the hospital — he couldn't deliver a baby, could he? He hadn't a clue. Did he need to find towels and boil water or was that just on television programmes?

Skye grabbed his free hand and squeezed so painfully he almost yelped, but it bought him back to the present moment.

'I think the baby is coming. The pain feels different, more intense.'

Adam gulped. 'Did you hear what Skye said? What do I do?'

'Above all, don't panic. Is there anyone else with you apart from the mum in labour?'

'It's only us here, heavy snow outside, and we can't seem to contact her parents.'

Adam was aware that his voice appeared to have acquired a new high-pitched sound.

The midwife on the other end of the line changed the tone of her own voice, and he guessed it was because she had realized there was no choice but to keep him calm — he was all she and Skye had.

'Okay, Adam. I'm just going to get an update on the ambulance, but I'll only be a few moments away.' Benita confirmed the address and then the line went quiet.

Adam smiled at Skye and stroked her arm. 'It will all be fine. I can't wait to meet your daughter.'

She smiled back, but her lip trembled.

Benita's voice came from the phone propped up on the table.

'So, tell me a little about yourselves. Your first baby then, Skye?'

'Yes, she's my first baby, my first pregnancy.'

'All will be fine,' Benita said in her now annoyingly calm voice. 'Have you children of your own, Adam?'

'No.'

'Brothers or sisters?'

'No.'

'So, you've never been near to babies or births?'

'No.' Adam was aware each *no* became more shrill.

'Do you watch medical dramas on television by any chance?'

'No!' That response was more of a wail, as Skye gripped his hand tightly again as she rode the pain of the contraction.

Benita waited until Skye said the pain had passed. 'I've just checked on the status of the ambulance and it is behind the snow plough coming into Borteen. Unfortunately, the team has to divert to a life-or-death situation. Someone has had a heart attack in Borteen. Another ambulance has just left on its way to you. I'm going to give you a couple of things to find, Adam.'

'Of course.'

'We will need towels. And set the kettle to boil so you have warm water ready.'

Adam asked Skye where he could find towels. In between panting on all fours on the floor, she directed him to the cupboard in the hallway.

As he collected the towels from the airing cupboard, he noticed some facecloths in a pile and took a couple of those too.

When he returned to the kitchen, Skye was talking to the midwife. She smiled a watery-eyed smile at him. Then her face contorted yet again.

'Another contraction, by any chance?'

'Yes, they seem to be coming faster.'

'Adam, first babies are normally slow to make their way into the world, but this one seems very keen. I suspect Skye has been in labour longer than she realized. It looks likely that you may have to help this little one into the world.'

Despite already recognizing the truth, Adam gulped. Was he up to the job? Could he really do this with no prior knowledge at all? He was finding it difficult enough that Skye, who he really cared about, was in such awful pain.

She looked up at him now with her forehead furrowed, flushed cheeks and concern in her eyes as the contraction passed. Adam couldn't contain a burst of irrational laughter.

'You're laughing at me?' The hurt in her eyes was raw.

'Not at you. Sorry, sorry. It just struck me that in all the scenes I imagined of romancing you, trying to win your heart, to get you to marry me after all . . . well, none of that started with helping you to give birth.' He waved his hand over the towels strewn around them.

Now Skye was laughing too. 'I don't think anything about giving birth is romantic. And . . . I'm so embarrassed that you're going to see me in this state. I mean, how will we ever get to romance again . . . when you've seen me like this?'

Adam was grinning from ear to ear.

'You're laughing at me again.'

'No, I'm elated that you're even talking, no considering, us getting together in the future.'

'Well, you did mention the marriage word again just now.'

Adam slid his hand behind her lovely head. He kissed her tenderly and it was all going well until Skye was wracked with another contraction.

'Here we go again . . .' gasped Skye.

'Remember to breathe,' said Benita.

Adam stood up and began to organize the things he'd gathered earlier. They had been thrust on the floor when Skye had had the previous contraction. *Pull yourself together, man.*

He put the towels in a pile on the kitchen counter and then went to soak one of the facecloths in cold water. Returning to Skye he mopped her forehead in a way he hoped was helpful and maybe soothing. Her weak smile told him he was on the right track.

Benita continued talking and he forced himself to focus on her words.

'You two sound close, which is lovely. The ambulance isn't far away now.'

Skye smiled at him. She answered Benita's questions and then Benita asked her to share what she was feeling.

'Look, guys, I know I'm not there to see, but from what Skye is describing, I think things are about to happen really fast. Now, you should be reassured that the ambulance is close, so you won't be on your own for much longer, but for now, Adam, you're the midwife. Can the paramedics get into the property if you're otherwise engaged when they arrive?'

'Yes, I was too busy concentrating on Skye earlier to lock the door. I hope no one has cleaned out Buzz's shop while we've been up here in the flat.'

Skye made a strange noise. 'Benita, something different is happening.'

'Right, I want you panting for a moment.'

'But I want to push.'

'Keep it calm. Adam, I want a nice thick towel beneath Skye's legs ready to catch the baby.'

'Catch the baby? Is she nearly here?' He grabbed a towel and realized his hands were shaking.

As if to answer Adam, Skye made a weird noise and then told Benita she believed the baby's head was out.

'Right, next contraction — push.'

Skye turned puce with the effort and Adam felt helpless once again. But then a miracle happened, and just like that, he found himself holding a baby.

Benita gave him instructions about clearing her airway and wrapping her in a towel. She made a little cry and Adam found tears on his cheeks as he placed her in Skye's waiting arms.

As soon as he had, he heard the sound of heavy footsteps on the staircase and two paramedics arrived in the kitchen.

Adam sighed with relief, his brain still feeling somewhat bewildered about what had just happened, what he'd witnessed and done. He found that he couldn't stop smiling.

One paramedic clamped and cut the cord, before checking the baby over and showing Skye that her daughter was perfect. Then the tiny bundle was placed in Adam's arms while they dealt with the afterbirth and cleaned Skye up.

Adam updated Benita and thanked her. She praised him before he ended the call.

As he stared down into the little baby's face and began to relax now the drama was over, he was aware that he'd fallen in love. This may not be his baby, but he felt an immediate bond with this little scrap of new humanity, especially as he'd been here when she came into the world.

More footsteps sounded on the staircase and Wynn burst into the room. 'Skye? The baby? Is everything okay?'

CHAPTER THIRTY-SIX

The paramedics insisted that Skye and the baby were taken to Sowden General Hospital to be checked over properly. Adam felt quite deflated as they were prepared to be taken away, as he didn't want to let Skye or the baby out of his sight.

Skye called him over and grabbed the front of his jumper to pull him in for a brief kiss.

'Thank you, Adam. You were a complete rock star,' she said.

'Glad to be of service.' He bowed and looked down at the two of them.

'I'd like you to name my daughter,' said Skye suddenly.

Adam clutched at his throat in shock. 'Really?'

'Yes, really.'

'But . . . but that's such a responsibility.'

'As I said, I'd like you to name her.' Skye pulled the blanket a little away from her daughter's face so that Adam could see her more clearly.

'Well, the name you talked about once, Iona, resonates with me. Would that be right?'

'Absolutely perfect. What do you think, Iona?' She snuggled the baby close and Adam was once again overwhelmed by feelings of love for the pair.

Wynn had been watching them and nodded with a smile.

He went to help Wynn clear up the flat after locking the shop door once the ambulance had pulled away. He picked up the towels that hadn't been used and returned them to the airing cupboard. Wynn pulled him into a hug as he came back into the kitchen.

'Thank goodness you were around when Skye needed you. Thank you for being there for her.'

'She couldn't get hold of you or Buzz. Where is Buzz, by the way?'

Adam felt his hair stand on end as Wynn told him the reason why they had both been absent. Wynn shed a tear as she described the tension of thinking she might have lost Buzz.

'Goodness, you have a lot to tell Skye.'

'I can't believe I got away without telling her just now, but thankfully she was wrapped up with the baby and you.' She winked. 'Adam, I hate to do this, but could I prevail on your good nature a little longer?'

'What can I do?'

'Could you take me over to Sowden General? Skye and the baby will need transporting home once they've been checked over.' She put her hand in the air as if something had occurred to her. 'Don't let me forget the baby seat. And Skye might as well show Buzz the baby while we're there as he will be in the hospital for tests for a bit longer. Sorry, I'm making assumptions . . . do you mind being a taxi? The roads have been cleared and gritted now. And I'm so tired, I'm afraid I might snore all the way to the hospital.'

Adam knew he was needed and would not have dreamed of turning down Wynn's request, however tired he now felt, but he would have to make a phone call first as he was due in Sowden at noon for his job interview.

He looked at the clock and couldn't believe where the time had gone since Skye had summoned him to Crazy Crystals in distress.

'Give me forty minutes for a shower and to sort a couple of things and I'll meet you . . . where? Here? Or your cottage?'

They agreed to meet at the shop as the baby seat was there.

* * *

Both Skye and her baby had been given the green light to return home, but Buzz, who they had visited before leaving the hospital, had to remain at Sowden General for more tests until the following week. The snow had disappeared as quickly as it had fallen.

Skye had been shocked and dismayed about Buzz's heart attack, but the signs were good for a full recovery as long as he changed certain things about his diet and lifestyle. She realized that she'd almost lost her father just as she had found him.

Wynn had stepped up to run Crazy Crystals while Buzz recovered and Skye had been delighted to notice she was wearing her wedding ring on her finger.

She soon realized the advantages of living close to both Wynn and Buzz. They made it a requirement that she had regular time away from the baby. Skye thought it amusing that their babysitting usually coincided with when Iona was asleep.

Seeing her parents staring at her daughter in her Moses basket warmed her heart. They would be doting and supportive grandparents. Iona was a lucky girl. Skye was reluctant at first to leave her daughter at all, but soon recognized that having regular breaks improved her mood and, of course, gave Wynn and Buzz time to bond with their granddaughter.

Leaving Iona in their care, she went for a walk to meet up with Christine, who was supervising the rebuilding of the café. Christine had been one of the first people she had told about the birth of her daughter. The café owner was keen to reassure Skye that she still had a job as soon as they were up and running again.

As she left the café building site, she bumped into Adam, who was just completing his daily run.

'My new routine starts next week when I take up my job in Sowden,' he said, panting slightly.

'You got it? You got the charity job?'

His smile was full of happiness. 'Yes, they finally got the funding and I got the job. It gives me some breathing space to think things through, to get myself back on track, and Nigel is keen I still live at the vicarage with him. He said something so touching — that I was the nearest thing to a son he would ever have.'

'Oh, that's so lovely. I won't see as much of you when you're working, I guess?'

'I wouldn't say that. Just you try to keep me away from seeing as much of Iona as I can.'

'Are you sure you're pleased about the new job? I mean, I thought you wanted a completely different direction?'

'Nigel helped me to see that I was floundering around after the foundations of my life had been shaken. And this job doesn't preclude me doing something different in the future, but for now it fulfils my need to work for a worthwhile cause. It's not exactly a return to the rat race in London.'

'But you had that lifestyle for a number of years, do you think you can be happy long term in a backwater like Borteen?'

'Why do you think I wanted to come back to Borteen, after I left that time?'

'Tell me, Adam. I think I need to hear why.'

'You.'

'Really?'

'It's that simple. I came back to see if there was any chance of there being an "us". I know what you said about it being too convenient, but when I went away that time, I was incomplete, as if a piece was missing from my jigsaw.'

Skye's stomach was doing loop-de-loops.

'I need to be near you to feel whole, Skye. I need you, full stop. But what I really need to know is if you're still adamant to go things alone with the baby or if you'll let me into your life, even a little bit — and, of course, Iona's life too?'

There was a busker on the end of the promenade and the sound of his music was carrying clearly down to the edge of the beach where they were standing.

'Dance with me?'

'That doesn't really answer my question.'

Skye laughed that it felt so different to snuggle up against Adam without her pregnancy bump, but also so right. She cupped his face with her hands as they sort of swayed together and she pressed her lips against his.

'That thing you said about feeling like a jigsaw with a piece missing — I recognize that so well. I don't think I've been properly warm since that time you went away after we argued. I felt as if I'd let go of something precious that day because I somehow didn't feel I really deserved it, but I mourned its loss — the loss of you, Adam. If you would only ask your question again — well, questions really — but I do understand if that ship has sailed and that I'm expecting too much of you.'

'Right, Miss Contrary Mary. Will you marry me, and can I please be Iona's daddy and the father of any other children you might happen to have . . . with me, of course?'

'Yes please,' answered Skye solemnly.

Adam picked her up and twirled her around. 'Did you really just say yes?'

'Yes, yes, yes.'

They ran up the road to Crazy Crystals to give their daughter a hug and tell her parents what they had decided about their future.

THE END

ACKNOWLEDGEMENTS

I wrote this novel through a period of great changes in my life, the birth of my grandson, Roman, to whom this novel is dedicated and the death of my mother, Patricia Jones (1933–2022). Mom, thankfully, got to meet her great grandson, Roman, and was overjoyed by his arrival.

As the writing of each book accompanies me through life's journey, the stories will forever be entwined with my own, and even though not visible to the reader, they evoke many memories for me.

Susan Wood's gift to my son many years ago of a heart-shaped pink bucket to make sandcastles on Llandanawg beach appears in this book and Buzz's shop, Crazy Crystals, was originally inspired by a visit to The Karma Shack in Worcester.

As always, there are too many people to thank for their invaluable support and guidance and I am always worried about missing anyone out. Thanks to my family and friends, to my writing tribes in the RNA, the Cariad group and my Tuesday Zoom writing group. Special thanks to the Choc Lit editorial team.

Thank you to the Choc Lit Tasting Panel for believing in my story.

I do hope readers will enjoy this my seventh book set in the fictional seaside town of Borteen. Please leave me a review to tell me what you particularly liked about it.

THE CHOC LIT STORY

Established in 2009, Choc Lit is an independent, award-winning publisher dedicated to creating a delicious selection of quality women's fiction.

We have won 18 awards, including Publisher of the Year and the Romantic Novel of the Year, and have been shortlisted for countless others. In 2023, we were shortlisted for Publisher of the Year by the Romantic Novelists' Association.

All our novels are selected by genuine readers. We are proud to publish talented first-time authors, as well as established writers whose books we love introducing to a new generation of readers.

In 2023, we became a Joffe Books company. Best known for publishing a wide range of commercial fiction, Joffe Books has its roots in women's fiction. Today it is one of the largest independent publishers in the UK.

We love to hear from you, so please email us about absolutely anything bookish at choc-lit@joffebooks.com

If you want to hear about all our bargain new releases, join our mailing list: www.choc-lit.com/contact

Milton Keynes UK
Ingram Content Group UK Ltd.
UKHW011140280124
436847UK00002BA/2